JEFF JACKSON
DESTROY ALL MONSTERS

Jeff Jackson is the author of *Mira Corpora*, a finalist for the Los Angeles Times Book Prize. His short fiction has appeared in *Guernica*, *VICE*, and *The Collagist*, and six of his plays have been produced by the Obie Award–winning Collapsable Giraffe theater company in New York City.

DESTROY ALL MONSTERS

SIDE A

MY DARK AGES

JEFF JACKSON

DESTROY ALL MONSTERS

THE LAST ROCK NOVEL

FSG Originals • Farrar, Straus and Giroux • New York

FSG Originals
Farrar, Straus and Giroux
175 Varick Street, New York 10014

Library of Congress Cataloging-in-Publication Data
Names: Jackson, Jeff, 1971 July 16– author.
Title: Destroy all monsters : the last rock novel / Jeff Jackson.
Description: First edition. | New York : Farrar, Straus and Giroux, 2018.
Identifiers: LCCN 2018011509 | ISBN 9780374537661 (softcover)
Classification: LCC PS3610.A3518 D47 2018 | DDC 813/.6—dc23
LC record available at https://lccn.loc.gov/2018011509

Designed by Richard Oriolo

Our books may be purchased in bulk for promotional, educational, or business
use. Please contact your local bookseller or the Macmillan Corporate and
Premium Sales Department at 1-800-221-7945, extension 5442, or by e-mail at
MacmillanSpecialMarkets@macmillan.com.

www.fsgoriginals.com • www.fsgbooks.com
Follow us on Twitter, Facebook, and Instagram at @fsgoriginals

1   3   5   7   9   10   8   6   4   2

Gratitude for advocacy and sage advice: Jaida Temperly, Jo Volpe, Devin
Ross, and the New Leaf Literary team, Jeremy M. Davies, Alethea Black,
D. Foy, Frank Lentricchia, Phillip Larrimore, Darragh McKeon, Giorgio Hiatt,
Michael Kimball, John Schacht, Gregory Howard, Sean Madigan Hoen, Irini
Spanidou, John W. Love Jr., Jim Findlay, John Cochrane, Scott Adlerberg,
Duvall Osteen, Virginia Center for the Creative Arts, MacDowell Colony,
Hambidge Center, Ben Marcus, Dennis Cooper, and Don DeLillo.

For Stephanie.

in memory of
JOHNNY ACE
the first rock-and-roll casualty
(June 9, 1929–December 25, 1954)

MY
DARK
AGES

FOLLOW THE TRAIL OF UNUSED TICKETS. They are scattered along the town's shuttered storefronts, lit by sporadic streetlamps, a path of yellow paper that winds down the sidewalk. They're all for tonight's show.

The boy in the blue hat scoops up one and keeps walking. He nods as he reads the name of the band printed on the front. The trail leads him to an unmarked metal door. No signs indicate whether this is the entrance to the club, but the boy tugs the handle and the heavy door swings wide.

Inside the darkened space, the smell of antiseptic cleanser stings his nostrils, barely masking the residue of stale beer. The boy in the blue hat holds out his ticket, but nobody is there to take it. He finds himself in a stark concrete room that resembles a converted meat locker. It's embellished only with a wrought-iron chandelier and a long tapestry hung on the wall, woven images of circling swallows and ceremonial fires. The club seems empty, but as he moves closer to the stage the boy spots spectators dressed in black. They're clustered along the edges of the room, waxen faces peering from the shadows.

At the back of the space, two bearded men in crimson robes stand over a bank of sequencers and synthesizers. They generate a lumbering beat and high-pitched wail that keeps cutting in and out of the speakers. The band mutters curses at the unseen soundman and mumbles apologies to the listless audience. They begin several times, never getting further than a few bars before something short-circuits. Finally, the song erupts from the sound system, the droning squall intensified as it recoils off the concrete walls.

The stage lights brighten. The piercing frequencies grow louder. The meager audience seems stunned by the sheer magnitude of the sound. As the bearded musicians chant a wordless melody, the boy in the blue hat swivels his neck and undulates his arms through the air. It's a spastic dance, or a moment of spiritual possession, or maybe an expulsion of nervous energy. It ends as abruptly as it began. From the back of his jeans, the boy produces a revolver, takes aim, and fires.

The music muffles the sound of the shots. There's only the sight of the two musicians collapsing to the floor. One of them pulls himself up by his bank of synthesizers. He's hunched over, frantically ripping the fabric of his robe. As he staggers toward the side of the stage, the boy in the blue hat shoots him in the head.

There are screams of terror, probably, but the distorted sounds spilling from the speakers are louder. The boy's attention shifts from the dark pool collecting under the corpse to the other musician, who's struggling to stand. The man wobbles upright for a moment, battling to maintain his balance, but the boy shoots him in the shoulder. He topples back onto the stage, pulling his mixer with him.

The boy in the blue hat finds the club is now deserted except for a trio of teenagers huddled against the wall. A boy with a silver nose ring, a boy wearing a studded leather vest, and a girl in a red wig. They stare at him with horror and fascination. Together they watch the bearded musician make another attempt to stand, gasping and heaving as he raises himself to his knees.

The boy in the blue hat turns the gun around and extends it to the teenagers. Their faces twitch and their eyes blaze. The revolver rests on the boy's palm, a gleam of polished steel, waiting to see who will accept its weight.

PRELUDE

A few encounters were like signals emanating from a more intense life, a life that has not really been found.

—GUY DEBORD

IT'S THE NIGHT THE MUSIC COMES HOME. That's how the concert is billed on the red flyers plastered along the telephone poles that lead into Arcadia. The notices accompany cars through the few blocks of dive bars, all-night diners, and ethnic restaurants that constitute the ragged downtown. Drivers cruise the streets in search of parking spaces, gliding past the ticket holders streaming toward the show and the onlookers loitering under streetlights. Normally people come to make the most of their hours away from jobs at the wheelchair factory, the tire warehouses, and construction gigs, but this crowd has flocked here for the homecoming show of a local band whose songs have gone viral. Their attention is riveted on the theater, its façade lit up like a beacon. A bustling queue of teenagers wraps along the building's perimeter, bodies pressed tight to keep a claim on their territory. They've camped out on the sidewalk for hours, dressed light in anticipation of spring weather that hasn't arrived, a sampling of what passes for an underground scene in this conservative industrial city. The strip-mall goths, the mod metalheads, the blue-collar ravers, the bathtub-shitting punks, the jaded aesthetes who consider themselves beyond category. Everyone in line has imagined a night that could crack open and transform their dreary realities. This is it.

●

Xenie clutches one of the red concert flyers while she watches the line grow. Teenagers swarm in tense cliques, unaccustomed to seeing one another away from the usual hangouts—the parking lot of the sandwich shop that sells alcohol to minors, the skate park haunted by the spirits of dead twins, the abandoned flag factory that's the site of ritualistic revels. Only one band could draw everyone here together. A steady stream of newcomers search for the end of the queue that's vanished around the corner. The overhead marquee doesn't bother to advertise the Carmelite Rifles. It simply says SOLD OUT.

Xenie smooths her tattered blouse and thrift-store skirt and scans the crowd, knocking her combat boots together for luck. Somebody has to have a spare ticket. She listens to some kids in tie-dye T-shirts and leather dog collars swapping stories about the band's incandescent live shows. The one where they dressed as the headlining band

and played their set note for note. The epic concert at Echo Echo whose encore spilled out into the courtyard.

—I was at their very first gig, she says. They played next to a washing machine in the drummer's basement.

Nobody replies or looks up. Maybe she didn't actually say anything out loud.

The sixteen-year-old keeps pacing in front of the theater. The scalpers skulking along the sidewalk keep a lookout for cops while chanting astronomical numbers under their breath. They assess her with sidelong glances both pitying and predatory.

Farther down the queue, she recognizes several faces from other shows, a tattooed girl with sleepy eyes and a blue-haired boy with pierced lips. Not that she's ever summoned the nerve to speak to them. Anybody got an extra ticket? she asks.

She holds up the concert flyer to emphasize her point, but it's the wrong side. She stands there facing the line, desperately waving a page of pure red.

●

Two teenage boys linger at the end of the line. They stand slightly apart from the shrinking queue. They try not to act alarmed by the low rumble of the opening act's set, but it's obvious the show has officially started. The tall skinny boy frantically empties the contents of his billfold onto the sidewalk. His face blazes crimson. I fucked up, he says. I really fucked up.

He turns to his friend Shaun and displays the empty expanse of wallet where their tickets should be.

—I must've left them at home, Florian says. I can call my mom. Maybe she'll bring them.

Shaun is sunk in thought. He casually shakes his long brown hair out of his eyes. Typically calm and unruffled. Still got the cassette? he asks.

—Right here, Florian says.

The demo tape contains several songs they wrote and recorded together. Their latest batch. The label doesn't list who played what because they share duties on vocals, guitars, everything. They've transferred the music to magnetic tape for maximum retro appeal. The case is spray-painted bright violet.

Shaun nods, then walks straight toward the front of the line, past the people impatiently shuffling their feet and the rows of silk-screened concert posters. Florian stumbles after him with his storklike steps, barely keeping up as they approach the security guard who clutches a wooden clipboard. The teardrop tattoos inked under his eyes make it even more difficult to imagine him crying.

—Hey, man, Shaun calls to the guard as if greeting an old confidant. I don't know what name he put us under. Maybe you can help us out.

—Who are you talking about? the guard says.

—You know, Mickey, the bass player. We're his cousins. Maybe it's under Mickey's name, maybe it's under mine, maybe my brother's.

The guard looks perplexed as he scrolls through the printed names on the guest list.

—There we are, Shaun says, peering over his shoulder and pointing to an unchecked name. That's me, and my brother's the plus-one.

The guard looks skeptical, but Shaun has already extended his wrist to receive a stamp. Florian follows his lead. He's used to his friend pulling off these sorts of stunts.

At the theater's entrance, Shaun notices a girl in a thrift-store ensemble and combat boots pacing the sidewalk. The spiky cut of her blonde hair doesn't entirely obscure her delicate features. She's singing one of the band's tunes under her breath, repeating the chorus in a lilting croon. Her lips barely move, but the shape of the song vibrates in her throat.

•

Xenie watches people file into the theater. Half the audience must be inside already. As the line steadily shortens, she can feel her options dwindling. A preppy girl from school struts past and pulls her lips into a knifelike smile: Not so cool without a ticket, are you? Xenie merely shrugs and mirrors her smile. Nobody is going to ruin this night for her.

She spots a boy leaving the theater for a smoke. He stands under the diffuse glow of the marquee, wearing an absent expression while he lights up. The spooky pink scar zigzagging down his cheek looks self-inflicted, but there's no time to be picky.

—I don't have a ticket, Xenie says, hoping she doesn't sound desperate. And I noticed your stamp.

The kid nods nonchalantly. No problem, he says.

She licks her wrist and holds it out to him. He presses the circular black stamp against her wet skin, and a glistening imprint of the stamp is transferred to her.

She thanks the boy profusely. He exhales a long plume of smoke. Good luck, he says, nodding at the security guard in the yellow staff shirt with the neck tattoo. One of the venue's infamous goons.

Xenie tries to keep her pale wrist from trembling, telling herself the stamp looks fine even as the circular outline grows fainter with each inspection.

●

Florian and Shaun follow the surging crowd through the lobby. They're overwhelmed by the number of people pushing a path toward the bar and jockeying for space along the wooden counter, waving worn credit cards and wrinkled currency. They marvel at the continuous swarm around the merchandise table, people sifting through the multicolored vinyl and screen-printed T-shirts featuring nuns brandishing automatic rifles.

—There's so many townies and college kids here, Florian says. Never seen any of these people at Carmelite Rifles shows before.

—It's cool, Shaun says. People are paying attention to

the scene. Other Arcadia bands are going to start making it, too.

They're both thinking about the cassette. Somewhere nearby the band members must be part of this crowd, socializing with old friends before they take the stage. Florian can feel it. He absorbs the charged hum of chatter, strangers striking up conversations, intertwined voices escalating toward a frenzied pitch. Sagging strands of colored lights are suspended across the ceiling, and even in their dim glow people's expressions seem amplified, their faces greedy with anticipation. Probably he looks exactly like them.

●

Xenie walks deeper into the theater. She weaves her way down the shadowy corridor through clusters of kids debating the band's penchant for dramatic openings. I heard Mister Charlie is joining them, a boy says. That homeless dude who lives in the woods and pays guys for their dirty underwear. Come on, a girl counters. I heard they're going to play some punk classic. No way, another girl says. My friend swears they're releasing a flock of birds into the audience. Xenie keeps her opinion to herself. She spots a discarded ticket stub on the floor and peels it from the concrete, pocketing it for her collection.

As she enters the darkened auditorium, she discovers the crowd amassed at the front, drawn to the bombastic blare of the speaker towers. They bob their heads and twitch their bodies, reptile brains in thrall to the throbbing frequencies. Onstage in a small spotlight, a deejay hunches over a turntable. The ballad he's spinning has never been a favorite, but right now as its snaking bass line and slow-burn chorus fill the cavernous room, it sounds exactly perfect.

Xenie spots the boy with the zigzag scar maneuvering toward the stage, using his shoulder to knife through clusters of people. She watches to see how well his approach works, then walks down the sloping floor to enter the intensifying heat, the crush of multiplying bodies, the communion of commingled limbs.

●

The lights flicker on as the deejay concludes his set. People shake off the sound and slowly disperse toward the bar and bathrooms. Florian stares up at the stage, taking in the ring of gleaming guitars and basses, the drum kit embossed with the band's logo, then looks down at the humble purple cassette in his palm. Maybe we should re-record this, he says. I should really redo my vocals. Or maybe you should sing my parts.

—Don't be so uptight, Shaun says. It's genius. Someday it'll be us up there.

Time is running short if they're going to connect with the Carmelite Rifles. They comb the crowd, scouting the length of the bar, searching the men's bathroom, consulting the taciturn woman working the merch table. Maybe they can give the tape to the band's manager. As they wander through the theater, Florian notices Shaun's determination is flagging. He seems more interested in the acquaintances he keeps running across—local musicians, older classmates, cute girls—who wave hello, shake hands, smother him in hugs.

After inspecting the remotest nooks of the theater, they return to the auditorium. Among the assembled throng, Shaun spots one of the faces he's been hoping to see.

—Hold up, he says. Look over there.

He points to the blonde girl in the thrift-store outfit. You know her? he asks.

—Is she with the band? Florian says.

—She was out front of the theater earlier.

—Oh, Florian says. I thought you were interested in Amber.

—Cheerleaders are boring.

As Shaun saunters toward Xenie, Florian stares at the cassette. He worries that it won't be long before Shaun loses interest in their music or gets lured away by a more established band. While his mind races, he inserts his finger into the reel and spools the magnetic tape, as if he's fast-forwarding.

●

Xenie keeps her eyes pinned on the stage. The tall red curtains flutter, but it's only a roadie coming out to adjust the height of a microphone. He stands at the center of the stage, testing the sound levels by reciting numbers in a practiced monotone. His poker face gives away nothing about the band's status. The restless audience responds with stamped feet and clapped hands.

—How do you think they'll start the show? the boy standing next to her asks.

She recognizes Shaun. The blandly handsome boy with long hair who seems to know everyone.

—What do you think they have planned? he says.

Normally Xenie might be self-conscious, but she's been waiting all night for someone to ask her this.

—They'll play the songs off their first single, she says. Both the A-side and the B-side.

—Not many people know that one, Shaun says. It was never re-pressed.

—That's the point, she says. They'll do it for the fans who've been there since the beginning. I mean, that's what I'd do.

Shaun gives her an appraising look that she doesn't know how to interpret.

—So which do you like better? he asks. A-side or B-side?

—B-side.

—The song with the scrambled riff where they only sing the chorus once? he says. That's a weird one. You always go for the B-sides?

—Most of the time, she says. I kind of like songs that take time to figure out.

—I'm always trying to write A-sides, Shaun says. But when I'm listening, I prefer the B-sides. They're the tunes where the bands bury their secrets.

—Their obsessions, she says.

Xenie has more theories, but she's never shared them with anyone.

—I bet you have an interesting music collection, Shaun says, smoothing his hair out of his face. I'd like to see it sometime.

He says this casually, not like a come-on. She likes how he listens, likes the easy cadence of their conversation. Despite herself, she moves a little closer, intrigued by his faint aroma of spicy cologne and sour sweat. It's not a bad smell.

●

While Florian waits for Shaun to return, he remains on the lookout for the band's manager. Instead he spots Randy, a boy from school with a small sinuous frame and pointed nose who's rumored to have a nice drum kit. Randy cracks jokes while circulating through the crowd, passing out flyers offering deep discounts at the Broken Ear, the local record store. Florian half wonders if he should give the cassette to him.

There's a commotion by the side of the stage. A muscle-bound security guard manhandles a teenager with a nest of brown hair, levering his left arm behind his back. Florian recognizes the skinny boy who twists and flails as he's frog-marched out of the auditorium. The boy tumbles to the floor and before he can stand up, the guard kicks him in the stomach.

Florian breaks through the ring of stunned onlookers

and steps in front of his friend to shield him from further blows.

—You okay, Eddie? he asks.

Eddie tries to nod, but can't stop coughing.

Florian faces the security guard, a giant whose bottom lip twitches spasmodically.

—Out of my way, the guard says. I'm tossing him out of here.

—He's not going anywhere, Florian says. You fucking assaulted him. Everybody saw it.

The guard stares at him with blank fury.

—You going to assault me, too? Florian says. Come on. I'm right here.

The audience members encircling them mumble taunting threats. The ring of people thickens as fresh faces push forward, straining for a better view.

The guard curses and backs away into the crowd, which closes around him. Florian lets loose a long breath, then helps Eddie off the ground.

—Damn, Eddie says. That guy could've killed us both.

—What the hell happened?

Eddie stares at his shoes. I didn't have a ticket, so I snuck in through the back, he says. I walked through the backstage without anybody noticing. I was so close, then that goon grabbed me.

His conservative cardigan sweater and pressed jeans are impressively out of place here.

—It's my folks' fault, Eddie continues. You know how they are. I thought I hid my ticket pretty well, but they found it and ripped it up. There's no way I could miss this show.

Florian remembers Eddie's controlling parents, their unpredictable alcoholic rages, their violent suspicion of music. They scared him as a kid.

—Come on, Florian says. Let's stake out a better spot.

Eddie coughs violently into his hands and discovers bright red spots. He stares at his speckled palms. That's hardly any blood, he says, so softly it sounds like a regret.

●

The lights cut out. Every face in the darkened theater turns toward the stage. As the footlights slowly brighten, the five members of the Carmelite Rifles step into view, marching single file, each of them wearing a white ski mask. Armed with their instruments, they confront the crowd: The boy with the zigzag scar pressed against the lip of the stage. Randy tapping out a syncopated beat on his chest. Eddie perched on his tiptoes to get a better view. Florian studying the posture of the lead singer. Shaun ruminating on the significance of the sinister masks. Xenie widening her eyes and holding her breath. The auditorium is hushed, performers and audience suspended together in this still moment.

●

In the years to come, this concert will be recounted by the entire community as the apex of the Arcadia music scene. The boy with the zigzag scar will focus on the reckless intensity of the band's performance. Randy will rave about the abandon of the crowd who treated the songs as if they were their own. Eddie will remember the violence of the singer smashing his guitar and slapping his own face. Florian will recall the audience clambering onstage during the encore, the mass of bodies engulfing the band. Shaun will marvel over the set lists he found taped to the monitors afterward, and how none of them matched the show.

●

When Xenie will think back on the concert, she'll always replay the band's entrance, the audience stunned into silence, the atmosphere saturated with expectation. She'll wish she could remain in this moment of wild possibility, her senses dilated, forever on the cusp of the distorted ripple of the first note.

part one
THE
EPIDEMIC

Anybody can shoot anybody.

—LYNETTE "SQUEAKY" FROMME

It was as if I knew it was going to happen. A dull feeling of dread had been gathering. The signs were getting harder to ignore. At the end of my street, I discovered a drum kit at the bottom of an overgrown ravine. Piece by piece, somebody had hurled it down the steep precipice and abandoned it there. A bass drum, snare, and cymbals were scattered in the shallow streambed, surrounded by tangled vines, rocks, and fallen branches, subtly rerouting the flow of the rippling water. My first thought wasn't to marvel at the strange sight, but to wonder why the rest of the band's equipment was missing.

I told my boyfriend Shaun about it, but he didn't see any deeper significance.

—Xenie, he said. It's probably some angry kid who didn't like his birthday present.

—It looked expensive, I said. Like a set a pro might play.

Something about this image made Shaun laugh.

—Xenie, he said. Drummers are practically feral. The best ones aren't even housebroken. Maybe that's just the guy's new practice space.

I tried to shake it off, but I kept thinking about how much had changed in Arcadia since I'd met Shaun. Over the past three years, the economy tanked and the wheelchair factory shut down. The Carmelite Rifles moved away to cash in on their success, and it wasn't long before several of the city's best musicians followed their lead, betting their fortunes lay elsewhere. The scene's heyday faded like a dull mirage. Nobody was surprised when Arcadia's only record store closed its doors. Outside the Broken Ear, the owner left piles of records, cassettes, and compact discs free for the taking. Weeks after the locks were changed and the windows covered with construction permits, the stacks remained untouched, blackening in the weather.

The clubs were still doing business, but there wasn't much excitement now around the shows. Even longtime landmarks like Echo Echo lost some of their allure. The theater downtown rarely booked homegrown acts, and it was easy to understand why. Most local musicians had little ambition, low standards, less taste. The bands that used to stun audiences and rampage across the stage— Taconic Parkway, Jerusalem Crickets, the 40 Thieves— had all broken up. Their members branched off in dozens of musical directions, forming projects that felt increasingly detached from their origins, part of a family tree of mediocrity. Nobody in the scene played for any stakes. People still came together in the night to get drunk and share gossip and hook up, but the music mattered less and less.

Whenever we went to see shows, Shaun always did his best to cheer me up. The more boring the band, the more he got turned on. His fingers would begin the set massaging my shoulders. If the music got worse, they'd steadily work their way down my body. Sometimes we spent most of the night making out in shadowy corners of the club, working the buttons on each other's jeans. If the band was really dire, we'd sneak off to a secluded bathroom stall and create our own competing soundtrack.

I was collecting more music than ever on my computer, but I rarely listened to it. I realized I was getting more pleasure from amassing the files than actually playing them. I'd spend hours obsessively accumulating an artist's entire discography, then promptly forget about it for months. Whenever I managed to spin my newly acquired songs, they rarely came across as more than modest diversions. It was hard to make myself believe any of it mattered. More troubling, even my favorite music was barely able to hold me in its sway, its pleasures easily eroded by the world around it.

One afternoon, I carried my hard drive full of songs through the street to the ravine. I let the plastic device drop and watched it careen down the weed-choked embankment and crash into the creek below. The battered black rectangle rested at the bottom of the stream, surrounded by the rusted drum kit whose punctured snare drum was now a nest for a family of sparrows. Several open red throats peeked from the spiral of dried grass and bent twigs, waiting to be fed.

That night, I dreamed about a group of boys emerging out of the darkness, following a path through the woods, one after the other. The boy with the shaved skull. The boy with the scraggly beard. The boy with the black overcoat. They each held an instrument—bone flute, rattling gourd, stick strung with a single metallic wire. There was a strange determination to their lurching steps as if they were in a trance. As they came closer, it became clear that they were covered in mud. Their clothes and faces caked in the stuff. Or rather, it was blood. A wet redness that refused to shimmer in the dim light. It obscured everything except the boys' lidless stares. Their eyes were white orbs, the exact shape of the absent moon.

DAY ONE

Nobody paid much attention to the account on the news of the first killing, but it made me feverish with anticipation and dread. I felt dizzy as I listened to the report of what had happened hundreds of miles away. My forehead was dotted with droplets of sweat. Shaun couldn't help noticing how distracted I'd become. As we sat there together on the couch, I stared at the television screen long after he turned it off.

—Xenie, he said. Are you okay?

I tried to nod my head, but my body wouldn't respond.

—You're so pale, he said. What's the matter?

Shaun was genuinely concerned. He rubbed my cold hands, trying to stimulate some circulation.

I wanted to tell him, but I was overwhelmed by the multiplying images of violence rattling through my mind. The teenage boy walking into the local battle of the bands in the rented veterans hall and pulling out a handgun. He aims his shots squarely at the group onstage. The drummer tumbles backward off his stool. There's blood on the wall. Another bullet brings the lead singer to his knees. There's a hole in his chest, but he reaches toward the scattering crowd, arms extended, as if he's trying to say something.

I needed to be alone. I went upstairs and locked myself in the bathroom. I sat on the floor and waited for the unsettling visions to subside, then I turned on the shower. Usually I loved to sing while I washed. I'd belt out tunes, lyrics half remembered, the sound of my voice obscured by the rush of water and the echo off the ceramic tiles.

But this time, I remained under the pelting stream until it ran ice cold, until my fingerprints vanished in folds of puckering skin. I only opened my mouth to let it fill with water, letting it overflow, until it felt like I was about to choke.

The boy with long hair wakes with a shout, knowing something is wrong. His hand thrashes around, probably searching for a lamp, but the bedside table is empty. He sits upright and clenches the sheets in his fists. He remains motionless while his breath slows and his eyes adjust to the darkness. He's having trouble remembering something. He combs his brown hair out of his face. He's fully dressed in strategically ripped jeans and a vintage cowboy shirt. Even his high-top sneakers are laced.

He takes several wobbly steps toward the window. He stretches the kinks out of his trim frame, then slides open the curtains, but no light streams into the room. It's pitch black outside. Down below, the shadowy expanse of grass, the stand of overgrown boxwoods, and the outline of a concrete pathway creep into focus. His chin drops to his chest. Memory comes flooding back. Oh shit, he's late.

The boy with long hair turns on his cell phone, winces at the glowing display of the time, and makes a call. Nobody answers. He hangs up without leaving a message. For several moments, he stares into the corner of the room, as if expecting some shape to materialize from the shadows.

He spots a note at the foot of the bed. He cautiously

uncreases the paper. The handwriting looks like it was executed underwater. The dissolving letters form a name and street address. Some sort of reminder to himself. At the bottom, he's inscribed a set of circles, one inside the other, that resembles a target. He seems hypnotized by this increasingly tight series of spirals . . .

DAY
NINE

Bands were being shot in the middle of their performances all across the country. The noise duo at the loft party in the Pacific Northwest. The garage rockers at the tavern in the New England suburbs. The jam band at the auditorium on the edge of the midwestern prairie. The bluegrass revivalists at the coffeehouse in the Deep South. There was never any fanfare. The killers simply walked into the clubs, took out their weapons, and started firing.

Everybody was slow to call it an epidemic. They didn't want to believe these deaths were connected. I tried to discuss it with my coworkers at the diner, but they reacted with raised eyebrows and sideways stares, treating me like the customer who only ordered glasses of chocolate milk and claimed that birds were trying to communicate with him. They keep following me, he said. They never shut their filthy fucking mouths.

I kept my ideas to myself, even though it was clear that the killers weren't acting in isolation. It was as if they'd all been infected by the same idea. They seemed to be obeying the same subconscious marching orders.

Somehow I knew each act of violence was a prelude to another. The night before each new shooting, I'd find myself closing the curtains throughout the house and pacing figure eights in the bedroom carpet without understanding why. These events seemed like something plucked from my most disturbing daydreams. Whenever I thought about the bodies of the dead musicians, my mind went blank.

Was there some kind of message?

I blew the dust off my old tarot deck. I laid a black cloth on the kitchen table, cut the cards, and arranged them. Each arcanum was illustrated with lurid gothic lines. No matter how many times I shuffled them, I was always confronted by the catastrophic image of the Tower, lightning striking a stone structure, fire leaping from the windows, human figures tumbling through space. It felt like a spell had been cast, giving shape to something formless floating in the air. Part of me worried that somehow I had unleashed it, as if I had accidentally uttered an incantation in my sleep.

The boy with long hair stumbles from the darkened bedroom into a narrow hallway. He lurches past the entrance to the bathroom and flicks a switch. A bare bulb illuminates the worn shag carpet, the old framed photograph, the faded red wallpaper. The walls seem sprayed with a disorienting pattern of violent splotches. Only on closer inspection do they reveal themselves as miniature roses, each interlocking petal intricately etched.

He starts down the staircase and trips on the first steps. Catching himself on the banister, he slows and descends one tentative step at a time. The ground floor of the house is dark. The only sounds are the hum of a distant dishwasher and the squeak of his sneakers across the wooden floorboards. As he navigates the living room, he narrowly avoids banging into the exercise bicycle. He unlocks the front door and sets foot in the yard. The beat-up sedan at the curb beckons.

The boy with long hair slides into the driver's seat and slaps himself in the face. His eyes flare to life as his cheeks redden. He turns the ignition, revs the engine, and peels into the empty street. The floor is scattered with CDs, but he doesn't put on any music. He rolls down the windows and lets himself be enveloped by the sounds of the night.

As he coasts downhill, swerving through a succession of dimly lit side streets, he consults the note with the address.

He arrives at a cul-de-sac lined with bungalows whose yards alternate between barren dirt patches and knee-high weeds. The car skids to a halt in front of a white stucco house. The front porch is bowed by a molting leather couch. Splintering planks are nailed across one of the windows. The porch light secretes a gauzy malarial glow. The boy sprints up the overgrown walkway and slams his fist against the front door, beating out an enigmatic rhythm . . .

DAY
27

The expressions of the national news commentators and expert consultants remained stubbornly blank as they speculated on the causes of the killings. What motivated the violence? Why were musicians the only targets? Why was it only happening in smaller venues?

The black metal band ripped apart by an automatic rifle in the basement of a scuzzy rock club. The psyche-delic band expertly picked off from the balcony of the ren-ovated movie theater. The hip-hop collective shot at close range at the sweaty warehouse show. The female punk rockers massacred in the college town's most cel-ebrated venue. The Afrobeat ensemble murdered when a grenade was rolled onto the stage of the international cen-ter. The indie rock show that turned into a blood-soaked melee in the cramped confines of a suburban house show.

Few of the bands were familiar to me. They were mostly small-time acts, locked in their own communities, but their names briefly became national headlines with photographs of the crime scenes serving as their publicity shots. It was always gruesome. Immobile bodies contorted in unnatural poses, instruments spackled with gore, the stage covered in dark pools that resembled bottomless shadows.

I warned Shaun about the killings, and he promised never to do anything reckless. He seemed to take it seriously, at least for my sake, and I wanted to believe him. But I could also tell he was more focused on his latest band, which was starting to make a name for itself in town. He and his bandmates sat in our living room for hours tweaking the mixes of their upcoming single and listening to demos of their latest tunes. They pored over maps as they plotted a tour itinerary, eager to take their music beyond the confines of Arcadia.

His bandmates were even more cavalier about the danger. I guess Shaun liked to surround himself with people willing to say the things he never wanted to speak aloud—those guys thought they had it all figured out. They were smug in their easy theories:

—The killers are just frustrated musicians.

—The killers are just settling personal grudges.

—The killers just got tired of post offices and schools and started shooting up rock clubs.

Over the next few weeks, I tried to block out the violence and made a point of avoiding the news. The first killings were terrifying, but as they gained momentum my reaction started to change. I saw it. There was a pattern. An idea behind what the killers were doing. I could feel their thoughts buzzing. I could almost trace the shadow cast by their actions.

Everyone at the diner had become swept up in the epidemic, arguing about the latest tragedy, stunned and tearful as the body count mounted. I was surprised that I never cried or watched the memorials or read about the victims. I was scared, but I had to admit it—part of me wanted the epidemic to continue.

The boy with long hair keeps knocking until somebody inside the house stirs. A woman cracks the front door just enough so that he can make out her green eyes and pinprick pupils. She squints at him as if looking through a rapidly rotating kaleidoscope. Nobody's here, she says.

—I've come for the package, says the boy with long hair.

—Johnny's already gone.

—I know I'm late, the boy says, but he said he got the delivery. I'm sure he left it. He knows I need it for tonight.

—He didn't say anything.

—Let me in and I'll look for it myself.

—Nobody's here.

—Look at me, says the boy. Do I seem like a guy who's going to cause trouble?

He pulls back his long hair to showcase his good looks, cherubic cheeks, long lashes. He adds a wink and a wolfish smile. The door slowly swings wide, and he comes face-to-face with an emaciated young woman with stringy brown hair. She's wrapped inside an enormous jacket with cascading leather fringe. Her sole reaction is a quavering fish-eyed stare.

—There isn't any left, she says.

—I'm not here for drugs, says the boy.

—You can't tell Johnny that I took them all.

—He'll never know.

The boy with long hair dashes past her and into the nearest bedroom. The stale air reeks of pot smoke. Algae scum floats across the top of a half-filled fish tank. He rifles through the piles of paper, stencil drawings, cutout images on the desk. Yanks open the dresser drawers. Crawls through the closet, frantically patting his palms along the floor. Flips over the mattress. On the coiled metal springs, he discovers a square cardboard box . . .

DAY
81

The city meeting didn't generate any solutions. Council members read carefully worded inconclusive statements, police officers offered commonsense safety tips, frightened parents shouted demands over one another. Nobody could figure out how to ensure the violence wouldn't spread to Arcadia. It was proposed that all concerts within municipal limits be temporarily suspended, but the plan was voted down. Motions for stricter security measures were passed, but it wasn't clear who was going to pay for them.

I stayed home that night. Shaun was at practice at the Bunker, hanging out and drinking with other musicians, and I wanted to be by myself. I looked through my records, running my fingers along the spines of the albums that had survived my recent purges, the remaining collection of genuine rarities and profound favorites that I'd accumulated over the years. I read their titles as if they fashioned an autobiography.

I hadn't been listening to much recently, but tonight I

needed something. I pulled out a record whose enigmatic cover featured two women in black housecoats and red scarves standing against a brick wall. They leer at the camera, almost leaping out of the photograph, their teeth smeared with red lipstick. I bought the album as a kid from someone selling a pile of them at the flea market and its tumbling rhythms, whiplash riffs, and shouted lyrics never failed to shock me out of my malaise. I put it on the turntable and slipped on my headphones. I steadily cranked the volume until the sound swelled inside my head. Until the song felt bigger than I did.

I reached the moment when I usually shut my eyes and started to sing. The music was always too loud to hear myself, but I would feel my voice vibrating in my throat and continue until I'd scraped my vocal cords raw. It was my ritual against the world.

But this time, I didn't feel inspired to even move my lips. The power of music had been steadily disintegrating, and now I realized the remaining scraps had started to curdle. As I stood alone in my bedroom, my headphones boring into my temples, there was a feeling of something rotting in my chest. Maybe whatever infected the killers had also infected me.

The boy with long hair hesitates before reaching for the cardboard box. He looks up at the hunting trophy mounted on the wall. The stuffed deer head meets his gaze, the glass eyes embedded in the animal's sleek brown fur staring with a fixed expression. It might as well be determination. The boy lifts the box and turns it in his hands. It's properly heavy, and the contents shift when he gives it an exploratory shake. He cracks open the top and peers inside.

—Found it, he shouts.

—I don't know, the woman says.

—It's okay, the boy with long hair says. I already paid for it.

—I don't know.

—Don't worry, he says. Nobody's here.

The boy hurtles down the walkway with the package tucked under his arm. The front door remains wide open, and a hazy light spills onto the empty porch. It forms a fuzzy rectangle that resembles a stain. The woman is nowhere to be seen.

He springs open the trunk of the car and places the package inside. Before he shuts it, he rummages through an assortment of shabby towels and folding chairs. He heaves them onto the ground, then stares into the emptiness. Something is missing.

As the boy drives away, he steers with one hand and dials his phone with the other. Nobody answers. He hangs up again without leaving a message.

He checks the time and curses. Shaping his hand like a gun, two fingers for the barrel and thumb as the hammer, he points it against his temple. His foot applies more pressure to the accelerator, maintaining his speed through several red lights. Eventually he's forced to stop behind a stalled semitrailer truck. He slams his palms against the steering wheel.

—I'm coming, I'm coming, he says . . .

DAY
100

There was a shooting at a concert across the state border. It was less than an hour from Arcadia. Emergency bulletins cut into regularly scheduled radio broadcasts. Staticky details about stampeding crowds. Reports of the drummer slumped over his kit, the singer's hemorrhaging body draped across a screeching amp. Speculations that there were several killers working in tandem, stashing weapons in the bathroom before the show. Interviews from the scene were ghosted by a muffled soundtrack of screams, sirens, sobs.

We heard the news as we were driving to see a show in another town, going to support one of Shaun's musician friends. I begged him to stop the car and turn around. I was terrified that I might lose him, the one person I loved, my deepest connection to this rotten planet.

I got out of the car and stood on the shoulder of the highway, staring into the blinding lights of oncoming sedans, feeling the ground rumble as container trucks careened past.

—You've got to cancel your show, I said. Postpone it. Whatever. You can blame me. Tell the guys I've gone mental. Tell them I'm a crazy fucking bitch. Tell them I don't have any family and you're the only person I've got left. Just don't do it.

I felt myself winding tighter until I could barely breathe.

—Promise me, I said. Promise you won't play any shows until this is finally over.

He held out his hand and stroked my face. His touch was always so gentle.

—You're so scared, he said. I didn't realize how much this had gotten to you. Is that why you won't help us out? Sing backup on a few songs?

I turned away and walked along the thin margin of grass next to the edge of the road. Somehow he didn't understand any of this. He even refused to accept that I didn't want to sing. No matter how many times I told him, he couldn't get it through his head.

—Come on, Xenie, he called after me. You know our first single comes out in a few weeks. It's important to me. I need to get out there and promote it.

—You're acting like you had a lobotomy, I shouted, but my words were carried away in the gusts of passing traffic.

Shaun came up behind me and wrapped me in his arms. It felt good to be held so tightly against his body, to be enfolded in his familiar smell. Despite myself, I felt safe.

When we got back in the car, he adjusted the radio until he tuned in to a station playing music. I used to think songs sounded best through trebly car speakers, the windows rolled down, the air rushing through the vents. Now the music didn't sound like anything. The melody was indistinguishable from the drone of the motor, the whine of the tires, the hiss of the wind. The suffocating noises of the world.

The boy with long hair speeds past a weathered mural. Its peeling letters announce he's entering Arcadia. The scenery shifts to a shimmering strip of clubs and restaurants. Rows of parked cars choke the narrow streets. People feed parking meters and couples bicker in crosswalks. Klatches of smokers loiter outside bars, their feet surrounded by halos of extinguished butts. On the edge of the neighborhood sits a theater whose half-lit marquee makes it difficult to decipher tonight's main attraction. Nobody is out front. The show must be under way.

The boy stops across the street at a red light. He watches as a woman throws open the doors of the theater and tumbles headfirst onto the pavement. She lies there rasping, her skirt ripped up the calf seam, her face a mask of glistening mascara. The woman pulls herself up and starts to run. She barely avoids the base of a nearby lamppost as she sprints along the sidewalk. She vanishes in the shadows, but appears under the next light, running just as fast. She reappears in the pooled light of each lamppost, materializing and evaporating, a frantic apparition.

The traffic signal turns green, but the boy keeps

watching to see if someone will pursue the woman or others will flee the venue. Nothing happens. He drives through the intersection, turns down the alley next to the theater, and pulls into a handicapped space by the loading bay.

After grabbing the cardboard box from the trunk, the boy ascends the groaning metal staircase to the theater's back entrance. He pounds on the rusted door.

—Surprise delivery for the band, he shouts.

There's no reply. He stares at the pattern of rust that's corroded the center of the door. The raised red flakes form a teasing shape, something exotic and sinister, that he can't quite place. He kicks the door so furiously that the metal rattles in its frame. Then he calmly steps back.

—Need a signature, he shouts.

The door creaks open. A young man with a blue Mohawk leans out. His face snaps into a grin. So you finally decided to grace us with your presence, he says.

—I'm always worth the wait, the boy with long hair replies.

They walk through a shadowy backstage storage area filled with stacked risers and monolithic speaker towers. The familiar bass line of a song by the 40 Thieves, one of the founders of the local scene, echoes from the auditorium. They bob their heads in time to its jagged syncopation as they spring up the concrete steps to a modest suite of dressing rooms. The band lounges on a sagging yellow sectional, fitfully draining beers from a nearby cooler. They make a point of barely glancing at the new arrival.

—I don't see your guitar, a guy with a curly black beard says.

—I swear I had it in the car, the boy with long hair says. Someone must have borrowed it.

—Fabulous, the bearded guy replies.

—I'll use one of yours tonight, the boy says. I've got something more important right here.

He produces the cardboard package and tears off the top. It's a box full of records. The label at the center of the disc displays the image of a disemboweled panda lying in a pile of bamboo leaves. Blood trickles between its bared teeth.

—Our first single, the boy with long hair says. Hot off the press.

The band gathers round the parcel. They reverentially remove copies of the record, tracing the lines of artwork with their fingernails, inspecting the vinyl discs between their palms, unconsciously nodding their heads in time to the riffs still locked inside the pristine grooves.

They're interrupted by a middle-aged man whose yellow staff shirt barely contains his bulging belly. Everyone's waiting, he says. Get onstage already. He swivels and glares at the boy with long hair. How'd he get in here? I told you everybody comes through the main entrance and gets frisked. His hands pantomime a choke hold aimed at each of the band members in turn, then he exits the room.

While everyone else stows their personal effects and gathers their instruments, the boy with long hair ducks into the tunnel to make another phone call. Nobody answers, but this time he leaves a lengthy message. He presses the phone against his lips. Although there's an urgency to his tone, his voice doesn't rise above a whisper.

The bearded musician shoves a battered Gretsch hollow-body guitar into the boy with long hair's arms. This'll have to do, he grunts. As the others file in beside them, the band promenades together down the tunnel, the noise of the crowd intensifying as they approach the stage . . .

TODAY

Somehow the epidemic didn't scare anyone in Arcadia away from the concert. Maybe fear was even spurring ticket sales. For the first time in ages, the best local bands were being showcased on a big stage. For Shaun, it was the spotlight he'd been craving. There were stories on the radio and in the local paper. One even featured a photograph of him, his face playfully obscured by his beautiful long hair.

Shaun knew I was upset, but he refused to drop out of the show. He tried to make it up to me with gifts. He bought me a single by a beloved soul singer, which I'd been trying to locate for years. I shattered it with the sole of my combat boot. He bought me an enormous bouquet of roses. I ground them up, one by one, shoving them bloom-first down the garbage disposal. I worried that I was on the verge of cracking up, and my freak-outs were upsetting Shaun. But I had to get through to him.

We stood together in the kitchen, the walls frescoed with shredded rose petals. I rolled up his shirtsleeve and ran my index finger along the scar on his wrist. The residue of a painful period before we met.

—We promised each other we wouldn't ever try it again, I said.

He traced the raised pink line of flesh that ran the length of my wrist as well.

—It's not the same thing, he said. If I thought this was dangerous, I wouldn't do it.

He kissed my neck.

—I can't stop performing because of a bunch of psychopaths, he said. I've been waiting months for this gig. It's sold out. All those people are coming to hear me.

—Don't worry, Xenie, he added softly. There'll be extra security. It'll be fine.

I tried my hardest to believe him, but the morning of the show, I was tormented by images of the killer's preparations. Descending the staircase to a basement filled with mementos of dead parents. Kneeling on a mildewed carpet to clean the weapon. Lining up an assortment of toothbrushes, rods, oils, and solvents. Inhaling the stinging smell of ammonia. Disassembling the guts of the handgun while softly chanting the names of the mechanical parts. The frame, the slide, the barrel, the chamber. Listening to the series of clicks as the pieces fall into place.

The houselights dim as the band climbs onto the rear of the stage. As they walk through the red curtains, the boy with long hair catches a fugitive glimpse of the audience massed shoulder to shoulder, their charged faces hovering above the edge of the platform, fervent eyes leveled in his direction.

It might be nerves, or nausea, or simply excitement that causes a tremor to ripple through his body. His shaky hands plug in the guitar, switch on the hand-painted green amp, and fine-tune its dials. He measures his steps until he's positioned precisely two paces behind the microphone. His feet register the energy pulsing across the stage and chart the placement of each support beam. He senses the resounding hollowness of where he's standing. If he stamped hard enough, he's certain he would fall straight through the floor.

As the band arranges themselves, the bearded musician shouts into his microphone. Hello Arcadia, he says. Great to be playing for a hometown crowd. He's interrupted by a scathing torrent of feedback, brought on by the bass player adjusting his levels.

In the ensuing silence, the Mohawked drummer taps his sticks together. Hey Shaun, he says. You ready?

Shaun nods. He clears his throat and bashfully mumbles in the microphone:

—This one is for Xenie.

The drummer counts off. The music swells as bass and lead guitar fall in behind the beat. The stage lights flash on. They're blindingly bright, but Shaun leans directly into them. He juts out his chin until he can feel their warmth. His vision is a swarm of bleached spots. The stage shrinks around him. The audience seems to have vanished, but then there's a surge of applause.

Shaun flings his arms open and starts to sing. Theatrical flashes of anger animate his face as he unfurls the verses. A keening rattles his throat and rushes out his mouth. His serenely ragged voice fills the cavernous room. He must be consumed by the moment because he doesn't notice the scene playing out a few steps offstage.

Behind the hem of the curtain kneels a boy with a pink zigzag scar on his cheek that looks self-inflicted. He wears a yellow staff shirt and a child's pointed birthday hat. Plunging a hand into a long cardboard box, he pulls out a rifle and hoists it against his shoulder.

The band is heading for the bridge when the first shot is fired. Shaun collapses, his body crashing to the floor, though the impact is little more than a flutter through his bones. Everything onstage shifts sideways, and his head feels like it's filling with bubbling water. When he tries to speak, the words taste like copper. There are more shots, but the noise fades as the bubbles in his head multiply and rush to the surface. This surging evanescence crowds out other sensations until the sound starts to disperse and it's impossible to tell if what he's hearing are the volleys of gunfire, or the residue of music, or merely the ringing of his own ears.

The first dead body I ever saw was in a parking lot. We stood over it and sang.

We arrived at the supermarket at dusk and headed toward the crowd at the far end of the lot. People were huddled in a circle, holding candles. Aunt Mary had been talking about the body and its tragic death the entire time we'd been walking. I dug in my heels and refused to go farther. I was maybe five years old.

—Xenie, she said. This is important.

I didn't care.

—There will be music and singing, she said.

I didn't want to sing.

—Don't be scared, she said.

Aunt Mary tried to distract me by pointing out a flock of birds pouring from the sky into a single tree. She said, Do you ever wonder why they're all gathering together like that?

I didn't answer.

Aunt Mary coaxed me closer to the crowd. A few people held up signs, and a couple clutched fresh flower bouquets. Everyone stood around the body. Aunt Mary had talked about a young man, but there was only a chalk outline. The arms and legs were spread wide. Inside the lines were dark splotches, like someone had rubbed red into the asphalt. I tried not to stare at the bits of hair and congealed clumps. There was less to a dead body than I had imagined. Maybe it had been absorbed by the ground, and the chalk marked the edges of a trapdoor it had vanished through.

Behind us, several musicians with beat-up horns and guitars began to play. It was a slow song that made the air feel heavy. People started to whisper the words, then sing them softly to themselves, as if they were afraid of puncturing the sadness.

Each time the song reached the end, it would restart. Each time, people's voices grew louder and their wet eyes shined. The sad song seemed to lift something chained inside everyone's chests. My aunt put her hands on my shoulders, coaxing me to join in.

I keep thinking about that parking lot. I remember how I didn't want to sing, how the tune was an itch in my skull. I remember when I finally opened my mouth, people's faces slowly turned in my direction. I remember they came up to me afterward with a startled look in their eyes.

They said: You have a beautiful voice.

part two

THE
ECHOES

To the novice, the voices of the dead sound like static. It takes a patient ear to discern their musical murmurings, which resolve with infinite slowness, like the notes in a strange and shimmering chord.

—VIVIAN DARKBLOOM

chapter one

THE ERASED

IT'S HARD TO TAKE ALL THIS SILENCE. The concrete corridors of the Bunker remain empty. Familiar practice rooms are mixed throughout the rows of storage spaces, but there are no mobs of musicians squatting in the halls, sharing flasks and six-packs, tuning guitars and tinkering with effects pedals. No raunchy gossip filtering through clouds of sweet-smelling pot smoke. No muffled feedback and sputtering grooves permeating the warehouse's passageways. There are only rows of wooden doors chained shut with rusty padlocks. Pools of brackish water collecting from unseen leaks. The stale stink of fermented socks. The Bunker is now a ghost site where even the ghosts seem half rotted. Its hallways are haunted by a solitary presence, a tall and gangly boy who grips the sides of a trash can with both hands. He can't seem to stop vomiting.

Florian spits out a final mouthful of spew. He feels ambushed by the tidal wave of nausea. It's left him light-headed and queasy, but it's not as serious as it looks. Even in his early twenties, he still walks with a storklike gait that makes it seem as if he's a few steps from toppling. He continues down the main loop of the Bunker, avoiding the labyrinthine passageways that veer off like tributaries. He pauses at a couple of practice spaces, spying through the gaps in the crumbling yellow foam that serve as soundproofing. If he peers long enough, the darkened rooms reveal their shapes: the billowing tapestries tacked to the walls and the instruments arranged on cast-off Oriental carpets emerge from murky memory. But when he tries to imagine the particular sounds of the musicians—

I can't hear anything. There's too much quiet.

He continues down the corridor until he reaches the room where Shaun's band used to rehearse. It's remained off-limits since Shaun was murdered and the other members seriously wounded. Florian has avoided coming here for months, dreading this final confirmation of his friend's death. He's been encased in a haze of depression, his waking hours smothered by a pervasive grayness, his nights stricken by vivid dreams. The rehearsal door, draped in cascading folds of shiny black fabric, reminds him of a casket.

•

Florian tries not to think about the farce of Shaun's funeral, a theatrical spectacle mobbed by ghoulish strangers who barely knew him. They had drifted apart in recent years. After the bassist of the 40 Thieves persuaded Shaun to join his new band, they only spoke when they ran into each other at shows. Florian didn't know whether it was guilt or love that spurred him to wade through the crowds, past the mayor and city council members, to attend the service. He tried not to focus on how everyone seemed obsessed with positioning themselves as close to the wooden casket as possible, performing some perverse pantomime of public grief. He managed to sit through the severe hymns that reminded him of the tunes his mother used to sing. He struggled to block out the sermon, which sounded like it was written for somebody else. The minister kept stumbling over phrases, perhaps sensing they weren't right, deepening the disconnect. Halfway through, Florian fled the church to find sanctuary in the bar across the street, figuring that while getting blind and blackout drunk in his old friend's name wasn't much, it was still a more fitting memorial.

•

Next to Shaun's rehearsal-room door, a newspaper is tacked to the wall. Beneath the local headlines about a possible chemical plant closing and a high school football victory in overtime, there's a collection of mug shots of the epidemic's most notorious assassins from across the country. Florian is surprised how many he recognizes by sight. The harelipped boy in the baseball cap who shot the cowgirl singer between the eyes. The bronzed surfer boy who sprayed a spastic volley of bullets at a costumed cover band. The skinny boy who sprang onto the night-club stage and stabbed the R & B diva. The freckled girl who blew apart the stoner rock trio in the historic audito-rium, then sat backstage to wait for the cops. The dread-locked boy with the backpack full of explosives who stood listening to the street-fair musicians play songs about an endless summer. Somebody's stuck this paper here in an infantile attempt at a transgressive gesture. Next to it, in what looks like black lipstick, they've scrawled the phrase YOU CAN'T KILL KILL. Florian rips down the newsprint and balls it in his fist, but for some reason he can't bring himself to throw it away.

●

Florian's face is twisted into an odd strangulated shape. He has a simian brow, but his minuscule eyes simmer with intelligence. His large expressive mouth seems to conceal a perpetual secret. Essential components of his onstage charisma. His band has been invited to headline a gig at Echo Echo, which has been shuttered since the shooting. It's a special concert to try to resuscitate the Arcadia music scene. An opportunity to pay a worthy and genuine trib-ute to Shaun. If only it didn't mean placing himself in the line of fire. Soon the other members of Florian's band will arrive, and they'll have to make a decision. As he navigates the empty hallways to their rehearsal room, he listens to the lonely echo of his footsteps. The crumpled paper in his hand begins to itch.

I have to do something for Shaun.

A cockroach squirms on its back. Abdomen exposed, legs madly paddling the air. Florian feels a pang of kinship with the panicked creature. He bends down and flips it over, waiting to see if the stunned insect will regain its composure. Its antennae gingerly probe the air, then it scurries away, vanishing beneath one of the countless darkened doors.

●

Florian sits in his usual wooden chair in the rehearsal room, unfolds the newspaper, and places it on a music stand. He isn't sure why, but he needs to take a better look at the smudged faces of the killers. Most people believe the epidemic has fizzled out, but Florian worries more murderers are out there. He can taste the sour residue of stomach acid as he stares at these steely portraits. Each one looks straight past the camera. Fish have more animated eyes.

●

The most disturbing face is the killer from Arcadia. The boy with the zigzag scar, wearing a child's birthday hat, who stood in the wings of the theater and fired his semi-automatic rifle until he'd shot through his ammunition. It happened only a few blocks from here. At his arraignment, with serene and unshifting eyes, the killer faced down the injured audience members, maimed musicians, next of kin. He pled not guilty, claiming extenuating circumstances, giving a rambling speech that few bothered to follow, something about how he felt assaulted by the difference between the music he heard in his head and the music he heard onstage. How the musicians had unleashed something contaminated and contagious upon the audience. He informed the jury: I acted in self-defense.

●

The Arcadia shooting was only a sliver of the national epidemic, but the tragedy still sank bone deep. The local imagination was stained with its own particularized images of tear-choked faces, victims in bloody T-shirts slumped on the sidewalk, blaring rows of ambulances rushing to the theater, columns of helmeted officers brandishing shotguns and creating a perimeter. There were sprawling memorial services, traumatic school assemblies, swarming influxes of professional grief counselors. A few national journalists flew in to file stories, but mostly the town was left to mourn alone. Its nightmares went unreported, children and parents screaming themselves awake in the chill of the night, their bodies wound in sheets they'd started to rip apart. After a few weeks, a shrine for Shaun spontaneously materialized at the site of the shooting. A teeming assemblage of photographs, homemade scrapbooks, handwritten testimonials. *You warped my life in the best ways. Your music will always live on. Your blood is the truth. It was a lucky shot. Stop playing dead. Please watch over us.* And there were bouquets of roses. Always roses. The scentless kind wrapped in plastic, bought from the bodega down the street. Behind the shrine, the theater sits empty on the edge of town, cordoned off like a collapsed mine shaft.

●

A few weeks ago, Florian was unable to sleep and seized by a compulsion to contribute to the shrine. He wanted to place something personal among the sentimental trash piled up by strangers, a totem his dead friend might actually treasure. He arrived at the theater in the obscure hours of the morning carrying a cassette of the first songs that he and Shaun wrote together as kids in his bedroom. In those days, they shared a method for judging music: the more times a song used the word *love*, the worse it was. As an inside joke, every song on this tape was a love song. Florian slipped the cassette between a teddy bear and a row of votive candles. Even partly obscured, the violet cover stood out. As he walked away, those songs spun round his head, their naïveté almost profound. The recording is colored by Shaun's enthusiasm, his contagious conviction that all his friends were secret geniuses. The boys trade off vocals, sounding so young that Florian often forgets which voice belongs to which body.

I still remember all the lyrics: The words we say,
they never fade away.

Florian finds himself obsessively cleaning the rehearsal space. The room is four stark white walls, devoid of personal touches like posters and any adornments apart from a couple of chairs and a rectangle of industrial carpet slid under the drum kit. He collects the few stray candy wrappers and cigarette butts, then grabs the broom. He tries to get lost in the rhythmic whisk of straw across the concrete floor, the dispersal of the clouds of dust that settled during the deserted months. When he reaches the far wall, he listens for some sign of the man who rehearses on the other side. Nobody in the band has seen him, but their schedules are often synched. This solitary phantom has been the subject of much laughter and speculation. They imagine he works either as ticket taker at the shabby independent movie theater or stocks shelves at the lone electronics store. They've dubbed him the Shit-Faced Robot because he plays note clusters on an analog synthesizer that constantly tumbles out of tune. Florian hopes he'll be there today to distract them. He raps his knuckles against the partition, but there's only a feeble echo. The silence of the screechy soundtrack adds to his unease. Another yawning absence.

●

Randy the Mongoose enters with his usual greeting. Yo Flo, he says. And Florian replies: Hey Goose. Normally there's something comforting about this exchange, a shorthand developed several years ago when they formed the band, but today Florian finds it annoying. They haven't been together in this room for months, yet they're pretending it's just another practice. Florian knows he should put away the newspaper, that it'll probably piss off Randy, but he can't bring himself to remove it. Neither of them mentions the gig.

Randy the Mongoose believes there's no mystery to the epidemic, that the killers are a pack of chemically unbalanced psychopaths. He's repulsed to see their faces but doesn't comment on the photos. He refuses to get drawn into it. His bandmates gave him the nickname for his sinuous frame and pointed nose, though he likes to think it's equally deserved for his discreet cunning.

Randy sticks to the routine, heading straight for his drum kit, picking up his sticks, testing out a new pattern. He speeds up the tempo, slows it down, adds and subtracts beats, letting himself get lost in the particulars. He pauses to tune the drums, knocking his palm against the Mylar heads and progressively tightening the metal rods, evaluating the depth of each hit.

●

Florian picks up his electric guitar, strums the strings, and mumbles some phrases over a languid riff. Sounds bad. Reworks the riff and syncopates it. Sounds worse. Hums a wisp of a melody until it shimmers into shape. Sounds like something he'd make fun of another band for playing.

Every song he writes these days feels false. He lays the guitar flat across his knees and stares at the newspaper. The vacant expressions loom in judgment. All his friends call the killers *zombies*, but Florian worries they might be something even more disturbing, true believers in pursuit of some ideal they can feel but can't name. Perhaps they represent the true essence of the audience. He simply refers to them as *fans*.

●

Randy breaks into a drumroll. Their unspoken signal for Florian to add a riff and start jamming. The unofficial launch of rehearsal. Florian looks down at his guitar but can't even bring himself to plug in his instrument. This ritual they've built over the past few years suddenly seems empty. Randy initiates the drumroll twice more, but he doesn't acknowledge the cue. He's paralyzed by the memory of Shaun sitting cross-legged on the floor, patiently counting off the openings of their songs because Florian was forever coming in too late. He remains motionless. The beat goes on without him.

●

Florian feels his temples tighten. A telltale sign a headache looms. When he was younger, stress made his skin break out in red blotches that left him self-conscious. Now his body has escalated to crippling headaches, less visible but more damaging. He takes out a pill bottle and swallows several capsules to ward off the migraine. His mind is a mess these days. He can't process more than a few moments at a time. He scoops a sandwich off the card table. Roast beef and Swiss cheese on pumpernickel, freshly wrapped in cellophane. Can't even remember having bought it. Since Shaun's death, his inner and outer worlds keep slipping further out of synch, invisibly grinding against each other like continental plates. Every item in the rehearsal room is arranged in its customary place, but the space feels entirely alien.

The epidemic has ruined everything, but everything still seems the same.

Eddie, who serves as the band's unofficial manager, appears in the doorway. He stands hunched, pulling at the threads of his tatty cardigan sweater, his stare resolutely trained on his sneakers. It's a familiar posture that Florian recognizes as meaning that something is up.

—Echo Echo called again, Eddie says. We have to let them know today about the show.

He shares the latest information about safety precautions, reciting the litany of the club's promises. A crack security team comprising prison guards and war veterans. State-of-the-art metal detectors. The latest frisking techniques. His high-pitched stammer betrays a discomfort with the epidemic, as if even speaking about the violence might put the impulses back into circulation and start the killings all over again. He doesn't approve of this gig, but he's silent after his speech, channeling his energy into cleaning the fishbowl lenses of his enormous eyeglasses.

●

Florian doesn't want to be the first to speak. His thoughts are too tangled. He unwraps the sandwich and takes a bite. Revolting tang of horseradish. Still no memory of buying it.

●

No matter how close he looks at the photographs, he's unable to chip loose any warnings about the future, not the slightest sliver of portent.

●

He can't stop thinking about the emptiness of the eyes.

●

Uninhabited.

●

Whistled notes drift in from the hallway. They're followed by the casually pursed lips of Derek D., a recent addition to the group. The band dandy wasn't recruited for his punctuality or bass-playing abilities. He's reliable for his expertly mussed coif, impeccably rumpled clothes, simultaneously scuffed and burnished boots. This afternoon, he sports a shredded black bandanna round his neck.

—Everybody's here now, Eddie says. So you guys let me know.

It takes Derek D. a moment to figure out what he's talking about. The epidemic has made less of a dent in his psyche. Occasionally he parrots the pundit opinion that the violence in the music itself prompted the killings. Mostly, he shrugs off the entire thing.

—The show, Derek D. says slowly. I think people are feeling safer and they're ready for things to get back to normal. There's been a lot of talk. Everyone seems excited about it. The timing's finally right, you know?

Derek D. picks up his electric bass and briefly tests out a pose with it, plucking a few random notes without bothering to plug it in. Satisfied, he sets the instrument down.

—Yeah, he says. It's good exposure. I think it's a cool thing to do.

He adjusts his bandanna so the fabric lies flush against his throat, effortlessly slipping together into an immaculate knot.

●

Randy snaps on a sweatband to corral his unruly curls. He speaks up now that the first vote has been cast, choosing his words with caution, careful not to look at Florian or appear like he's trying to convince him. We should do it, he says. Show people we're not afraid. Stop those monsters from getting their way. And with Flo's connection to Shaun, we're the perfect band. It'll really mean something. We'll finally get heard.

·

Florian feels everyone's gaze focused on him. There's a ratcheting tension about the next words.

·

—I want to do something for Shaun, Florian says. But maybe this isn't the best way. Maybe it's not the right show.

He starts to pace. A few steps in each direction, trying not to be overtaken by his thoughts. His chin juts outward as if braving a stiff wind.

—We're not ready. We haven't practiced in forever, Florian says. It's too soon anyhow. People are still in shock. No matter how well we played, it wouldn't have an impact.

Randy and Derek D. remain silent. They're used to giving their bandmate's anxieties a wide berth, though it's clear from their furrowed expressions that they're having trouble believing him.

—We're hardly the first band the club asked, Florian says. There's a reason people have been turning this gig down. They don't think it's worth it.

Florian can sense his nausea returning. He quickens his steps and clasps his hands behind his back, compacting his elongated frame. Even walking in place, he feels himself losing ground.

—Those bands weren't scared, he says. They just weren't stupid.

The newspaper remains spread on the music stand, visible to everyone, the smudged faces peering from the print.

●

Florian scratches madly at his left forearm. His tattoo itches. The design is a stylized cursive depiction of the letter *J*. The first letter of his dead mother's name. Hard to believe she's been gone almost three years now. Florian called her Jean when he wanted to irritate her. His father called her Jeanie when he was drunk. Her friends called her Jet when they needed a favor. She acknowledged them all with a curt nod and forbearing smile. Her name was Jeanette. The bright emerald ink of the tattoo blurs around the edges as if spreading like mold spores beneath the skin. It would be typical of his luck if his protective talisman were slowly poisoning him.

I don't want us to play that day.
That day especially.

Florian scans the room and spots it. His electric guitar, propped against the chair, still unplugged. A black cable lies next to it, coiled in a loose circle, the silver connector splayed on the floor. It's the physical confirmation of all his objections. He can't believe it didn't occur to him sooner.

—Even if I thought the show was a good idea, he says. I couldn't do it. I don't have my amp.

His bandmates look increasingly ticked off. They don't bother to conceal the rolled whites of their eyes.

—You lost it? Randy says. You broke it? So we'll find it. We'll fix it.

—I lent it to Shaun's band. Don't you remember? They used it at the show. *That* show.

Randy is unmoved.

—So buy another amp, he says. Borrow one.

—It's a vintage tube amp, Florian says. I've spent hundreds getting it hand wired. The circuit is customized to distort at a lower volume. It's completely mine. It's my sound.

—You spend too much time chasing some tone that's half imaginary, Derek D. says, creasing his fingers through the back of his coif. My friends are always saying we get too complicated and lose the tunes. We should rock out more.

—Nobody cares about your trust-fund friends, Florian says, or their so-called musical opinions.

—They're the ones who come to all our shows, Derek D. says. So, you know, food for thought.

—Look, I'm sorry, Florian says. I can't do the show without that amp. It would be a disaster.

Randy stands up from behind his kit. He stretches his compact frame with studied casualness. He scratches his lower back with the splintering tip of one of his drumsticks.

—Fine, he says. Let's go get your amp.

Florian struggles to decrypt the undercurrent in

Randy's voice. He can't decide if he's bluffing. Nothing in the drummer's posture provides the remotest clue.

—That's impossible, Florian says.

—It's easy, Randy says. Most of the instruments are still at the theater. I heard the police didn't remove them all. We'll break in.

This time it's Eddie who interjects: We're going to steal it?

—Who's stealing? Randy says. It's our amp.

—I don't know about this, Eddie says.

—It's a tribute, Randy says. We'll be using our amp, which was briefly Shaun's amp, which will be our amp again, to honor them and their music. It's the best sort of homage. It's practically poetic.

The earnest inflection, the circuitous logic, and the hint of duty coalesce into an intoxicating sentiment that could justify any action. Before Florian knows it, the idea is engraved in the air.

●

—Okay, fuck it, Florian says. Let's go. I don't believe the amp is there. I don't believe any equipment is there. In fact, I don't even think we can break into the theater. But I'll humor you. I haven't had a good laugh in forever.

Randy and Derek D. head into the hallway without further comment.

Florian doesn't move. He sighs and shakes his head.

—Sorry, Eddie says.

Florian reaches out and takes Eddie's arm in a gentle

but complex grip, the kind of position he might use to form an unusual chord.

—Listen, he says, I need your help convincing these guys.

—I'm not a member of the band.

Florian isn't used to Eddie's oversize glasses. Ever since he got them, he's seemed withdrawn and secretive. His moods more camouflaged. Florian wishes he knew what his friend sees now when he looks through those lenses.

—Come on, man, Florian says. You're part of this. You're here because you've got more sense than those two combined.

—They're not going to listen to me.

—You just need to step up. Make yourself heard. Make them pay attention.

Eddie picks up the roast beef sandwich and notices the crescent-shaped bite. Someone's been eating my sandwich, he says. He inspects the scalloped arc of teeth marks as if these indentations might foretell the future.

●

The hallways of the Bunker are silent except for the fibrillating pulse of the overhead fluorescent lights.

●

Florian leads the procession to recover his amp, refusing to appear unsettled by the mission. The overcast sky presses down as they walk through the half-abandoned industrial park. They make their way up the hill to the theater, past the tire warehouse with its soaring towers of steel-belt radials, the perpetually shuttered art galley advertising open studios, the sheet-metal storage facility with the half-finished mural of a herd of deer, their lower halves nothing more than outlines, as if they're emerging from the bricks. Hands in pockets, the band leans their faces into the lashing wind. Everyone maintains his own brand of silence. Florian can feel the others psyching themselves up for the burglary. Their movements have become more skulking. Hyperaware of every sound. The slide of sweaty feet in sneakers. The ragged inhalations of breath. The asphalt road feels like an extension of the Bunker, part of the same circuit of wounds.

●

They pause at the railroad tracks. Florian used to hang out here with Shaun, pressing their ears to the metal lines, listening for oncoming trains. The soles of his sneakers register a distinct tremor relayed through the rail. Something is approaching, but he can't see any locomotive, not even the slightest shimmer on the horizon. Florian can't remember how long it's been since their games of chicken, seeing who could hold his ground long enough to make the engineer pull the emergency brake.

> Shaun always won. No matter how many times I tried,
> I could never match his nerve.

Randy whistles one of the band's tunes. Derek D. joins him with a harmony so brutally off-key even Eddie winces. A gust of wind shreds the song into rasping shrills and gasping tatters. As they crest the hill, the theater rises into view, emerging a few steps at a time. It looms like a beacon at the edge of downtown. The sight makes Florian's stomach churn. He tries to spit, but a squall knocks the saliva straight back into his throat.

●

Downtown Arcadia used to be well trafficked, but few choose to linger here now. The bodega does steady business selling flowers for the memorial, but the pizza parlor, the Indian buffet, and the twenty-four-hour coffee shop have permanently shuttered, and the sports bars are little more than darkened shells, desolate rooms with derelict pool tables and soundless televisions, the stools empty except for the staunchest regulars. The cement planters that line the sidewalks are overgrown with rude weeds. Even the trash cans seem forsaken. The band notices the heavy somnambulance that hovers over these blocks, the entire neighborhood suspended in a state of uneasy slumber.

●

The outside of the theater teems with thick shingles of ivy. The edges of the leaves are curled and blackened. Vines that once marauded across the walls have become limp and sallow; their rotting tendrils lie listlessly against the concrete. The town treats the theater like holy ground, but nobody wants to consider whether the rest of Arcadia is being poisoned by its purity.

●

Florian scoops up a handful of loose gravel from the street. He slings the rocks at the front of the theater, which remains encased in an intricate architecture of yellow police tape. The others follow suit, raining stones on the façade, pelting the oversize poster that warns this is a crime scene. A preemptive strike against this imposing structure. The band stands under the unlit marquee that's stripped of every bit of alphabet except remnants of the letter E. They try to determine the current state of the theater, but the windows are scabbed over with multi-color band posters, illustrated concert schedules, official venue announcements. Strata from an antediluvian era.

●

A patrol car rolls slowly past the theater. An officer glares at the band, which has swiftly adopted the pose of pilgrims here to pay respects. They pretend to be so absorbed by the shrine that they're oblivious to the authorities. As Florian combs through the latest contributions, he finds himself genuinely overcome by a photograph of Shaun with his long hair obscuring his face. In it, Shaun displays the same V-shaped gesture with each hand—the one closest to the camera extends the peace sign while the other offers the two-finger salute. This characteristic bit of mischievousness now scans as a more conflicted and complicated gesture. An unexpectedly profound portrait. The band stands before the image for several long moments, breath caged, throats dry. None of them notice when the cop rounds the corner.

●

The most conspicuous additions to the shrine are the folded sheets of paper left by fans. Most are scrawled with snatches of song lyrics. They were just another local band while Shaun was alive, but death has conferred an unlikely aura of importance upon them. Florian is amazed how Shaun's music suddenly radiates meaning for these strangers, their handwritten notes tucked in the crevices like prayers. In the corner, he glimpses the cover of the cassette he contributed to the shrine. Somehow, among this entire expanse of offerings, it's the only flash of violet.

Shaun was always obsessed with that color.

The only time Florian has seen this many mementos was at his mother's grave. The mound of remembrances that ringed her headstone in the old family cemetery. She still glides through his dreams, her pockets leaking birdseed, singing the same three notes in a halting rhythm, and he keeps forgetting she's gone, believing for a few tangible moments each morning he's waking into an unbroken world.

•

Jet, Jeanie, Jeanette.

•

Whiskey bottles line the shrine's perimeter like sentinels. Shaun's favorite drink. One bottle miraculously remains half full. An inviting tide of burnished amber. Perfect to fortify them for their task. Randy hoists the bottle and proposes they each take a swig.

—To the departed, he says.

He and Derek D. each take a healthy hit off the bottle.

Eddie refuses and waves it off. This whole thing is a bad idea, he says.

Last is Florian. His hands clamp the bottle like he's about to smash it, then he takes a longer throat-searing swallow than anybody else.

•

They turn down the alley that leads to the theater's loading bay. Eddie hangs back a few paces to watch for circling cops. One by one, they disappear around the corner and dash up the metal staircase to the rear entrance. Derek D. pulls on the door, tilting backward with all his weight, but it doesn't budge. Randy runs his fingers along the latch, but there's not even a lock to pick. Sealed from the inside, he says. Florian can't look away from the pattern of rust that's corroded the center of the door. Against the brushed steel, the accumulation of raised red flakes stands out as a distinct configuration. It reminds him of the contours of a remote atoll, or the outline of exotic blooming flora, or maybe the shape of a cancerous sarcoma invisibly spreading in the intestine.

●

There must be another way inside. They round the corner of the theater and walk past the row of boarded-up windows. Randy halts at the last one. Stepping closer, he inspects the piece of plywood from several angles. He places his hands on either side to ensure a steady grip and lifts the panel without the slightest resistance. The nails had been removed. It was simply propped against the sill. You've got the radar of a true thief, Florian says. You should be using your skills to steal us a van so we can tour. The band marvels at how the window frame has been cleared away. It's nothing more than a large hole. Florian stares into the beckoning portal.

> I hope the amp isn't here.
> The theater empty.
> The equipment gone.
> Nothing but dust and darkness.

The others climb inside, but Florian can't bring himself to cross the threshold. He unzips his fly. As he listens to his piss splash against the theater wall, something about the sound emboldens him to join his bandmates. He watches his urine flow away from the building, streaming down the cracked blacktop, branching into golden tributaries.

●

On the other side of the opening, they've landed in the theater's business office. Everything remains in its place, the perpendicular arrangement of metal desks, the red leather sofa, the framed silver records hung on the wall. Only the line of file cabinets has been incinerated. The metal is blackened and scorched. The drawers pulled out and emptied. Strewn papers blanket the floor. Over the door that leads to the lobby, someone has carved two words in welcome: KILL CITY. As they shuffle through a wake of charred receipts, contracts, and concert riders, the ashen scraps stubbornly stick to the bottoms of their feet.

●

The lobby is pitch black. The band's pupils are slow to dilate. They feel their way along the walls with their shoulders, stuttering a few steps at a time, until they reach the opening that leads to the auditorium. They've entered this room many times, but now they're met by silence. Gradually it gains texture. The wind rattling the roof tiles. The metal crossbeams sighing. The concrete support columns shifting. Florian can sense the ceiling rising far above. He recalls the theater's contours, but the space feels larger than memory. The massive soundboard stands next to them, shrouded beneath a black tarp.

Soft flap of wings. The band freezes as an unseen bird flies overhead through the auditorium. The flapping reverberates in Florian's mind, echoing so loudly through the empty space that he can hear the creak of gristle in its joints, envision the outstretched wings as large as helicopter blades, kicking up all the settled dust. The bird lands somewhere in the rafters, nestling into the patchy insulation. Florian tries to guess the species. Feral pigeon, mourning dove, sparrow hawk. He waits for it to sing, but the creature keeps its song to itself.

●

Deeper into the hushed chamber. The slope of the inclined floor feels unexpectedly steep. They descend through levels of increasingly strong smells. Spilled beer, stale sweat, musky piss. Faint note of mothballs. Undercurrent of incense. Their outstretched phones light the way. The scattered lumens catch snatches of beer cans, rat turds, hobbled barstools. Plastic wrappers clumped in weird hieroglyphs. It's impossible to tell where shadows end and walls begin. Unseen items crunch underfoot. Florian brandishes the whiskey bottle from the shrine like a protective talisman. He's afraid to shine his light through the rubble, to witness the true scale of the disaster, to confront an infinitely extending field of wreckage.

●

People have been here before them. Florian encounters a balled-up and still-soggy sweatshirt. A boom box ringed with freshly discarded batteries. Pizza boxes with grotty leftovers barely a day old. He pretends to not be spooked, but it feels like they've breached some inner sanctum, tomb raiders who arrived too late. He's shocked to discover an entire drama has been unfolding here in secret. He wonders whether this space has served as a hidden refuge for runaways, a tourist spot for ghouls engorged by the epidemic, or even a site of arcane necromantic rituals. Or perhaps it's simply that part of the Arcadia music scene was drawn here, the grief-choked core groping toward one another, seeking solace.

> *I should've known about this.*
> *I should've started something like this.*
> *I should've been here.*

They hoist themselves onto the stage. Somebody has stacked singles from Shaun's band, the label featuring the picture of a freshly disemboweled panda, in a wobbly tower. The vinyl is surrounded by a circle of votive candles. Wicks recently blackened. Tallow soft to the touch. A few steps farther, they encounter an archipelago of musical equipment. The police forensics team did its work on-site. The instruments, microphones, and monitors have been tagged, but they haven't been shifted since that night. Their positions now seem as inevitable as sculptures. Florian stumbles over a coil of cords. Before him, his vintage tube amp gleams, its surface hand-painted a livid emerald green.

●

Something stops the band from reaching for the amp. A noise emanating from backstage. The sound resembles static-tape hiss. Then, a throbbing exotic beat. Finally, it's revealed as the actual and unmistakable sobs of a human being. A sort of convulsive aria.

●

It's as if the wailing is trapped in the walls, embedded in the pores of the theater, broadcasting on a frequency to which they're only now attuned. The hiccupping cry becomes more strangulated and increasingly anguished. It transforms into something feral and furious. A lacerating howl that refuses to dissipate. Transmitting in ever-widening sets of ripples.

●

Through the billowing red curtains, a girl emerges at the back of the stage. Her face floats through the feeble light. Cheeks runny with mascara. Lips ensnarled. Eyes wild.

This bedraggled wraith stumbles a few steps forward, then stops as soon as she spots the boys. Each is bewildered by the other's presence. The band is unsure how to react.

—We should leave, Eddie whispers. Right now.

Nobody moves. The band has invaded a moment so private, it feels like they've managed to break into somebody else's dream.

•

The woman's features come into focus. Her skin is unusually pale, lunar and luminous. There's something coltish about her, from the enormous eyes to the flared nostrils. She cradles a white dress that resembles a uniform, except the skirt and sleeves have been shredded. The cuts look controlled, splitting the fabric into savagely even strips. At her side, she grips a steel paring knife. The boys' apprehensive reaction prompts her to examine these objects. The woman acts surprised to be holding them. She lets them both drop and they're swallowed by the shadows.

•

Florian finally recognizes the woman. The shaved sides of her head culminate in a messy patch of blonde hair. Her ramshackle style can't disguise her attractive features. The curves of her body are barely concealed beneath a baggy purple sweater. As she scrubs the mascara from her eyes with a few deft strokes of her palm, her face hardens. She teeters in place, arms hugging ribs, holding herself together.

Florian has known her for years from various shows and backstage scenarios where she typically kept to herself. He can only recall a handful of cursory conversations with her. There was always an unspoken static between them, and they steered clear of each other's orbit. They're the two people who knew Shaun best, and maybe that's what kept them apart. Even at the funeral, he didn't have an opportunity to offer his condolences.

She was Shaun's girlfriend.

●

Florian would like to ask Xenie about the shredded uniform and the paring knife, but he realizes this isn't the time. He hangs back in the deepest shadows of the stage and keeps his mouth shut.

—What are you guys doing here? Xenie says. Looking for mementos from the fallen rock star? Don't you know it's bad luck to steal from the dead?

She shapes fingers into tiny fists. Spittle collects in the corners of her lips. She's a mix of twitching vulnerability and truculent hostility. A startled doe with a foaming mouth.

—Or do you just get off on watching girls cry? she says.

●

Randy the Mongoose flattens his bristly hair and steps forward. We were Shaun's friends, he says. We all hung out in the Bunker. We played some of the same shows as his band. Eddie tugs at Randy's arm, trying to get him to back off, but he continues to talk. We came for that green amp, he says. Shaun and the guys borrowed it from us.

Xenie looks like she doesn't understand. She squints

in Randy's direction as if a clearer view of his features will fine-tune the translation of his words.

—You're fucking kidding me, she says.

—It *is* ours, Derek D. says.

—Just get out of here, she says. Leave me alone. Please.

●

Florian moves into the murky light, whiskey bottle clutched to his chest. He reminds himself Xenie's been more deeply affected than any of them and keeps his thoughts centered on Shaun. When he speaks, his voice is faint and frayed.

—I'm sorry, Xenie, Florian says. I was at the show. It was awful.

He can't tell how she's received his words. She looks down at her black boots and scours away the residue of makeup with the hem of her sweater. When she turns back to Florian, her resolute stare is utterly undone.

●

Florian looks closer. He's pierced by Xenie's dirt-encrusted purple sweater. This shabby item once belonged to Shaun. Her pained expression is also familiar, a battered reflection of his own emotions, and he realizes they might share more than he imagined.

—I keep having dreams about Shaun, he says.

—We were best friends when we were kids, he says, but the dreams are never about those times.

—I always see him singing the opening number from that night, he says. I hear the way his voice fills the theater when he gets to the chorus.

—Maybe you've been having those same dreams, he says.

> When I close my eyes at night, my hands shine
> with Shaun's blood.

Florian is confused by Xenie's reaction. She simmers with resentment. Taking a few tentative steps toward him, she thrusts her face forward and talks through bared teeth.

—Don't talk to me about that night, she says. Don't talk to me about that show. You think you know my dreams? You don't know anything about me.

—But I know something about you, she says. You wish you were the one who was famous. You're upset you didn't get shot in the head.

—Take your amp, she says. I don't care anymore.

Xenie flees the stage, her sprinting feet reverberating through the theater's unseen chambers.

●

Derek D. lets loose a high whistle. That's one cracked bitch, he says, half in contempt and half in amazement.

The others look away from Florian as he glares at the red curtain, its folds still rippling from her exit. Bitch is right, he mutters. He can't believe he felt sorry for Xenie.

He could never understand what Shaun saw in her. She's as arrogant as he always suspected.

—Come on, Randy says. Let's grab the amp and get the hell out of here. He picks up the vintage machine by the handle, grunting at its surprising weight.

Florian lingers on the stage. He kneels to pick up the paring knife and turns it over in his palm, testing the sharpness of the steel blade. A reminder of Shaun's penchant for collecting complicated friends. Outsiders who nurse a perpetual grudge against the world. Of course, *some* people take it too far.

He realizes the knife lies in the precise spot where Shaun stood that night. Florian raps his knuckles against the platform and is greeted by a hollow echo. There's a fissure in the floorboards and he presses his index finger into the hole, pushing straight through the stage, until he can almost touch the emptiness.

> *If Shaun was in my place, there would be*
> *no question.*
> *He'd play the show. He'd do it for me.*

The band retraces their steps, sticking to the rutted trails they blazed through the trash, their eyes focused on the glow produced by their phones. Florian follows their dim beacons through the darkness. He holds his breath through the waves of sickly smells. He wonders if the dust particles from that night could have fermented, becoming an airborne form of contagion.

—Hurry up, Randy shouts. His panicked words rebound against the walls, adding to the urgency.

The band finds themselves running, tumbling into the rubbish, dashing blindly toward the office. It's as if they've removed something load bearing that they fear will compromise the stability of the entire structure.

●

The unseen bird starts to chirp. A succession of notes without human inflection. Its song untranslatable.

●

As they slink down the sidewalk, a fresh contribution to the shrine flaps in the breeze. A colored-pencil drawing of the town's historic emblem: a stag in a meadow with a golden crown hovering above its antlers.

Across the street, a police officer stares at the band. He leans against a parked patrol car with his boots crossed, hands cradling his mirrored sunglasses, intently chewing gum. There's a sadness to his posture as he evaluates the boys, weighing his options, deciding whether they should be treated as potential thieves caught trespassing.

The band halts. Randy slides the amp behind his back. The others wait to see what will happen, but Florian marches straight toward the officer. You spare some gum? he asks. The cop hesitates, then puts on his mirrored sunglasses, concealing his eyes. He holds out a shiny foil pack. Florian removes a stick, unpeels the silver paper, and pops it in his mouth. He thanks the officer and heads down the street, not waiting for the others to fall in behind. Once they're out of sight, Florian spits on the pavement.

—I hate grape, he says.

His saliva has a violet tinge.

•

Florian shouts his name, but Eddie is nowhere in sight. He must have slipped away in the theater when things got awkward, Florian says, shaking his head as they cross the railroad tracks. He hates that sort of confrontation. He's too sensitive.

—I used to be that way, Derek D. says. My stepbrother was a bully and I was always hiding from him. I never stood up for myself. One day, he slammed my head into a metal door and ran away laughing. There was this huge gash and it bled like crazy.

He sweeps the hair from his forehead to showcase a faint sliver of scar tissue.

—I used my shirt to soak up all the blood, Derek D. continues. I held it against my head until the thing was drenched. Then I stuffed the bloody shirt under the covers of my stepbrother's bed so he'd find it that night and freak out.

Randy and Florian look startled by this revelation, but Derek D. continues in the same unflustered tone, as if he's reporting the weather.

—You don't have to fight, he says, but you do have to send a message.

●

As they enter the Bunker, Florian looks down at his hands and realizes he's no longer clutching the whiskey bottle from the shrine.

> *Maybe the memorials don't mean shit*
> *until we add our bodies to the pyre.*

Without discussing it, they set up for rehearsal. Florian wipes away the layer of dust from his amp before turning it on. It's no coincidence this machine and the tattoo of his mother's initial share the exact shade of emerald green. She was the only person he allowed to call him by his real name. He wonders what she would've thought about playing this concert. He shuts his eyes and tries to summon her words of advice. For a startling second, he hears it. Not his mother's words but her voice, not recalled but actually heard, that slight and lilting lisp.

●

Florian experiments with each of the amp's dials. There isn't one that can alleviate the weight of playing a worthy show for Shaun. His sound still isn't quite right, but there are no more settings left to try.

●

Nobody talks during the cacophony of tuning instruments and adjusting levels. Randy revisits the earlier drum pattern and slows it down, as if in a reverie. Derek D. refashions his bandanna to a rakish angle and experiments with half-remembered riffs from the last time they practiced. Their noises gradually intertwine, bathing them in a brace of dissonance. Florian detects something budding. He prowls the edges of the room, listening with eyelids shut and lips pursed. He increases the volume on Derek D.'s amp until the bass frequencies thrum through their bones. He taps Randy's cymbal with his fingers, prompting the drummer to play a terse martial rhythm. Florian launches into a hiccupping riff, his tall body twitching in time to the racket, channeling the sound like a conductor's baton. The barrage escalates, locked into an improbable groove, cresting toward an ecstatic din. At its peak, Florian wrings a series of keening phrases from his guitar. He lets the notes sustain, and drift, and slowly decay. He stops and signals Derek D. to wind down. Then he motions to Randy, who shifts into a decelerating drum-roll, escorting the wash of sound as it ebbs from the room.

●

Florian is encouraged, though he knows those moments are almost impossible to repeat. He unplugs his guitar and listens to the faint plink of raindrops against the Bunker's roof. They tap out an irregular rhythm, a spattering with sudden surges. A storm blows through the streets, past the empty theater, soaking the huddled contents of the shrine. Even nestled at the back, the cassette of Shaun and Florian's music won't be immune to the weather. The edges of the violet label will dampen and curl, warping the handwritten titles. Florian thinks about how fast things have changed. He's confident nobody would want to hear those tunes now. The epidemic has made love songs irrelevant.

> *The boy with the revolver enters the warehouse,*
> *winding through the labyrinthine hallways,*
> *past one empty practice room after another,*
> *tracking the source of the music.*

Florian walks over to the newspaper. He methodically rips up the assortment of mug shots, letting the fragments sift through his fingers and flutter into the trash can. One of the tattered images lands on the concrete floor. His band-mates are awaiting some word about the concert, but he can't bring himself to look away from the acne-scarred boy in the sweatshirt. The boy whose gun accidentally discharged and blew off his own foot before he could injure anyone else. Like a handful of other killers, this boy was a musician. The usual excuses for his violence don't seem to apply. He wasn't jealous of the band. He didn't feel left out. But still, his faraway stare is the same as the others'. Florian previously assumed this would-be assassin was acting out of blind idiot hatred, but now he wonders if maybe, like a few crackpots claim, the boy was motivated by some misguided love of music. He's transfixed by the boy's absolute inexpression. As he replugs his guitar into the amp, he's seized by a desire to translate what's behind those glassy eyes. He's haunted by a premonition that the concert will be meaningless until he can connect with the exact level of that fathomless blankness.

THE BIRDS

Daybreak. A solitary bird, perched in a grove on the edge of town, carries on a multipart melody. Three notes, each lower than the last, repeated in a halting rhythm. There are many songbirds in this area, but this one sounds like a sparrow. House sparrow? Russet sparrow? Parrot-billed sparrow? No, hold on, this bird is a white-throated sparrow. The creature puffs its breast and extends its chin. It unleashes a series of insistent trills. The song reprises with small variations, surges in volume and ornamental fillips. It's tempting to read some emotion into the furrowed yellow patches over the sparrow's eyes. Is she watching over her nest? Is she calling to her child? There's a long pause, an uninflected silence, maybe a calculated rest in the sparrow's composition. Then the song resumes its strange beckoning. If only there was some way to get inside these sounds, to use this music to send you a message of my own.

chapter
two
THE EQUALS

XENIE HEADS STRAIGHT FOR THE WOODS. She strides purposefully across the empty expanse of the theater parking lot. Her tears have evaporated, but her breath retains a slight wheeze. She tries to smooth her tufts of blonde hair and knock the crumbs from her crusty purple sweater. In the haze of twilight, she can barely distinguish the jagged tops of the trees ahead. She should stick to the streets, but it's quicker to cut through the forest on the edge of town. It offers the added benefit of being a haven for unstable homeless, the site of gruesome rapes, a dumping ground for stolen corpses. This fits her mood perfectly. Charcoal clouds loom overhead. Moisture saturates the air. Encroaching thunder clatters. Let it come down.

●

Xenie sings to herself, a gently soaring tune, half recalled and half invented. She's barely aware of this reflex, this old pleasure she can't seem to suppress. The closer she gets to the darkened opening of the woods, the louder her voice grows. The multipart melody emboldens her to continue. She's beguiled by her own siren song.

●

Somebody calls out behind her. Xenie stops singing, shoves fists in pockets, and quickens the pace. Her eyes fixed straight ahead. Soon a boy is running beside her.

—Hold up, the boy says.

It's one of the guys who broke into the theater. The skinny one with enormous glasses. He's waving something at her. In its ragged way, it resembles a white flag.

Xenie stops and snatches it away from him. She examines the bundle of white cloth with a twinge of revulsion, as if it's coated in unknown secretions.

—Thanks, she says. I wasn't finished shredding it.

The boy blushes. He must be seeing the outfit's frayed strips for the first time. The precise patchwork of energetic cuts, sawed and jagged.

●

He says: Sorry about what happened back there. I told them it was wrong to break in, but sometimes they're real pricks.

He says: We were all really shook up about, you know, his death.

He says: You're his girlfriend, right?

—I was, Xenie says.

> Don't say his name. I can't stand to hear
> another one of you say his name.

Xenie starts walking again to reset the rhythm of her thoughts. There's the sound of her boots scuffing the asphalt. The deepening sky. The beckoning woods. The boy lagging a few paces behind.

—Where are you going? he says.

—Home.

—Those woods can be dangerous, he says. I could give you a ride.

—That sounds a whole lot safer. No thanks.

—Okay, okay, he says. But don't walk through the woods alone.

—I'm getting the hell out of here as fast as possible.

—Let me walk with you, the boy says. I feel awful. It's the least I can do.

The boy speaks in a distressed mumble. His voice has the softness of someone unused to making demands, and his pleading tone possesses an alarming sincerity. These days, she's unaccustomed to any sort of understanding. If she pays too close attention, it could prove seriously disorienting.

They linger at the trailhead. A weed-choked strip littered with crushed beer cans. Xenie pulls her hands inside her sweater and hugs the bunched white fabric to her chest.

—So, she says, what instrument do you play?

The boy looks perplexed.

—I don't play anything, he says.

—You're not in the band?

—I'm sort of their manager.

She examines him more thoroughly: Messy nest of brown hair, collared shirt, moth-eaten cardigan. Short and skinny. Fragile but intense. Maybe she's underestimated him.

—You can never tell these days, she says. Everybody is in a fucking band.

The boy must think he's being insulted. He effects a lockjaw expression and stands straighter, but this accomplishes nothing more than making the argyle pattern of his cardigan seem crooked.

—I know I look preppy, he says, but I'm pretty punk rock in my own way.

Xenie tries to stifle her laughter, but the sound keeps bubbling to the surface. A series of high-pitched giggles, springing loose through clenched teeth, rising in a steady spiral of escalating titters.

And I thought I was delusional.

She lets the boy accompany her into the forest. She starts out before second thoughts can settle in. They tramp across pine needles and knobby roots. Surrounded by the stickiness of abandoned webs. The pulsations of insects. Distant birdsong.

—My name is Xenie, she says. For the record.

—I'm Eddie, the boy says.

—Eddie, she says. That's a kid's name. I'm calling you Edward.

Xenie remains a few paces ahead. Since Shaun's death, it's felt like a slight to his memory to spend time alone with anyone. Now even a simple walk through the woods is suspect, threatening to loosen the scorching throb in her throat. The secret she's swallowed these many months.

•

The breeze carries a chill, as if the woods are establishing their own climate. The trees squeeze together and the meager light filtering through the canopy progressively pales. As the shadows thicken, the trail becomes more theoretical.

—You know the way, right?

—Relax, Edward, she says.

She leads them over the fallen branches obscuring the path, through the dead leaves that crackle underfoot. Her boots stomp ahead, heedless.

•

The paths keep forking in front of them. There are routes rutted by dirt bikes, trampled by ambling teenagers, blazed long ago as part of forgotten official thoroughfares. Xenie tries to muster the energy to recall the trails she knew in her youth when she drifted through here in search of illicit treasure. Unused fireworks, abandoned porno magazines, unopened cans of beer. The treehouse she discovered one afternoon in a remote quadrant of the forest, camouflaged high in the branches. She feels impossibly distant from that more innocent person and wonders whether these woods hold anything she might still consider to have value.

●

Odd flowers peer out beneath the weeds and underbrush. Their twisting stems culminate in strange suppurating blooms. A fresh mutation struggling to manifest itself. A furtive efflorescence of the forest floor.

●

Without realizing it, they keep accelerating the pace. They're both trying not to think about the most infamous rumor involving these woods. How several years ago a group of drifters stole corpses from a nearby morgue and hauled them back to their encampment. There were persistent speculations about a black market in human organs. Supposedly the police found a collection of dismembered heads, limbs, torsos. Some claim this is pure legend, but the story became a permanent part of Arcadia's lore. Some of her friends swear they've seen the classified police photographs detailing the carnage in these woods. One of the news images from the early days of the epidemic showed corpses arranged on a sidewalk outside a punk club, covered with tarps, awaiting the coroner. Xenie imagines the scene was similar, flesh arranged in neat columns, tagged and numbered, awkward stumps of meat cradled in white cloth.

We're both either really brave or really stupid.

Eddie hums under his breath. She figures it's an attempt to maintain his courage. The sound is less song than soft moan, a barely melodic exhalation of breath, an increasingly annoying nervous tic. It never resolves into a recognizable refrain, remaining an unconscious broadcast of muddled private reflections.

—Can I ask you something? he says. About what happened back at the theater?

Xenie balls the white fabric between her hands. Bunched among the folds, the letters of her name are embroidered in raised blue stitches. A customization she had to cover from her first paycheck.

—It's not a dress, she says. It's a waitress uniform.

—I got fired this morning, she says, if you must know.

—I was attacked by my manager and had to defend myself, she says. It's lucky I was able to get my hands on a knife.

—I'm so sorry, Eddie says. I might know some people who could talk to that bastard. Maybe get your job back.

Xenie doesn't reply. As they walk on, Eddie continues to intone indistinct sounds, stunted vibrations far from any actual tune.

●

Xenie tries to block out the wind rustling through the trees. It sounds too much like the whispering voices at the diner, the other waitresses who were spooked by her dark moods, the cashier who kept leaving her brochures for grief counseling, the hostess who avoided speaking to her for fear the conversation might turn to her dead boyfriend. Xenie became an unwelcome reminder of the town tragedy. The pariah who always collected the largest tips. Her coworkers sincerely pitied her plight and sincerely wanted her to disappear from their lives.

●

Xenie says: My manager didn't exactly attack me. He told me I couldn't wear this sweater anymore.

—My manager told me it smelled, she says. He said it was disgusting. He said he was sorry, but it was freaking out the entire diner. Customers were complaining. My coworkers couldn't take it.

—I didn't think it was any of his business what I wore, she says. So I grabbed a knife and expressed my point of view. If the cook hadn't stopped me, I swear to Christ I'd have carved him a new pair of nostrils.

●

Xenie tears off a fresh strip of white fabric from the uniform. She wraps it round her middle finger until it throbs. She remembers staring at her hands while her manager lectured her in the kitchen. Surrounded by the smell of seared meat and grilled onions. The unrelenting percolation of the coffeemaker. Her coworkers had vanished, and the only person she could see was the man with the comb-over in the corner booth, picking at his scrambled eggs while fixated on his murder mystery. She felt lightheaded listening to her manager's words. As she steadied herself on the counter, her fingers encountered a steel paring knife. With the tip of her thumb, she evaluated the sharpness of the blade.

●

Eddie seems like he wants to say something, but he remains silent. These days Xenie is well versed in the various expressions and unlikely combinations of pity, disgust, and anger, but he looks at her with a countenance that she can't define. Maybe it's empathy, because she has only the roughest guess what that might possibly look like.

●

Xenie pulls the purple sweater over her mouth and inhales deeply. The odor makes her eyes water. A rank mixture of spilled whiskey, spicy cologne, and sour perspiration that adds up to something indefinable. The smell of Shaun. It gives her a flash of the first time he visited her bedroom. Him sprawled on the carpet, combing through her music collection as if it were her diary. They both understood the bond created by appreciating the qualities of certain bands, the emotional shorthand of adoring certain songs. She watched closely to see which album he'd select from the shelves, pleased when he plucked an obscure compilation of early rock-and-roll ballads, a record few people would've noticed. It wasn't a choice calculated to impress, and he was genuinely moved by those quietly soulful songs. He played the album over and over, his pinkie tracing the various titles, as if trying to commit the tunes to memory. She knew then they'd be together for a long time. She loved how transported he looked as the music spun, absorbed by the sound of those voices, so yearning and disembodied.

Promise me, darling, your love in return.
May this fire in my soul, dear, forever burn.

Thunder rumbles overhead, loud as cannon shot. They pause to listen as the sound rolls across the sky in waves. Eddie stops humming. Or maybe he's stopped for a while.

—I actually wanted to ask you something else about the theater, Eddie says. Why did you let them take the amp?

—Because Florian is an asshole, Xenie says. He's never liked me. He and Shaun drifted apart after I came into the picture. I know he thinks it's my fault.

—That stuff happens all the time. He wouldn't blame you.

—I wasn't at Shaun's last show, Xenie says. I should've gone that night, but I wasn't there. A lot of people know that. I'm sure Florian knows it, too. He was needling me.

—I don't think that's what he was saying.

—He was making a point, Xenie says. He was trying to make me feel like shit.

●

The trail is carpeted with blackened balls of yellow fruit. They're everywhere underfoot. When Xenie steps on them, the rotted ovals either rupture or sink deeper into the porous earth. The entire ground looks bruised.

●

—I've known Florian since we were ten years old, Eddie says. Maybe he's the sort of asshole who'd break into a theater to get an amp, but he wouldn't try to humiliate you. He's not that kind of asshole.

He removes his glasses and wipes them with the hem of his shirt. His exposed eyes seem smaller, his molelike squint unexpectedly steely.

—Not many people know this, he says, but his real name is Bruce. He started calling himself Florian in junior high. His family is poor and he's always wanted to seem exotic. A couple of years ago, his mother was shot by somebody who broke into their house. Florian passed out at her funeral. It was awful. He's been high-strung ever since. Now sometimes he's an asshole even though he isn't one.

I don't want to know about Florian.

I don't care about Florian.

There's a rustling sound nearby. A few yards ahead, a trio of deer hurtles past, heedlessly tearing through the forest, zipping around trees and lilting over branches. The white flags of their tails streak in and out of view. These frightened animals must be fleeing something, but the predators are nowhere to be seen.

●

Xenie and Eddie remain tensed. The entire forest sounds amplified. The charged air crackles, threatening to feed back. A current bristles through the treetops. Maybe it's the sound of raindrops spattering the highest leaves, or the sway of wind-frazzled twigs, or nervous birds shifting in their nests. Gradually, the noises subside until there's only the shallow exhalations of their own pinched lungs. They don't see anyone, but they spot something unusual in a nearby stand of maples. Dangling from the branches, attached by twine, are bars of white soap. They're tattooed with teeth marks, almost gnawed in half.

●

A sparrow delivers a sequence of shrill calls and thrashes its wings. Xenie wonders if it's a message of distress, a warning that's being relayed through the forest from some distant sector. She watches the song repeat, the sound rippling through the creature's slender distended throat.

•

The keening voices of those old ballads Shaun loved. She wonders if she ever understood what those songs truly contained.

•

They stop at a split in the path. Xenie scoops up a palmful of dried pellets and sifts them through her fingers, watching how they tumble onto the pine needles, trying to divine their arrangement like tea leaves. Something about these deer droppings isn't right. Many are misshapen and ghostly pale. She shuts her eyes, takes a succession of deep breaths, then steps straight ahead. She's not concerned with strictly following the path as much as tapping into that invisible route that feels like the path.

> I can't afford to get lost.
> I don't know this place anymore.

The sporadic trail transforms into a furrowed thoroughfare. Soon they find themselves entering an expansive clearing. Xenie and Eddie instinctively crouch behind some bushes. They're on the cusp of what appears to be an immense homeless encampment.

The camp is uninhabited, for the moment. Threadbare quilts are strung from a network of clotheslines, demarcating the different spaces. Some are staged with eviscerated sofas and battered Barcaloungers, others with skeletal tents containing vestigial scraps of canvas. A full-length mirror leans against an oak. Strewn throughout the sparse grass are plastic bases from a children's kickball game.

They notice how everything is gathered around a fire pit, a scorched stretch of earth encircled by busted metal stools. In the distance rests the burned-out hull of a car, its charred hood covered with bouquets of faded plastic roses.

●

Neither of them speaks. The panic scribbled across their features effaces everything else. Xenie is determined not to be the first to open her mouth. This is a test for Eddie. The path to true camaraderie is narrow. It allows only one correct response.

He sizes up the situation. His voice sounds dubious, but he manages to force the words past his teeth.

—Probably be smarter to turn back, Eddie whispers. Or cut around the camp. But I say we go for it.

Xenie can't help but smile, emboldened by the fake bravado he's summoned on her behalf.

—Right, she says. Let's do it.

●

Xenie leads them into the clearing. They advance as soundlessly as possible, careful to avoid the crinkling candy wrappers, bulbous condoms. The baby pram stacked with rusted cans of cat food. They weave slowly between the quilts, making sure the roughly patched fabric remains motionless, trying not to ruffle the air.

●

It's not a natural feature of the woods. As they get closer, it becomes clear the mound of dirt in the center of the camp is man-made. It rises to their waists. The mound has been constructed from countless shovelfuls, carefully tamped down, adorned with small round stones. Xenie feels a cold rush in her veins. It's a grave.

—Who do you think is buried here? Eddie whispers.

She circles the mound, running her fingers along the contours, calculating the proportions.

—I know he was cremated, Xenie says.

—I know it can't be him, she says.

She scoops up a handful of dirt and inhales its scent. She must be imagining the familiar hint of spicy cologne. Flecks of soil stick to her flaring nostrils.

●

Hoots and hisses erupt from the surrounding bushes. There's a pounding rhythm of whipping leaves and throttled branches. Sounds made by humans. Eddie and Xenie are afraid to look too closely. The napes of their necks prickle. Their stomachs make a fist. They've stupidly walked into a trap, and the layer of dirt beneath their feet suddenly feels perilously thin, as if the forest floor is hinged.

They stand back-to-back. Eddie picks up several sharp rocks and hurls them into the bushes. He emits a series of wordless shrieks and thumps his fists against his skinny collarbone. He acts unexpectedly possessed. His face transforms into a mask of pure ferocity. A wild scarlet pucker.

●

Xenie steps toward the noises. She hoists her tattered waitress uniform aloft. The shredded dress appears to signify the aftermath of an unspeakable assault. The defiant cape of a gored matador. We're right here, she bellows. Come and get us. More hoots from the bushes. Lower and more sinister. Accompanied by the swish of rattling sticks. Her feet are fixed firmly in the clearing, unflinched.

●

There are scattered growls, but nobody shows themselves. It's easy to picture men with peeling parchment skin and biblical beards, women with patchy scalps and zealous eyes, each of their frames held together with thick ropes and ensnarled rags. But Xenie wonders if maybe these unseen vagrants are more frightened than she is. Instead of organ butchers and feral perverts, they're pathetic creatures too timid to appear.

●

With defiant slowness, Xenie places her uniform atop the dirt mound. She smooths the edges of the dress so it covers as much of the exposed earth as possible. The tattered fabric serves as an offering, a crucial step in a ceremony she doesn't know how to name.

Maybe this is where it belongs.

As they exit the camp, Xenie steps on a soggy cloth that sticks to the bottom of her boot.

It turns out to be a miniature sweater. A peculiar herringbone pattern. A garment knitted with exquisite care and delicacy.

A sweater perfectly proportioned for a squirrel.

●

Dusk has fallen and the scenery feels two-dimensional, the expanse of surrounding trees flattened into wallpaper. Their silence has a preoccupied quality. A search for words to make the incident comprehensible. They act as if nothing unusual happened, but Eddie still clutches a handful of stones and Xenie's wrists won't stop trembling. She wants to touch Eddie but doesn't trust herself. If she takes his hand to steady herself, she'll surely unravel.

●

Xenie says: I wasn't scared.

—Me neither.

Xenie says: I was pretty sure they wouldn't do anything.

Besides, I could tell you were itching for it. Looking for an excuse to let loose.

—What do you mean?

Xenie says: The rocks, the screaming. It was primal. You've obviously got a lot of pent-up violence.

—What? Eddie stammers. Of course not. I mean, that's not me. I mean, I've never done something like that before.

Xenie's creased lips form an oblique curve. She says: I see you, Edward. I see you clearly.

It's like looking in a mirror.

The evening keeps losing texture. The trail has widened, and it won't be long before the path deposits them back in town, but Xenie isn't eager for this to end. She finds she's enlivened by the darkness that erases their expressions and absorbs their gestures. There's only the tenor of their voices to navigate, and this makes it easier to talk. Her secret hovers on the edges of their conversation, the impulse she's barely admitted to herself. She feels compelled to speak to Eddie about the epidemic, though she isn't sure how to start.

●

Xenie says: Most of the people I know are in bands. All these so-called creative people are always telling me to join their group or start my own. They're always trying to get me to see their shows, listen to their songs, buy their stuff. It's like everything has to be public, everything has to be validated by a crowd, or it doesn't exist.

—Everybody craves the spotlight, she says, but then they're so mediocre. It's pathetic. These days, it takes more guts *not* to be in a band. We're probably the last two people who aren't.

—We're probably the only two people, she says, who really get it.

Do you get it? Please tell me you get it.

—You're right, Eddie says. I try to be supportive and it's nice the musicians are trying, but you're right. The local bands aren't that good anymore. Florian is better than most of them. I've seen him pull off amazing things in rehearsal, but his sound still hasn't come together. The bands here don't seem to realize how far they have to go. In fact, most of them are a joke.

—Exactly, Xenie says. The entire scene has devolved. It's totally delusional. Everyone is convinced they're doing something special. If somebody truly great came along now, nobody would even recognize it.

—What about Shaun?

Xenie halts. She stares in Eddie's direction, attempting to discern his attitude in the dimming light.

—Are you really asking me that? Did you know Shaun?

—Not that well, Eddie says. Not personally.

—But you saw him play?

—Sure, Eddie says. A bunch of times.

—Then you know, she says.

Xenie plucks out one of her eyelashes. It makes her wince, but she keeps plucking lash after lash after lash.

—You know, she says, that he wasn't that good.

●

Eyelashes collect on her fingertips. Shaun used to scold her about this nervous habit held over from childhood and sometimes he'd clasp her hands between his own, trying to calm her until the compulsion passed. But now there's something reassuring about accumulating the stray black squiggles. She craves each painful twinge.

●

—It's not just the local bands, she says. There's so much lifeless music everywhere and it keeps multiplying. It's polluting everything.

—These bands are poisoning something that used to be meaningful, she says. Their music is actually toxic.

—Nobody wants to talk about any connection between the bands that have been targeted, she says, but most of them have been terrible. I'm not so sure that's a coincidence.

> The shitty noise duo in the Pacific Northwest.
> The smarmy bluegrass revivalists in the Deep South.
> The listless jam band in the Midwest.

They stumble through the brush. Thorny vines pull through their hair, and leaves lash against their faces, but neither pulls out a phone to illuminate the path. There's an unspoken understanding that any amount of light would rupture the fragile mood. They prefer to remain together in the same darkness.

●

—I used to have a huge music collection, Xenie says. I was obsessed and even saved my concert stubs in a red cardboard box. Sometimes I'd open the box, and just touching the tickets was enough to give me a rush.

—Over the years, I kept accumulating huge amounts of music, she says. I had access to almost everything, but I listened less and less. I finally had to admit that music no longer excited me. So I've given away most of my albums. Even the great ones have been tainted. They feel worthless like all the others. They're just more noise.

—These days I crave silence, she says.

There's a wordless pause, filled by the rhythmic exhalations of their breath.

—I'm sorry, Eddie says. I know you've been through a lot.

—Everyone always thinks everything is about Shaun, Xenie says.

Eddie doesn't reply, though she can feel his thoughts churning, calculating her half confessions, recharting the conversation.

—Oh, he says. You felt this way before the epidemic even began.

—Months, she says, before anyone fired a shot.

•

Her body feels hollowed out, thrumming, the same as the time she wandered through that gigantic chain store in a half trance, compulsively circling the same unfamiliar aisle.

•

Eddie tells her a story, speaking in such a soft and halting voice that it's as if he's talking to himself. So I had a record player when I was younger, he says. I'd get fixated on an album and play it over and over. There was this death metal record I listened to for weeks. My dad kept complaining it was too negative. One night, he got drunk and smashed the record player with a baseball bat. He beat the shit out of it until everything was broken into pieces, then he smashed the pieces into smaller pieces. My mom watched the entire thing and laughed her ass off. After that, I went over to Florian's and listened to his copy of the album. Eventually I memorized every note, but I was disappointed the songs didn't live up to what was happening in my life. The music never felt negative enough.

In the darkness, Xenie nods her head, furiously.

—If it doesn't give you what you need, she says, it's useless.

•

They move closer to each other as they walk. Xenie can't see Eddie's body, but she can feel his heat.

She's seized by a vision that they're surrounded by piles of discarded tapes, compact discs, computer hard drives. The refuse is purposefully stacked into primitive cairns, towers that dot the landscape, arranged in obscure ritual patterns. These mysterious totems hover in the shadows, but she can almost feel their presence. Evidence of some ancient civilization that ransacked its temples and cast out the gods.

●

She imagines the trail paved with excess vinyl, countless unheard records from bands soon to be forgotten. The discs crack underfoot, leaving fragments in their wake, each unwanted record another stepping-stone, a shattered black path that leads them out of the forest.

●

It must have rained while they were in the woods. The asphalt street, the cars in driveways, the tidy bungalows are all freshly slicked with droplets of water. Even the tangled network of telephone wires shimmers overhead. There's a fresh tang in the breeze. The sweetness of mown grass, the sourness of gasoline, the headiness of dirt. She can taste the sharpness in the air. The birdsong has been staunched for the night. Everything is silent except for the breeze absently mumbling through the trees. The drowsy glow of distant porch lights makes it seem like hours have vanished and the entire town has fallen asleep, sinking deeper into its unsettling dreams. It feels like they're the only waking souls.

—My place is close by, Xenie says.

She tries to sound nonchalant, but a quiver clings to her voice.

—Want to walk me home?

She curls her hands inside the purple sweater, and her shoulder blades shudder. She's surprised by her own pantomime, these gestures of flirtatious vulnerability that she never imagined could belong to her.

●

Xenie leads them up the hill. The headlights of passing cars refract in the puddles, lending the blacktop a phosphorescent sheen. A city bus drives by, empty of passengers, lit up like an operating room.

—I knew something was going to happen, Xenie says. I knew sooner or later the epidemic would come to Arcadia.

—I've never told anybody this, she says, but I'm the one who brought it here. I didn't want to, but somehow I willed it to happen.

—Deep down, she says, I know it's my fault.

Eddie reprises his low hum as they walk.

—You probably don't want to hear this, he says, but it's not your fault.

Xenie listens to the rainwater trickle through the gutter grates and drain into the sewer pipes. Gushing sounds resound beneath her feet, feeding a network of unseen torrents.

> *If you knew what I really thought.*
> *If you knew how bad I feel.*
> *If you knew how close I came.*

The streets narrow as they crest the hill. Xenie pauses under a streetlamp, bathing her body in a harsh white light that scours away all shadow. Her bleached blonde hair appears more electric than ever. She stares up at the searing corona and wishes she could become one of those pure bright particles, her corporeal form consumed, atomized and liberated.

●

It's the only house on the block that's completely dark. A modest two-story bungalow whose front yard is framed by overgrown boxwoods. They follow the concrete pathway to the front door. Xenie kicks over the corner of the welcome mat and stares at the silver key.

—Come inside, she says. I need to show you something.

She can feel her nerves crackling, but there's also an unfamiliar sensation of hopefulness, a raw spark of excitement that causes her legs to wobble. She reaches out and grabs Eddie's belt buckle. Half steadying herself and half pulling him closer. His face has been scratched from the thorns and branches. Marks of quiet determination borne without a word. She runs her finger along one of his cuts, tracing the ragged contours of the incision. She finds the abrasions unexpectedly attractive.

Nobody visits since he died.

The living room is steeped in weeks' worth of trash. Balled clothes, battered sofa cushions. Dishes furred with mold. Glasses rimmed with gelatinous residue. An exercise bicycle with sprained handlebars. Xenie is too embarrassed to turn on the lights, but even the shadows are in shambles. The depth of the mess is profound, uncomfortably reminiscent of the campsite in the woods.

Eddie turns away from Xenie. She can sense him processing the full ramifications of this room. Sadness permeates the air. Takeout boxes from the diner are piled everywhere, signs of meals eaten alone, upright and hunched over, food barely tasted, the depression too heavy to do more than choke down a few swallows and abandon the containers where they lay.

—I keep telling myself that I can be sad for one more week, she says. And then I'll get my shit together. But it never happens.

—I know I'm impossible, she says. In old times they forced grieving people to live on the outskirts of the villages. Nobody could stand to be around them. I get that custom. I really do.

—I just want to feel normal again, she says.

•

She's impressed that Eddie hasn't fled. He stands in the thick of her disaster and doesn't deliver scolding words, reproving looks, coping advice. Somehow he seems accepting, maybe even interested in her. As they navigate the chaos of the living room, pushing a path through the capsized lamps and the pots of wilted ferns, she extends her hand to Eddie. Her grasp is surprisingly tender.

•

Xenie leads him up the staircase. Her fingertips linger along the wooden banister, touching the knots and indentations as if they're notations in a score she once knew. My Aunt Mary left me this house, she tells him. It's my one bit of good luck. When they reach the second floor, she flips a switch. A bare light bulb illuminates the worn shag carpet, the faded rose wallpaper, the framed photograph of a middle-aged woman with her hair in a polka-dot scarf. Aunt Mary, who camouflaged her kind soul behind muttered curses and cigarette smoke, the one person who always believed Xenie, who understood what she was trying to say even when her explanations faltered. Mary's image is obscured behind a patina of dust thick as glaucoma. It's an old snapshot, not a shrine. Xenie gave up pretending long ago that somebody could be watching over her.

•

They pass the bathroom where several days after Shaun's death she found one of his brown hairs clinging tightly to the bristles of her toothbrush. A single strand live as electric current. It's still there, untouchable.

●

The elongated hallway leads to her bedroom. She's nervous but focuses on the intoxicating warmth of Eddie's palm. There's a look in his eyes as if he's shuffling through every possible scenario and each one ends with them under her sheets. For a moment, she wonders if she misjudged him and what might happen if he decided to attack her. In her fantasy, Xenie doesn't fight back, and almost invites the assault, until he realizes too late this is not a violation but a trap.

●

She sits on the edge of the mattress. The bedroom is saturated with the smell of her sleep, an oily musk of perspiration and perfume. Her hands gather up the tarot cards from the bedside table. She shuffles the deck, listening to its oracular whisper about those moments where her destiny forked and led down a different path. A version of her life where she doesn't know anybody touched by the epidemic, where she's unafraid of consequences and feels the pull of a higher calling, where one night she's walking to an anonymous club, her strut a bit lopsided, thrown off by the extra weight in her purse.

She needs insight into how this moment will play out between her and Eddie. Maybe she's made a mistake bringing him here. She lays out a trio of cards on the comforter. There's the romantic Two of Cups, the apocalyptic arcana of the Tower, the Ten of Wands signifying a massive conflagration. The combination is inconclusive and disturbing, the divination muddled.

She reshuffles the deck. Deals another spread. The messages come like hailstones—

> *Trust him.*
>
> *Tell him.*
>
> *Try to explain.*

—When the epidemic started, she says, I followed it obsessively. I couldn't help myself. It felt like the bubble I'd been living in had been punctured. For the first time in forever, something real was happening.

—Everyone said the killers were like zombies, she says, but I think they were wrong. These crimes were intentional. They had meaning.

—The killers wanted music to matter again, she says. They wanted to purify it. It's like they were thinning the herd, putting wounded animals out of their misery.

She looks down at her fingernails where the black polish has been fretfully chewed away.

—It's an insane idea, Xenie says. I know that it's wrong. It's sick.

Eddie runs his hands through his squirrelly whirl of hair, trying to flatten it as if that might tamp down his thoughts. He squints through his oversize glasses. Everyone has their own way of dealing with these things, he says. It's totally—. He searches for the right word. Natural, he says.

It's not the right word.

●

Emotions flicker across her face, like a radio frantically surfing between stations. Her eyes remain locked on the window that surveys the front lawn. Her body seems to shrink, disappearing into itself. We had a big fight before his last show, she says. I left Shaun asleep here in my room and stole his guitar. Now the only things I have left of him are a hard drive full of his songs and that glorified slab of wood.

●

She can't bring herself to look at the silhouette of the instrument. The contours of the electric guitar are warped by the shadows. It stubbornly refuses to resolve into a familiar shape. The instrument looks uncanny, like some ancient object used in forgotten rituals to coax the rotation of seasons, the harvesting of crops, the cessation of plagues.

Come closer.

Eddie puts his arm around Xenie. She tries to speak, but her voice splinters. The only thing she manages to say is: I really loved Shaun. Her mind shuffles through his habit of writing himself notes that she'd find stuck in the crevices of his car, stuffed in his pockets, stowed in his pillowcase. Odd fragments with appointment reminders, stray lyrics, motivational exhortations. *Pickup at 405 Ashburn. Dream what you've forgotten. Practice more.* Their dates getting drunk at the laundromat. Their long showers together. The bottle of hair dye they picked out every month and rubbed into each other's scalps over the bathroom sink. The matching scars on their wrists, desperate mementos they rarely discussed but weren't surprised they shared. The sharp spice of his skin. His sour sweat. She's terrified she's going to forget his smell.

●

Xenie says: This is my worst secret.

She says: I've never shown this to anyone.

She says: Nobody even knows I've had these thoughts.

She says: I'm so sorry Shaun was shot.

She says: You have to believe that.

●

She removes a red cardboard box from her nightstand and cradles it in her lap. She nestles closer to Eddie, wanting to feel the reassuring thrum of his pulse.

—It was this strange compulsion, she says. I barely remember buying it.

Her shoulders won't stop twitching, but she manages to hold back the tears.

—A couple of weeks before the first shooting, she says, I found myself walking the aisles of a store in a half trance. As I made my purchase, it felt like I was preparing for something, but I didn't know what. Then the killings started and things crystallized. I stood on the sidelines and watched like everybody else, but some part of me agreed with the killers.

She can barely bring herself to speak. The words are little more than a rumble in her throat.

—Even as the violence got worse, she says, I couldn't shake the thought that the killers were right. Those bands all got what they deserved.

I hate feeling this way, but this is the way I feel.

She opens the box and produces an object enfolded in violet felt. With convulsing fingers, she unwraps the cloth to reveal the revolver. Black mascara runs down her cheeks, but her eyes shine like polished steel. She thrusts the weapon toward him, the loaded barrel balanced on her palm, a freshly oiled offering.

THE BIRDS

Noontime. The white-throated sparrow is perched in the center of its nest with a tiny fledgling. The two birds are singing, but the song keeps slipping out of tune. The timbre sounds pinched, and the pitch shifts ever so slightly. The white-throated sparrow is undisturbed as it reiterates the warbling pattern to its offspring. She waits for the wisp of fuzzy gray feathers, his small beak upturned, to repeat the sequence to her. He learns it a few notes at a time, volleying stray phrases back and forth. He slowly intuits the tune's hidden complexities. It reminds me of instructing you, Bruce, to listen to the birds and try to memorize their songs. The fledgling only needs to have courage and keep repeating the song. Easy does it. Remember that you can sustain the contours of the sound, even when you can't hold on to the melody.

chapter three

THE ELECT

**Each night, for Xenie and Florian, the epidemic unfolds
in their dreams, the killings beginning all over again.**

The boy with the shaved skull moves like a sleepwalker—a strange determination to his lurching steps—locked into the dull repeating throb coming from down the street—he crunches across a gravel parking lot, heading straight toward a windowless concrete building, a shabby veterans hall—the source of the sound—he joins the line to buy tickets—a girl hands him a notice about tonight's show, a battle of the bands whose list of performers looks endless, the bubbly handwriting at the bottom indicating yet another group added to the bill—and the boy with the shaved skull folds the flyer in half, in quarters, in eighths, making the creases perfect until the paper is reduced to an immaculate square—he throws it onto the ground—gives

the cashier a few crumpled bills from his pocket—walks
through the club's empty foyer and follows the echoing
rumble until he enters the darkened performance area—
music blares from the speakers, but the small wooden
stage is bare except for an amp, a drum kit, and a solitary
microphone—everyone's facing the stage—their attention
focused on the video projected onto the white bedsheet
tacked against the wall, a shimmering image of a dirt road
winding through the forest at night, the camera moving
relentlessly along a fitfully illuminated path—the boy
scans the packed room—the audience is mostly composed
of musicians—a motley assemblage of hippies in tie-dye
shirts and denim jackets, punks with ratty coifs and ripped
jeans, bearded indie rockers with color-coordinated headbands, long-haired kids with immaculately applied
corpse paint, girls in secondhand Catholic-school
uniforms clasping keyboards under their arms like
purses—a low murmur of conversation, the hum of
expectation—some people strike poses to simulate patience, others don't bother to obscure their fidgeting
limbs—everyone restless to perform—as the boy with
the shaved skull stumbles to the front, a trio in bowling-
league shirts and high-top sneakers bounds onto the
stage—as if they've been waiting for his cue to start the
show—launching into a frenetic brand of garage rock,
throttling their instruments and cranking their amps—
and the boy suddenly looks lost, surprised to find himself here among these shadowy faces, watching the
guitarist windmill his arm and the singer strangle his

microphone stand in time to the spastic beat—then the boy calms as his eyes latch on to the video projection—the image has grown darker, though he can still make out the bobbing headlights, the twilight woods, the vacant dirt road—he's drawn toward the frame, as if he could step directly into the sheet and follow the deepening nocturnal trail—his hand reaches into the small of his back, a gesture that appears rehearsed—and now he's pointing a revolver at the stage—the weapon hovering in the bright beam of the projection, its shadow eclipsing the entire band.

While Xenie and Florian struggle to wake up, the epidemic escalates.

The crowd slams into one another as the band plays, bodies ricocheting through the cramped space, spinning toward the rear of the club and getting shoved back into the centrifugal melee—the skinny boy with big hair stands at the edge of the mosh pit, droplets of sweat beading his forehead, barely reacting when people pinball off him—instead he's watching how the musicians' neck veins bulge as they pound out the precise riffs, their tightly wound songs scrubbed of extraneous notes—he's focusing on the singer, who barks lyrics at a frenzied clip, his agitated sounds matching the music's hurtling martial cadence—concluding each tune with a piercing shriek—the audience pants and stretches, wringing out sweat-soaked T-shirts like washcloths, generating a haze of rank perspiration that hovers along the ceiling of the club like its own weather system—a tropical depression of pale boys with crew cuts and long-haired girls with medieval tattoos—the skinny boy with big hair reaches into his pocket with a studied swagger, only to discover the gun is already in his hand—the recoil of the first shot staggers him backward, kicking his arm over his head—ceiling tiles crash to the floor, downy flakes of plaster powder the air—somehow he keeps firing—one shot blows apart the massive amplifier—another knocks the guitar player off his feet and deposits a sucking red cavity in the center of his chest—another finds the fleeing drummer, exploding his kneecap and leaving him writhing on the ground, clutching at the muddle of bone and cartilage—the slithering singer is flattened against the platform, pulling himself along on his stomach by his raw fingernails—a bright red plume smeared across the bass drum points the way offstage—the crowd huddles on the ground, presses against the walls, stampedes past the shooter—and maybe because everything is happening fast, the skinny boy steps slowly across the beer slicks and cracked plastic cups, taking purposeful strides toward the bleeding band members until he's halted by an earsplitting shriek—his own—though he doesn't recognize the voice.

They twist and tremble in their beds, though their expressions remain perfectly blank.

The two girls stand over the bodies of the dead musicians, holding Magnum revolvers of enormous caliber—the echo of their shots reverberate in their ears as loud as mortar volleys—they're surrounded by hot shell casings and the acrid smell of gunpowder—the living room of this house show is silent, the furniture pushed against the walls, the overhead lights switched off, the walls spattered with permanent shadows—the two girls are spackled with gore, their skin wet and sticky, spongy particles lodged in their teeth—the blonde's glasses are splashed crimson, tinting her view of the room, but she doesn't wipe them off—the brunette's eyes resemble scuffed marbles, her gaze steady and unblinking—she turns and shoots the blonde in the head, not watching the descent of the corpse as it crumples to the carpet—then she places the barrel of the revolver against her own temple and presses the trigger—but nothing happens—the blood from her hair steadily trickles down her smooth forehead and she starts to blink—furiously—the only sound is the repetition of the girl's index finger pressing the trigger, the steady rotation of the empty chambers, and the rhythmic click of the hammer—those three interlocking sounds, in continual sequence, again and again and again.

THE BIRDS

Midday. A small flock of white-throated sparrows now populates the grove of trees on the edge of town. They twitter as they rustle through the leaves and hop from branch to branch. The sunlight catches glints of the stark black-and-white stripes on their heads. Each sparrow offers its own rhythmic call. Some swing up the scale and some skid down. They appear to be singing in a round or engaging in a colloquy. The components of the tune get redistributed as furious counterpoints, but then the overlapping voices become more aggressive. The song begins to sound increasingly alien, without any human feeling. It's important that you never lose your connection to the music. Lean in and listen closer. Don't be afraid, even as the foreign sounds grow louder, the intricate aria shrills and swells, threatening to become an undifferentiated din.

chapter
four

THE EXITS

HE STANDS IN THE MIDDLE OF THE STREET, GUITAR IN one hand, amp in the other. There's a distant whine of traffic, but the road remains empty. Florian surveys the converted house with its cracked paint, bricked-over windows, and bleached sign perched along the ridge of the roof. Blinking away the shimmer of afternoon sun, he's struck by the raggedness of this two-story structure. A sagging razor-wire fence encloses the gravel parking lot, a vain attempt to isolate the building from the rest of the neighborhood. In the daytime, Echo Echo isn't so different from the surrounding shacks with their rickety foundations and peeling tar-paper roofs. Dusk will initiate a transformation. Tonight, for the first time in months, the building will be juiced with enough wattage to make a club materialize, a luminous mirage flickering in the center of the slum.

On the side of Echo Echo, the torn trash bags are piled three deep. Their spilled contents marinate in a pool of their own blackened juices. Even from a distance, Florian finds the odor overpowering. A noxious mix of rank leftovers, month-old Szechuan beef and spoiled papayas. His heightened sense of smell is an early warning that a crippling migraine is on the way. Hours from now, he'll be flattened against a mattress, hammered with pain, his head trying to cancel itself out. Florian doesn't bother to take one of his meds. Instead, he walks over and tosses the pill bottle atop the festering heap. He wrinkles his nose and inhales again, deeply.

●

After his mother died, Florian was the one who filled garbage bags with her possessions, emptying the house of her coats and dresses, romance novels and rosaries, toiletries and perfumes. He found himself seized by a compulsion to get rid of everything she'd touched. Suffocated by the very sight of her stuff. He knew that she'd understand. Early one morning Florian sat next to the towers of trash bags that lined the curb, the firmament lightening as he listened for the rumbling garbage trucks, holding his breath for minutes at a time, waiting to make sure every last item was ferried away.

Today.

Today of all days.

Florian enters the club. He's surprised to find it pitch black. His eyes detect a slight glimmer, and he trails that faint illumination past the ticket booth. As he turns into the hallway, it grows brighter. Arriving in the bar area, he sees the glass case full of beer bottles at the far end, which bathes the room in a limpid glow and supplies the stammering mechanical hum that's the venue's only soundtrack.

—Anybody here? Florian shouts.

Above his head, he makes out the soft clomp of footsteps. It must be the twins who run the club.

—Florian? calls a voice from the ceiling.

—Yeah.

—You're early.

—Not really, Florian says.

There's the muffled sound of conversation that resembles a throat-clearing contest. It builds to an inconclusive crescendo.

—We'll be down in a few minutes, the voice says.

Florian pushes open the doors to the performance area and tentatively steps into the shadowy space. From the fugitive gaps in the walls, the room is shot through with shafts of light. As his eyes adjust, the club reveals its contours. One errant sunbeam outlines the lip of the stage.

•

Florian paces the perimeter of the low wooden stage. He keeps muttering the word *fans* as he marks out the exact distance to the nearest exit. He begins to measure the other exits, counting off the number of footsteps, then realizes what he's doing. He stops himself midmeasurement. Enough, he says. But in his mind, his feet are still moving.

I can't let myself get carried away.

Florian turns on the soundboard console. He's brought a recording of a deep electronic drone for the band's pre-show music. It's part of his strategy to remain calm. The music has the gaseous quality of an expanding cloud. The tones thicken the atmosphere, building toward an inevitability that never arrives. This drone is designed to replicate the soul's journey through the different phases of death and create a sense of acceptance in the listener. If Florian listens closely enough, maybe it will recalibrate his attitude. He imagines this sound subtly altering the color of the club's atmosphere. With a properly attuned mind, maybe he could perceive the precise shade.

●

The twins stomp downstairs, clutching microphone stands and cursing each other. They both have stocky lumberjack frames, black metal T-shirts, and combat boots. A.C. has loose black curls, while B.C. sports a military crew cut. They resemble not-very-clever variations on a theme.

Both acknowledge Florian with a terse nod. They flip on the overhead fluorescents and throw open the patio door. The performance space floods with light, revealing the collection of graffiti scrawled across the walls and ceiling. The room is a turbulent fresco comprising the names of iconic bands and local legends, signatures amassed across the decades, adorned with aerosol cans and Magic Markers. They've become an integral part of the club's lore. The teeming textures of the club's walls could be cataloged as archaeological layers. Florian has daydreamed about the exact spot he'd add his own mark. It's not far from where the Carmelite Rifles and Jerusalem Crickets left their tags years ago. An unblemished area along the back wall. A few square inches that corral years of longing.

●

Another layer of writing lurks throughout the crevices of the club. Slogans and messages furtively etched into the bar, inked underneath the booths, concealed behind the stage, manifestations of the institution's unruly id.

●

You are entering an occupied territory. Put your cell phone on vibrator. Be your own anarchy. No more rape jokes. Here comes the something. Go into exile. Eat your makeup. Under the paving stones, more concrete. Anybody can shoot anybody. Please limit your set to 30 seconds.

●

The twins survey the performance space as if they're unsure how to begin. A.C. stumbles onto the stage and stomps his feet several times, evaluating the echo. Part of the security plan, he assures Florian. Explain it to you later. B.C. sits behind the soundboard and starts to adjust speaker levels, only to realize he's missing a couple of crucial adapters. The twins bought the club several years ago and live in the overhead apartment. It's their entire life, and right now their life is either badly hungover or struggling to sober up.

●

The activity in the club steadily escalates. B.C. crawls around the baseboards, attempting to trace the source of some whistling static. Echo Echo is renowned for its stellar sound, making it a coveted venue for bands to play, but right now the main audio is a series of listless grunts. A.C. leaves belligerent voice mails for the security team to find out why they haven't arrived. He tallies the online ticket sales and realizes tonight's show is oversold.

Lisa-Lisa, the bartender, breezes into the club and immediately discovers a profound shortage of bourbon. How much did you fucking monkeys drink? she bellows. It's been so long since they've produced a show that everyone is off their game.

Florian sits with his head sunk between his knees to block out the surrounding commotion. He's trying to visualize performing a worthy tribute to Shaun. He is determined not to settle for mediocrity like the other bands on the local scene. He shuts his eyes and envisions the audience surging in front of him, absorbing every shuddering note, waiting to get knocked clean out of their bodies.

Tonight I'll be good enough.

Florian removes a ballpoint pen from his bag. He sits on a barstool and rolls up his sleeve, revealing the emerald lines of his tattoo. He reinforces the blurred edges of the initial *J* with a few stabs of black ink. This needs to be prominent. He recalls how his mother eased him out of anxiety as a child. She'd remind him about the birds who never know where they're getting their next meal, migrate thousands of miles, yet never stop singing. Think about their songs, she'd say. Together they'd recite the names of various songbirds. They'd repeat them until he was calm.

—Easy does it, Bruce, she'd say.

●

Under a pile of tottering boxes, Eddie appears with the latest copy of the guest list. Florian notices something different about his old friend, but he's too busy marveling over all the requests to pin it down. For this first local show since the epidemic ended, the list is crammed with columns of names. It's crazy how many people have reached out the past few days, Eddie says. It's all coming together. Florian suppresses a smile. Scattered among the band's support network is a roll call of the most respected musi-cians and critics on the local scene. Arcadia will be here tonight.

●

Florian begins his show preparations. He positions his freshly painted green amp on the stage. He picks up a broom and starts to sweep. After weeks of obsessive prac-tice, he's unaware that his left hand treats the wooden handle like a fretboard, his fingers forming a succession of riffs.

●

There's the hum of an unseen presence in the room, prick-ling the hairs in his nostrils, then Florian realizes the drone is still playing.

●

Clanging doors, shouted greetings. Yo Flo, Randy the Mongoose calls as he hops onto the stage. Florian feels surprisingly soothed reciting his part of the exchange. Hey Goose, he says. Randy begins to assemble his kit piece by piece. Soon he's tuning the snare, tightening the cymbals, testing the volume. He essays a few delicate rolls, then beats the drums with increasing fury. He concentrates on hurling his full weight into each thundering blow. The sound shudders through the club's walls, and he seems determined to make the hits reverberate as loud as mortar volleys.

Nobody expects Derek D. to be on time, much less arrive early. But here he is, strolling into Echo Echo, bass tucked under his arm. He drags a hand along the graffitied walls, running his fingertips against the rough texture, luxuriating in the splinter and scratch. He's decked out in black leather pants and a black shirt, hair coifed for the occasion in a shocking-pink pompadour.

—Fancy look, says Randy. Does the rug match the drapes?

—I see you're your same sloppy self, Derek D. says. But I guess there's nothing too special about tonight.

—I've set my sights higher, says Randy. I brought us some mojo.

He removes a black rope from around his neck. It's adorned with a bright green circle.

—Amulet of protection, says Randy. The lady at the New Age store swore it possessed ancient powers. And it was on sale for two dollars.

—You were robbed, Florian says.

—Nothing's too good for you guys, says Randy.

He ceremoniously lashes the amulet to his cymbal stand. He tries to conceal that its pattern of multipronged swords is meticulously engraved in agate.

●

The band stands shoulder to shoulder on the stage and looks out at the club. It's tighter quarters up here than they expected. Florian senses the mood growing solemn. To puncture the tension, he unbuttons his long-sleeve top. Underneath, he's wearing a T-shirt with a bright bull's-eye.

—Thought I'd get into the spirit, he says with a grin. In case our fans have bad eyesight.

—Hey, this is a band, not a solo act, Randy says. Hope you're not planning to hog all the bullets.

—Don't worry, Florian says. There'll be plenty to go around.

—I'm not sure this is funny, Derek D. says.

—If we can't laugh at our own deaths, Florian says, what can we laugh at?

Derek D. looks perplexed, as if his bandmates have lapsed into a foreign language.

—But you're not laughing, he says.

●

A shadow at the edge of the room yawns. Xenie stretches her arms as she takes in the show preparations. She looks funereal, her pallid skin offset by a motley black outfit. Her cheeks are powdered, lips darkened, eyebrows etched in razor-sharp lines. Shock of blonde hair exquisitely styled in a wave. Nobody can tell whether her elegant appearance is an attempt at disguise or is her way of playacting some private role. Her black blazer obscures a ratty flash of purple wool.

Florian curses under his breath. Randy lets loose a raspy whistle. Even Derek D. doesn't hide his confusion.

Only the twins don't seem shocked to see her, each offering a friendly wave.

Eddie's heart surges. He and Xenie have grown so close over the past few weeks that he steps into the center of the room without hesitation, pretending he knows what she's doing here.

—She's with me, he announces. I needed someone to handle the merch table.

Xenie clasps her hands and curtsies toward the band.

—Consider this an apology, she says. For freaking out about the amp.

She remains inscrutable. Florian watches her purse and pucker, applying a fresh coat of black lipstick, intensifying the hue of her mouth.

What does she really want?

As the band sets up, they study Xenie without bothering to conceal their stares. Eddie grabs a stack of vinyl singles and gestures to a box spilling over with T-shirts. She grabs it, grateful for his improvisational ingenuity, which smoothed her entrance. They ferry the merchandise into the next room and set everything on one of the booths across from the bar.

—You said you weren't coming, he whispers.

Xenie offers a snaggletooth grin.

—I changed my mind, Edward, she says. I knew you'd need my help.

—Come on, he says. I'm not an idiot.

In a deft sequence, Xenie picks up a T-shirt by the shoulders, snaps it to remove the wrinkles, then folds the fabric into a neat square.

—I started thinking it might be good for me to get out, she says. Be around people.

—Xenie, he says.

She lays down the T-shirt and meets Eddie's eyes. Her first impulse is to act defiantly impassive, but then she realizes he's sincerely concerned. Beneath the caked makeup, her cheeks flush.

—Okay, she says. A.C. and B.C. asked me to say something about Shaun. Give a little speech.

—When?

—Before the band plays. Or after. Whatever seems right. I think I'm going to do it. I have to do something to get some closure.

She's already told him more than she planned. If she says much more, she's afraid her resolve will crumble altogether.

—I don't want Florian and the other guys to know, she says. Okay?

Eddie seems unsure how to process this news, but he wants to trust her. He nods his head.

She surreptitiously slides her hand down the front of his jeans and gives his cock a light squeeze, then plants a lingering kiss on his cheek. Your hair looks really great, she murmurs. She ruffles and rearranges his part. Eddie leans his head back, letting her tease her fingernails along his tingling scalp.

●

Xenie's nails are painted a black without depth or reflection, the coats of lacquer precisely applied, as if in preparation for some midnight ritual.

●

Florian points to the guest list, but his eyes are trained on the next room. There are too many people on the list, he tells Eddie. We're already oversold. Maybe we should get rid of some of the obvious freaks. He glares meaningfully in the direction of Xenie.

Eddie pretends not to notice and takes back the list. I'm on it, he says. I'll work it out.

Florian searches for some clue to his unexpected attitude, but Eddie heads back toward the bar without meeting his eyes. With a jolt, Florian realizes what's different about his friend.

●

Eddie lays out the T-shirts in precise rows according to size and fans out the records in a scalloped arc. He's proud of the configuration he's created, which has proven to draw people's attention to the table.

—It's amazing how you actually enjoy this, Xenie says. I heard you last night folding sleeves and coloring artwork for the singles.

He looks up, surprised she was paying such close attention.

—I thought you were asleep, he says.

—You lost track of time. You were so engrossed in it.

—It's nice to be part of something. Part of the show.

—I've done this stuff, too, she says. There's no magic to it. You're just a gofer for those guys.

—It's not a big statement, he says. I'm good at it. It's something I like to do.

He hunches over the booth and pores over the names on the guest list.

—You forgot some singles in the other room, she says. I'll grab that last stack.

As Xenie sashays away, Eddie notices the odd asymmetry of her ass. There's a question he isn't sure how to ask about the unnatural ripple of her black skirt.

●

B.C. announces that the professional security team will arrive shortly. They'll be equipped with metal-detection wands, frisk each body that walks through the doors, and circulate through the crowd during the concert to isolate suspicious persons. We want you guys to be able to relax and have fun, he says.

—We want this to be a great show, A.C. adds. That's what everyone needs right now.

—We even got protection for you while you play, B.C. says with a devious grin. A.C. produces a trio of bulletproof vests. It's a joke, sort of. Florian winces.

The twins rustle around backstage and return hoisting a large piece of Plexiglas. They arrange the shield in front of the drum kit. The band gathers around the transparent plastic. As it wobbles, the air itself appears to shimmer. Florian stares at their frail reflections, warped and wavy spirits observing them from the other side.

●

There's more. B.C. points out the hinged rectangle carved into the center of the stage. We built a trapdoor, he says. You trigger it by stomping on this button. You'll land on a pile of mattresses in the basement.

—It's an escape hatch, A.C. says. Just in case things get weird.

This time, the twins are more somber. They spent serious time considering and constructing this. The precision of the emergency exit punctures the good-humored mood. It too clearly suggests the stakes of the epidemic.

When the twins motion for a volunteer, Randy and Derek D. both back away from the stage. Dry tongued and throat constricted, Florian is determined to defy his fear. He steps forward, offering an uncomfortable smile as he positions his storklike frame squarely over the trapdoor. He raises his foot to trigger the device. One moment he stares straight ahead, fretful lines scribbled across his face, and the next—

●

It takes Florian a second to remember how he arrived in this darkness. His bones feel like they're ringing. His breath hovers a few inches above his chest. He lies flat on his back, staring up at a rectangle of milky light. Spinning dust motes drift downward. Time seems to dilate. The world is slow to fasten around him. Objects creep into focus on the periphery—crates of beer bottles, broken speaker cabinets, stacks of folding chairs. Floating faces eventually appear overhead wearing querulous expressions. The timbre of their voices is familiar, but by the time their muffled sounds reach him, the sense of their sentences has decayed.

I wonder if this is what it feels like to be dead.

During the sound check, Florian suggests they play their first song wearing the bulletproof vests. A bit of brazen theater. They launch into the opening number, but their movements are stiff and the music sounds pinched. Despite the countless rehearsal hours they've clocked, the instruments feel limp in their hands. Even the electricity coursing through the cords has gone sour.

Halfway through the song, Florian waves them off.

—Forget it, he says. This is fucked.

—I know one problem, Randy says. He hefts the Plexiglas shield and hurls it offstage.

Florian strips off his vest and punts it toward the mixing board. You can't think about this shit and make music, he says. It's literally impossible.

—Forget the protection, Derek D. says. We should just play in our underwear.

Randy and Florian look to see if he's joking, but Derek's never been known for his sense of humor. They simultaneously strip off their shirts and pants. They toss their clothes at the foot of the stage in an escalating heap, crowned by three pairs of sweaty socks.

●

Randy counts off the tune. As Florian adjusts the dial on the green amp, a liquid mercury tone bursts from the speakers. The band plays slightly out of phase, propelled by grinding beats and terse bass lines, resembling a machine that spits out iridescent arcs of broken glass. Their bodies become siphons for the spasms of the song. A.C. and B.C. bob their heads in approval. Eddie and Lisa-Lisa shuffle toward the stage as if magnetized. Beside the bar in the next room, even Xenie's ears begin to twitch. Florian's eyes are shut and his mind is blank, letting himself experience the sound flowing through his pores.

> That's almost it. The sound that's been stuck in
> my head all these years.
> I can start to hear it.

While the others put away their instruments, Florian remains on the stage. He wants to stay in the flush of the moment, keep the sound circulating through his veins. He takes his time putting on his clothes. Sweeps away the dust that's accumulated on the platform. Rearranges the order of the guitar pedals. Tweaks the amp settings. But the realities of the room keep intruding. The quiet conversation of A.C. and B.C. in conference with Xenie, the infectious cackle of Lisa-Lisa, the questions about lighting adjustments, the small talk about encore selections. He can't shut out these clumsy siren songs of the mundane.

●

The presence of that silvery sound progressively seeps away.

●

Xenie seats herself on the wooden stage next to Florian. She scoops up a fallen capo from the floor and hands it to him. He looks at it warily, unsure whether it's meant as peace offering or provocation.

—Ready for tonight? she says.

Florian takes the capo and clamps it to the top of his guitar, then checks the instrument's tuning once again.

—Sure, he says.

—You're lucky, she says. Headlining a show like this is something local bands dream about.

—Yeah, well, Florian mutters, I've been having some dreams about it.

Behind him, he imagines a bright red plume smeared across the bass drum, pointing the way offstage.

—Me too, she says softly.

They silently stare at the wooden platform, realizing they're revisiting the same distressing vision, seeing the surface of the stage splashed crimson, spattered with permanent shadows.

●

Xenie fastens her arms round her knees, lacing her fingers together. Florian notices she's scraped the black polish off the nail of her pinkie. She drops her chin and speaks quietly, as if she's afraid of being overheard.

—Can I ask you a question? she says. Why are you doing this?

Florian's been waiting for something like this. How about this for a question, he says. Why are you here? Why have you decided to grace us with your presence?

Xenie's gaze is genuinely probing, not confrontational but not convinced.

—I'm not trying to pick a fight, she says. I'd just like to know why you're doing the show. Is it for Shaun? Or for you?

Florian tries to catch the attention of someone in the club who might provide an excuse to end this conversation, but everyone is preoccupied with their own preparations.

—You've got a lot of nerve, he says in a low voice. I knew Shaun since we were little kids.

—So?

—So I knew him before he started to change. I watched how he became more aloof and competitive.

—Maybe he was growing up. Maybe he outgrew you.

—That's your projection of Shaun. That's not what happened.

—What happened?

Florian flashes on the last few times he saw Shaun, how he seemed guarded and distracted, comparing notes on equipment, talking recording dates and touring plans, offering his familiar smile but treating him more like a colleague than his closest childhood friend.

—You poisoned him.

—That's ridiculous, Xenie says. I had nothing to do with it.

—Really?

—You don't understand me at all. You barely even see me. I'm just somebody's girlfriend to you.

—How could I miss you? he says. You've wrapped yourself in your grief to make sure you're the center of attention.

A cockroach scuttles across the stage between them, its antennae flicking at the wood. Just as Florian spots the insect, Xenie smashes it with the flat of her hand. She wipes the paste of guts, wings, and abdomen onto the floor.

—So violent, Florian says. That's the difference between you and me. I would never do something like that.

—It's just a bug, Florian, she says. Not a metaphor.

Xenie pushes up off the stage and rises to her feet.

—You still never answered my question, she says.

●

Lisa-Lisa isn't at the bar, so Florian sets up the shot glasses. He feels so sober it makes him queasy. He wordlessly salutes both Randy and Eddie with the whiskey bottle. The three of them toss back the alcohol and slam down their glasses in tandem.

Florian watches the two security guards who were recently briefed by A.C. and B.C. They resemble marines who've gotten profoundly stoned. They lounge on the patio, feet propped on benches, a cigarette circulating between them. The first pangs of Florian's migraine twitch in his temples.

—Look at those guys, Florian says. We're supposed to feel safe with them?

Randy and Eddie can't stop smirking at each other.

—This isn't funny, Florian says, causing them both to burst into peals of laughter.

•

Randy the Mongoose says: What's the difference between Echo Echo's toilet and a Puerto Rican whore?

Florian shrugs, his attention locked on the security guards.

Randy says: In an emergency, you can shit on a Puerto Rican whore.

Xenie looks up from refolding T-shirts. You're a pig, she says.

—Hey! Randy says. My mother's Puerto Rican, so I can tell that joke. It's not my problem you're uptight.

●

The door to the notoriously nauseating bathroom swings open. Lisa-Lisa tumbles out, blouse askew, hair frizzier than usual, hoop earrings swaying with each loopy step. Derek D. follows, smoothing the edges of his pink pompadour.

—Never would've believed it possible, Randy says. He plucks a twenty-dollar bill from his wallet and presents it to Derek D.

—She was eager, Derek D. says. I think she knows I fucked her boyfriend behind the supermarket last week. He fastidiously folds the money and snaps it in the elastic waistband of his underwear. Nobody appreciates how complicated it is to be bisexual, he says.

—You make it look easy, Randy says.

●

A tall man with a gray-flecked beard wanders into the club. His denim overalls appear freshly pressed. He removes his minor-league baseball cap and looks around, bewildered.

—What the fuck, Florian says. His head sinks into his hands.

Eddie jumps up and stops the man from coming any farther. Sorry, he says. The club's still closed.

—The door was open, the man says.

A.C. yells at the security guards slacking on the patio. Sorry about that, he says.

—I'll handle this, Eddie says, and shuffles the man around the corner, back toward the entrance.

The pressure in Florian's head tightens several notches.

—This is too much, he says. Any stranger can walk in here and you're telling us we're safe? You're all too distracted by bullshit to realize that we could actually get killed.

Florian hurls the three shot glasses against the wall, one after another after another. They explode in a series of brittle ricocheting sprays.

Everybody thinks this is a joke.

Florian blusters out of the bar, stomping past the box-office alcove, and heading toward the entrance that's mercifully obscured from the rest of the club. His head is a hive of roiling thoughts. His strangulated face resembles a punctuation mark in a foreign alphabet. Eddie stands on the steps engaged in polite conversation with the bearded man. Florian interrupts.

He says: What the hell are you doing here, Dad?

●

Florian's father removes his baseball cap and fiddles with the brim, cracking it in half and reshaping it with his thumb. He's taller and stockier than his son but presents a less imposing presence.

—I'm here to check out your band, he says with an abashed smile.

Florian looks around for Eddie, but he's vanished.

—The show is sold out, he says.

—Can't my son get me a ticket?

—Since when have you cared about my music?

—I came to support you, his father says. I know this is a rough night.

—I know what night it is.

—Three years, his father says. Hard to believe she's been gone that long.

—I'm fine.

—The last two anniversaries you went on benders that lasted almost a week, his father says. I don't want you to do something stupid.

—You never took it very well either. I'm surprised you're still sober. I'm surprised you're still standing.

—I'm worried about you, his father says. I'm worried about you doing this show tonight.

—It's not a big deal.

—Your mom, his father says. You were everything to her. She'd want you to be safe.

Florian chokes down the lump of mucus that's formed in the back of his throat. He blinks the redness out of his eyes.

—Bruce, his father says.

He reaches out his hand, but his son recoils.

—You know only Mom could call me that, Florian says. It's Florian to you.

●

Florian scratches at his tattoo. Maybe it's the twilight, but the design seems to keep fading. The extra layer of ink has sweated away, and the green letter floats under his skin like a ghostly bacterial growth.

●

Florian and his father look into each other's eyes and listen to the filament buzz of the overhead light. The silence is reminiscent of the months after the funeral, alone in the house together, sitting at the dinner table and unable to fathom the first thing about the person opposite. During that stretch, his father was either catatonic or absent. He'd vanish for days at a time, letting the place grow filthy and leaving Florian to scour away the accumulated mess, along with the residue of toxic memories that were contaminating them.

—Your mother used to sing in bands, his father says. Before you were born. She played all over the place. She was pretty popular.

—I've heard all those stories. You made her stop singing.

—She didn't want to do it anymore. I didn't have anything to do with it.

—The show is sold out, Florian says. The show is sold out. The show is . . .

He repeats himself over and over, the same tempo and intonation, like a needle trapped in a run-out groove.

●

His father replaces the baseball cap on his head. You should drop by the house sometime, he says. You're always welcome. Then he reluctantly returns to his truck, gripping the steering wheel for a long minute before igniting the engine. The tires churn up loose gravel as they furrow a path through the parking lot.

Florian follows a few paces behind, making sure the vehicle turns onto the street and heads toward the highway. He watches until the glare of the taillights gutters away. Then he walks back to the club, tracing the channels his father's truck carved in the gravel, obeying some obscure impulse to ensure his feet fall precisely within their tracks.

Three years since I stood over her dead body.
Couldn't get the blood out of the carpet.
Ripped it up and added it to the trash.
Never replaced it. Just avoided the living room.
It still reeks of rust.

There are so many ghosts here tonight.
I can feel them around every corner.

I owe them all something.

Florian sits alone on the front steps of the club. He roots through his pockets, hunting for a lighter and hand-rolled cigarette. He locates them, along with some scattered seed pellets. The only possessions of his mother's that he didn't remove were the bird feeders she'd hung throughout the backyard. They were her pride, and she spent hours cataloging the flashes of feathers that circled around them. Florian still sneaks back to the house to keep the feeders stocked, making sure he avoids his father, who probably doesn't even realize they're being refilled. It's been a few weeks since he's gone. As he licks the seam of the cigarette paper, he notices a smattering of tan and black food pellets stuck to his fingertips.

●

Somewhere in the waning twilight, those bird feeders sway in the breeze. Tall plastic cylinders with metal perches and wooden domes. Strung at varying heights from tree branches. Clinking softly on their lines. An intricate archipelago winding through the yard as they recede from sight.

●

A single reverberating shot startles Florian out of his reverie. He wants to believe it's a backfiring car. There's no subsequent scream or siren. He cranes his neck into the encroaching darkness, struggling to see the sound. The echo is slow to dissipate, its vibration rippling through the air, scratched onto the surface of the night. He tries to believe it belongs to a story unfolding in another Arcadia, a drama unconnected to him.

●

Eddie's patient shadow hovers at the corner of the building. He watches Florian take a long drag, inhale a mouthful of smoke, and add to the tiny pyramid of ash rising between his feet.

—I thought you quit, Eddie says.

—I did, Florian says. This is hash.

—A.C. and B.C. want everybody inside.

—They can wait, Florian says. They can wait forever.

•

As Florian and Eddie pass the joint back and forth, the sensations around them become amplified. The teasing breeze. The dervishes of smoke. The cadences of unseen birdsong. Those three notes are naggingly familiar, each lower than the last, repeated in halting rhythm. In reply, Florian silently recites the names of songbirds from memory. The tune superimposes itself over the canopy of stars that just snapped into glittering focus.

•

—She dyed your hair, Florian says, didn't she?

—What?

—Your hair is blond, Florian says. It's the same shade as hers. You probably thought I didn't notice.

—You mean Xenie?

—If you're sharing hair dye, you're in over your head. That girl is seriously damaged.

—Who isn't?

—She's way more fucked up and smarter than you think, Florian says. I don't know if even I could handle her.

—Oh, even you?

—I know I sound like an asshole, but I'm your friend. I worry about you. I'm talking as a worried friend.

Florian waits for Eddie to share some stories, but he keeps his thoughts about Xenie to himself, clearly even more infatuated than Florian suspected.

—Come on, Eddie says. You're worried about the show. You're freaking out, but it's going to be great.

—I worry about it all.

—Remember the time I ran away, Eddie says. I hid in the forest and was terrified by every sound.

—I brought you food and we hung out.

—You talked me out of going back home to my parents. You made sure I stayed the night.

Florian pictures them sitting together in the dark woods. Probably stoned. His skinny friend nestled among the pine needles, bundled in two sweatshirts, hands clutching a rapidly dimming flashlight.

—Sometimes you have to teach them a lesson, Florian says. Take a stand.

—This is your night. Your stand.

—This is going to be a circus. Everybody is coming here for Shaun. No matter how well we play, he's what they'll remember.

—Play for yourself. Everything else will fall into place.

—I don't know, Florian says, I want the set to be something that would make Shaun proud.

—Shaun is gone, Eddie says. This is your night. You deserve it.

Florian looks over at his friend. The appropriate words are far beyond him right now, so he tries to express his gratitude by forming a circle with his mouth and blowing two smoke rings, one ring inside the other.

> *Maybe it'll be a show people will talk about for years.*
> *Maybe I'll finally be heard.*

It's past time to open the doors. Everyone scurries through the club. The twins make the security team recite their step-by-step instructions. Lisa-Lisa counts out the cash drawers. The band untangles cords while Florian rearranges his equipment one last time. Eddie calls out adjustments to Xenie, who stands tiptoe on a barstool, tightening the corners of the plastic banner behind the stage.

—Two minutes, Lisa-Lisa shouts.

They all huddle together at the bar. A bottle of bourbon is passed around, and they each take a swallow. The shattered remnants of the shot glasses still litter the floor. Their shards give off an intense sparkle.

•

Nobody makes a toast, so Florian figures he should hoist the bottle and provide the benediction:

Into the void.

•

The parking lot within the razor-wire fence is full. Cars line the streets next to the club, packing the nearby grass lots, pulling into ragged rows on dead lawns. Drivers transfer valuables to the trunk and pray their rides are shitty enough that nobody steals them. This neighborhood is a haven for cheap crack. Or as the twins have it, at night the vampires come out. A mad crush of people funnels into a slow-snaking entrance queue. A number of them carry handmade shrines and memorials for Shaun. In less than an hour, the place will be over capacity. The security guards thoroughly frisk every physique, turning out pockets, patting inseams, tracing the buzzing contours of each body with a magnetic wand.

•

The crowd slips their IDs under the black light and presents their right hands to get stamped. They remember the routine, but they're unusually reserved as they're herded through the entrance hallway toward the bar. People alternate between nervous pauses and awkward laughter as they line up to order the cheapest cans of beer. Everybody seems conflicted about what tone to adopt, if this show is the somber culmination of the past few months or their cue to shed circumspection. They're unsure whether they want tonight's concert to cast off the past or seal them inside it.

●

As people step into the performance area, they confront the banner suspended across the back of the stage: a photograph of a bloodied panda lying in a pile of bamboo leaves. It's the logo of a respected independent music label, sponsor of tonight's event, but the image still makes people wince. Some say it originated from Chinese dissidents who mutilated the cuddly state symbol to protest censorship. Others say that even as an emblem of extreme free speech, it's in poor taste. The label is giving away music by Shaun's band. Stacks of their single rise on tables throughout the room. A hit parade of Shaun's favorite songs detonates from the speakers and livens up the crowd. A deejay hunches in the narrow space behind the soundboard. Every time he flips a record, the axis of the room shifts ever so slightly.

●

Florian sits on the back patio and keeps watch for trouble. People gather around the picnic tables and hanging paper lanterns, stubbing out cigarette butts in the sand-filled planters. Florian shakes hands and makes small talk with friends and fellow musicians. It means a lot to be playing tonight, he finds himself saying. Tonight of all nights. As he speaks, his mind roams elsewhere. Though he can't spot any actual flowers, he's distracted by the pervasive scent of roses.

An elfin woman wearing a beret breaks through the ring of well-wishers. She places her hand on Florian's wrist, a light but persistent touch. He does a double take, startled by the stranger's profile. She bears a slight resemblance to his ex-girlfriend Jade, who moved out of town but not before telling all their friends that he had trouble getting it up in bed.

—You look like you could use a drink, the elfin woman says.

—A beer would be great, Florian says. Thank you.

—I adore your music, she says. I'd love to talk to you about it sometime. Maybe after the show tonight?

—Uh, sure, he says. That'd be cool.

—I'll be back with that beer, she says with a solicitous smile.

The woman drifts away in the direction of the bar. Florian notices the amused looks she collects from his friends as she moons her way through the mob of people. Her frizzy black hair is braided into a thick strand that stretches the length of her back. With each step, it swings like a pendulum.

—Well, well, Randy says. You should pay more attention to that one.

—I was being polite, Florian says.

—Plenty of time to get in a quick one before the show.

—I can't think about that sort of thing right now.

—That's the brooding magnetism the ladies love, Randy says. Keep cultivating it.

—I'm not brooding.

—You attract the weirdest groupies, Randy marvels.

●

Florian filters through the audience, scanning for the faraway expressions of those who might consider themselves his biggest fan. The pock-faced boy in a hoodie, the black kid sporting a bicycle chain as a necklace, the sullen girl in a puffy rainbow wig. Each seems a likely candidate. In photographs, the killers' uninhabited stares generate a sort of negative gravity, an implosive pull that destabilizes their surroundings. But close-up, none of these kids are intimidating. Florian physically towers over each of them. Or maybe he's mistaking photographs for reality. Maybe gravity isn't achieved until the trigger is pulled.

●

Florian keeps watch on Xenie. She's shed the black blazer and rolled up the sleeves of her purple sweater. She hovers around the alcove at the back of the club that contains the homemade shrines, a ramshackle collection of collages, assemblages, paintings. There's one photograph she keeps tracing with her index finger. Florian can easily imagine why she's drawn to this particular image. In it, Shaun raises his sprained and splinted wrist and flashes a smile, his easygoing spirit saturating the print. The way Xenie distractedly flattens the photo, Florian can't tell whether she's trying to absorb some of Shaun's optimism or erase it. Maybe she doesn't know herself. She seems caught in some inner conflict, her thoughts collapsing in on her, threatening to bury her inside her own indecision. She outlines the image so often that it bubbles from the wall. With every touch, the adhesive loses more of its stick.

●

Xenie probes the card for clues. It's an illustration of a man hanging from a tree, strung up by his ankle, hands bound behind his back, head radiant with a burning halo. She places this talisman from the tarot deck next to a photograph of Shaun, but any resemblance between them remains obscure.

Eddie approaches and gently puts his hands on her shoulders.

—That's a haunting song, he says. What is it?

—What are you talking about?

—The song you were singing to yourself, he says.

—I wasn't singing.

—You don't have to be embarrassed, he says. It was mesmerizing. It made my neck hairs stand on end.

—I wasn't singing, she repeats.

—Okay, Eddie says. Okay.

He runs his fingers along the small of her back. She tenses, then eases into his touch. She's amazed how readily her body responds to him, how quickly his caress can calm her.

—It must be hard having all these pictures of Shaun here, he says.

She continues to search for some presentiment of tragedy in the photos, but even in the one taken a few days before his death she's struck by his effortless grin.

—The worst thing, she says, is that he looks exactly the same.

—How do you mean?

—I'll go on and on, she says. And he'll stay frozen here. He probably wouldn't recognize me now. I've been so warped by all this sadness.

As they walk to the bar, her mind returns to the tarot. She can't decide whether the Hanged Man is augur or omen, symbol of past predicament or unfulfilled prophecy. Everything remains inscrutable except the sensation of the world turned upside down.

●

Too many familiar faces. Florian is uncomfortable seeing so many people who were at Shaun's funeral. As the club grows more crowded, it recalls the circuslike atmosphere of that service, people constantly bumping into one another, acting either uptight or unhinged. Strangers tipping over the enormous floral arrangements, jockeying for prime seats in the front pews, erupting into spontaneous sobs. The tense ceremony, full of doomy hymns, put everyone on edge. Flasks circulated through the room as the pastor stumbled through the saccharine eulogy. Florian is still amazed that he managed to last through half of it.

When it was over, the mourners seized on the same idea as him. They thronged across the street to the bar to start drinking in earnest. Bottles of alcohol soon lined the full length of the wooden counter, bodies three deep, spirits decanted.

●

Lisa-Lisa can't serve fast enough. Her hands are constantly in motion, filling the increasingly voluble orders for hard liquor, switching between brightly labeled bottles, splashing out refills, counting crinkled bills, making change. Each movement is soundtracked by the insistent clang of empty glasses.

●

Everyone at the bar tries not to stare at the willowy woman with stringy brown hair. As she orders a beer, the conversations around her dissolve into silence, and even the most cynical members of the scene strain to remain aloof. Everybody is shamed by her presence. Her swollen left cheek is scarred from a recent gunshot wound. She must have been one of those injured at the show. Lisa-Lisa pours her a beer and quietly says the drink is on the house.

●

The spirals of the woman's scar tissue make Florian dizzy. For a moment, he imagines dropping the needle of a record player into the puckered grooves of her wound. He wonders if it could broadcast the pain of that night. The disorienting spasms of shots and screams. The racking waves of adrenaline and nausea. The sensation of a stomach determined to wring itself inside out.

> *Shaun collapses, his body crashing to the stage.*
> *He tries to speak, but the words taste like copper.*
> *His head feels like it's filled with bubbling water.*

Florian slams the bathroom door behind him. He kneels in front of the toilet and starts to retch. He's too sick to be disgusted by the bowl's oozing cracks and moldering shit stains. He can see through the fractured floorboards to the expanse of dirt below. The network of exposed pipes, rutty weeds, weird blooms of fecal flowers. He keeps heaving, but nothing comes out. His lip jerks and drools. A sinewy rope of saliva swings from his chin. He pants deeply, trying to regain control of his equilibrium.

●

Florian's eyes are fixed on the toilet's water tank. Half in a trance, he reaches for the ceramic lid. Unsure what he might find when he removes it.

He swallows his breath for several seconds, then flips it over.

●

On the underside of the toilet lid, crisscrossed by silver duct tape, somebody has placed an object wrapped in newspaper.

Florian cautiously peels back the thin sheets of smudged print.

Inside sits a revolver.

●

Florian replaces the lid. He rinses the residue of ink from his hands and confronts his brooding reflection in the mirror. His oddly proportioned and unappealing face. His features are in flux, projecting different versions of himself like a frantic slideshow. His heart thrums to a hiccupping rhythm.

He removes the toilet lid and flips it over again. Fingers the duct tape that holds the revolver in place. Peels back the newsprint. Runs his hands along the polished steel of the cylinders. Reconfirms it's real. The weight feels right. It's as heavy as his head.

●

He leaves the revolver where it is.

Now he knows the worst is going to happen.

He's almost relieved.

> *This is what's coming.*
> *It's been coming all along.*
> *It's pointless trying to outrun it.*

He bends toward the mirror. Seized by a desire to fix himself in this fleeting moment. To treat this shiny surface like a headstone. He extracts his apartment key from his front pocket. The veins in his forearm bulge as he etches eight letters across the center of his reflection. The only eight letters that make sense right now.

•

As Florian steps into the hallway, several girls at the bar burst into applause and cheer his name in unison. In other circumstances, their shrill drunken cries might not sound like the call of destiny.

•

Florian pulls Eddie away from the congested merch table. It's hard to hear much beyond the throttling riffs spilling from the sound system. The deejay is building his set to a punishing crescendo with a pile-driving song by local legend Taconic Parkway. A few more punk anthems and it'll be time for the show to begin.

Florian hollers: There's something I need you to do.

—If anything happens to me, he says.

—When something happens to me, he says.

He shouts straight into his friend's ear. Eddie nods and digs his compulsively gnawed fingernails into Florian's shoulder, almost breaking the skin.

•

Xenie keeps a low profile. Mostly she sits in the booth by the bar and collects cash for T-shirts. She blows her nose and discovers the napkin is engorged with bloody mucus. She borrows a handkerchief and presses it against her face, alarmed to watch the white fabric bloom red. Lisa-Lisa scurries over with a box of tissues.

—You okay? she says. You sure you should be here?

Xenie struggles not to get swallowed by the question.

—I'll be fine, she says. It'll stop soon.

She pinches the bridge of her nose and wads up several tissues, stuffing them inside her nostrils. The bloody handkerchief lies coiled on the seat next to her, resembling some larval discharge.

—Tonight must be hard for you, Lisa-Lisa ventures.

—I'm convinced those shrines are making me sick, Xenie says. I don't know why people bothered if they were going to do such a terrible job. If another person tells me they're beautiful, I'm going to scream.

—They are pretty ugly, Lisa-Lisa says.

—I know I'm awful, Xenie says. I must sound like some elitist snob.

As she removes a drenched tissue, more crimson dribbles down her lips. She's terrified by the sight of all this blood.

—Maybe I shouldn't be here, she murmurs. Maybe this was a mistake.

She wills her body to behave, but the blood is unstaunchable. She tilts her head back and pinches her nose with renewed fury. Her feet are encircled by an expanding ring of red-stained tissues.

●

People migrate toward the stage. The heat escalates from the mass of bodies. The security guards scan the audience for potential troublemakers, circulating through the crowd in the pattern of a figure eight. A squirrelly boy sporting a child's birthday hat shapes his hand like a gun. Two raised fingers for the barrel and the thumb as hammer. He walks behind people, takes aim, and shouts, Bang! Most roll their eyes and shove him away. One guy's head recoils in slow motion, the fluttering movement of his hand mimicking the decelerated spray of blown brains as his body crumples to the floor. The guy bounces back to life with a half bow and a sheepish smile. Scattered laughter crackles through the room, but it sounds brittle. The boy in the birthday hat stares in astonishment at his outstretched fingers.

●

Florian needs air. He wedges himself through the barricaded front door and stands alone facing the street. The stretch of asphalt is absent of any traffic. The racket of the club is subdued enough that he can hear his own thoughts. His mind keeps returning to the one time his mother beat him as a kid. She had trusted him to stay alone in the house. He had pulled the curtains, turned off the lights, and lit some candles. He put on a favorite album, found at a flea market, whose cover featured two women in black housecoats and red scarves standing against a brick wall. It looked like they'd been cornered, but they snarled defiantly at the camera and bared their red teeth.

He played it at obliterating volume until he felt himself dissolving inside the ecstatic din. When he opened his eyes, he wasn't surprised to see the living room was on fire. The flames climbing the curtains made sense, a physical manifestation of the music, ignited by forces deep within the song. Florian doesn't dwell on how he managed to smother the blaze or the belt whipping that left welts. His keenest memory is the several seconds after he opened his eyes, sitting motionless on the carpet, enraptured by the undulating fronds of orange flame, flickering in time to the rhythm. This was the moment he knew he wanted to be a musician.

●

Whenever Florian shares this story, he tells it with a sense of wonder. He emphasizes it was worth the danger and the beating. But it's also a memory of failure. If he had better understood the music, if he had been brave enough to heed its call, Florian knows that he would've turned up the stereo, walked out onto the lawn, and let his house be consumed by the fire.

●

His bandmates are probably searching for him, but Florian lingers outside a little longer. Down the block, a streetlight flickers to life. Under its fuzzy illumination, standing on the sidewalk, he spots a deer. They lock eyes for a moment, then the animal bolts, galloping away on tall spindly legs into the shadows. Florian can't decide whether he should follow its lead, whether it's being skittish or if it's smart to run. He watches as the doe materializes under the pooled light of each successive lamppost, smaller at each reappearance, until it disappears altogether.

> *Mom, if you're listening to me.*
> *If you're watching over me.*
> *I don't believe it, but I'm asking anyway.*

Backstage, Florian joins Derek D. and Randy the Mongoose. He bobs on the balls of his feet, trying to shake the tension out of his body. The cramped space is furnished with a sagging couch, but the band clusters together near the wooden riser that holds their instruments and steals a glimpse of the massed faces. Sweat shined, alcohol aglow, glistening with expectation.

●

—It's gone, Randy says. My amulet is gone. I tied it to my cymbal stand and now it's gone.

—That trinket you bought at the New Age store? Florian says.

—It's a family heirloom, Randy says. Sacred amulet of protection. I brought it here for all of us.

His complexion is pasty and pale. His voice has eroded to a shaky rasp.

—I keep having these nightmares, he says. They're pretty violent.

—Sorry about the amulet, Derek D. says.

—Maybe we should wear the bulletproof vests, Randy says.

—You're joking, Florian says.

He's not joking.

Florian puts his hand on Randy's shoulder. He can feel the tissue and tendons quailing throughout his friend's body.

—We have to do this, Florian says softly.

The audience starts to clap and holler. Soon they'll be stamping their feet.

—There's nothing between us and them, Randy says.

●

The lights go out. The band can no longer see one another's faces, but their emotions are so palpable they might as well be the graffiti sprayed across the walls. Florian shuffles his feet in a small circle, determined not to buckle under the fear.

—This is our fucking moment, he says.

—I was going to say we should play in our underwear again, he says. But that's not enough. We're not some precious teases.

—I think we should take it all off, he says.

Without another word, they strip off their clothes. It feels good to make a defiant gesture like this, but they're slightly self-conscious before peeling away the final layer. Derek D. goes first.

—I know you guys think I'm not committed, he says.

Standing amid a heap of black leather, Derek showcases his latest look. To match his pompadour, his pubic hair has indeed been dyed bright pink.

●

In a final ceremonial flourish, Florian produces a tube of red lipstick. He adorns each of their foreheads. Though the marks resemble third eyes, they're really targets.

I want to be worthy of their ammunition.

The vintage lamps set on the amplifiers dim to an anticipatory glow. The recording of the electronic drone announces their entrance. The deep tones tint the atmosphere, laying a translucent scrim over the space. Florian's senses must be sharpened because he can now see clearly how the entire club is a shimmering violet.

●

As the naked band climbs onto the stage, there are gasps and hoots. Florian leaps up and latches on to a hanging speaker, swinging back and forth before landing in front of the audience. Bursts of laughter erupt from the crowd, then a galvanizing round of applause quakes the walls. Florian straps on his guitar and strums with a dramatic flourish. He's determined to ignore the mounting pain of his migraine. Guided by a premonition that he's stepping into a performance soon to be lodged in local legend, he flips the switch on the green amp and cranks the volume a few extra notches so there's no chance he won't be heard.

●

Florian positions his bare feet directly above the trapdoor. His body feels attuned to the club's structure, as if he can perceive the maze of plumbing beneath the floorboards and trace the rush of fluids through the metal pipes, which culminates in the tide of brackish water rising inside the toilet tank.

Above it all levitates the revolver.

He silently chants the number of its chambers.

A sort of pacifying koan.

One, two, three, four, five, six.

Randy cues the band. He clicks his drumsticks and they launch into the first song. Florian wonders how far they'll make it into the set. If they'll manage to play longer than Shaun. If this will be more than a ritual reenactment of that night. After a tentative first few seconds, the adrenaline surge takes over. They make it past the first chorus, the second chorus, the bridge, and then they're into terra incognita. The perspiration slides off their skin and hits the stage with its own distinct rhythm.

●

The band can feel the audience alongside them. The crowd has become a single unified organism, no longer tentative but leaning into the music, abandoning themselves to the sound, willing the musicians to live up to the moment they're immersed in together.

They're all gathered under the watchful gaze of the bleeding panda. With its impassive black eyes, it resembles some remote deity. Florian scans the crowd. Among the throng, there's the pock-faced boy in the hoodie, the black kid sporting the bicycle-chain necklace, the sullen girl in the puffy rainbow wig. This is their moment, too.

Their faces stare up at him, blistered with sweat, emphatically blank.

●

Eddie stands on the periphery. Even as he's drawn to the mass of bodies lurching on its heels to the pulsating push-pull of the rhythms, he keeps checking over his shoulder. He tries not to seem clinging, but he's concerned about Xenie. She sits alone at the bar, stationed in front of the closed-circuit monitor, watching the grainy images of the performance happening on the other side of the wall. Florian leaning over his guitar, lost in an extended solo, simultaneously spooling out a thread of notes and unraveling them. Eddie notices the stray flecks of paper clinging to Xenie's nostrils. There's no more flow, but she still clutches one of the stained tissues, restlessly turning it over in her hands, examining the scarlet smears as though they were different sides of some foreign coin.

●

The amp starts to crackle. Florian adjusts the dials, but the thin sound is harsh and scratchy. He attempts to coax it back to life with a series of gentle kicks, but the pitch remains ear wrenchingly awful. It's happening too fast. The song is speeding away from him. The relentless tempo pulls him out of the moment, but he's still tethered to the tune and it feels like he's being dragged along by his ankles, skinned and skidding.

●

The others don't notice the technical troubles. Randy is subsumed by his sheer momentum. Derek D. is in his preening element. Florian is the sole reason the band's sound keeps taking longer to reach the audience. The delay from stage to synapses returns the crowd to their bodies. People notice how the air feels more saturated with heat than sound. They're distracted by the oppressive humidity, the perspiration collecting in cracks and pits, the salty excretions of every pore.

●

As the dull pressure escalates behind his eyes, Florian ratchets up his volume. He sings louder than usual, trying to fill every particle of the room. Toward the back of the crowd, he spots the elfin woman with the beret. She looks bored, not entirely present, as though her shadow has wandered off. Florian is flooded by a sudden desire to make love to her, the need to establish a corporeal connection, to feel the sticky slip of their forms merging, to return her beating heart to the present moment, to fuck her shadow back into her skin.

•

Florian strums the opening of the next song faster, sending the band hurtling after him. He's desperate to make something happen. His voice is hoarse and he's sliding out of tune. Several people start to retreat outside to the patio. The black kid with the bicycle-chain necklace is among the first to defect. Florian finds himself barking lyrics at the backs of their receding heads.

•

Florian is increasingly aware of his naked body. His thin frame, elongated arms, and flipperlike feet can't sustain the audience's attention. He starts to feel truly exposed. He tries to let himself get swept away in the moment, to allow the performance to become a single continuous gesture, a blissful blur later recalled by listeners as one long soaring song. But he can't do it. Surges of pure being sputter to a halt. Songs continue to let out the tension. The band's set is a leaking ship, taking on water with every verse, and the crowd has stopped bailing. The sullen girl removes her puffy rainbow wig and slinks toward the smoke-filled patio. She shakes the black sweat from her drenched locks and joins the sea of cigarettes and cell phones, rapt faces absorbed in digital displays.

•

Florian plays purposefully choppy, changes lyrics, generates reefs of feedback. Between songs, he thumps the microphone stand against the stage and curses out his bandmates. He pretends to be angry to ratchet some tension back into the music, but he fakes it so convincingly that he finds he's actually motherfucking furious.

As more people filter outside, he starts to viciously slap his own face.

Come back.

Don't start screaming. I won't be able to stop.
The scream will start screaming me.

Maybe they changed their mind.

Maybe I'm not even worth killing.

Three years tonight.

The house sparrow.

The russet sparrow.

The parrot-billed sparrow.

The white-throated sparrow.

Cha-cha-cha-cah.

Wheet-wheet'eo.

Vrdi, vreed, vreed.

Tee-si, tee-si, tee-si.

To-ree, to-ree, to-ree.

Ta-wit, ta-wit, ta-wit, tee-yo.

Easy, Bruce. Take it easy.

His head might be inflating. It feels filled with tiny bubbles, as if helium is being pumped into his cranium, multiplying with every breath, swarming against the knitted ridges of his skull. Florian's mouth is pressed against the microphone and he opens it to relieve the excruciating pressure. He's surprised to hear himself screaming:

—Shoot me! Shoot me! Shoot me!

●

A current of panic surges through the room. People snap out of their heat-induced stupor. Spines rigid, eyeballs widened, assholes clenched. The words spook Florian as well. His face leaps around on his skull. His pained expression resembles someone struggling to bench-press a terrific weight.

He's not sure whether it's an instinct to end with a

crescendo or save his skin that prompts him to activate the trapdoor.

He shuts his eyes, summons his weight, and stomps on the button.

●

Florian opens his eyes to find himself in the same space. He's bewildered, goggling at the crowd as if they're other-worldly beings. He keeps stomping on the button, but he's stranded onstage.

●

On the monitor by the bar, the black-and-white image of Florian raises his guitar over his head. The spectators at the counter draw closer to the flickering video feed. They're huddled tight, swaying slightly, drunkenly enthralled. Their number has steadily increased over the course of the evening. Eddie is uneasy that Xenie is no longer among them. A second before the pixelated picture of Florian's guitar slams into the stage, they hear the resounding thud and feel the aftershock ripple through the floorboards.

●

Florian bashes his guitar against the trapdoor, but the wood barely splinters. It remains stubbornly shut, deny-ing passage. Randy shouts at him to stop. Derek D. backs away in alarm. From the soundboard, A.C. waves his arms, sending urgent signals that not even he understands.

Florian musters all his mad fervor. He swings the guitar in a wild arc directly at the trapdoor and brings it down squarely on his own foot. He howls, hopping in a frenzied circle, clutching at his broken toes. Toppling face-first, he lands with his nose pressed against the outline of the exit.

Crawling offstage on hands and knees, he drags the guitar behind him, its cord towing the green amp after it. He's pursued by screeching waves of feedback.

●

Randy and Derek D. barely seem aware they're still playing. It's a reflex born out of pure habit. They look to Florian for some cue, but he's crumpled backstage, tangled in the guitar strap, moaning into his fist. They end the tune with an upsurge, a half-hearted attempt to make it sound like a planned finale. They drop their instruments and walk away, bare assed, no backward glance.

●

The chaos and commotion draw everyone from the patio. People stand in the darkness and point at the dimly lit stage, stillborn gestures and stunted phrases struggling to reconstruct what just happened. Even the deejay is too stunned to start any music. The room is a chorus of confused murmurs.

●

A figure hovers at the back of the stage. Emerging from the shadows, it floats a few steps toward the audience. In the murk and muddle, people need several moments to process the uncanny sight.

As the impossible image coalesces, the crowd is confronted by a familiar boy with long hair.

It's Shaun.

●

Shaun carries a boom box. He places it at his feet and presses PLAY. A song with a hypnotically slow tempo and a chiming piano riff begins. An old tune that feels broadcast from another dimension. Shaun opens his mouth wide, creating the illusion that what leaps from his throat is the beseeching voice of a soul singer. He holds a flashlight under his chin like a microphone, the beam of light bleaching his features. His lips are in synch with the singer's lilting croon, miming the desperate undertones of yearning and devotion.

●

It's an eerie likeness, and people are only now beginning to realize this is Xenie. She wears Shaun's ratty clothes and a wig with a flat plastic sheen. The familiar purple sweater sticks out under a flannel shirt. None of this breaks the collective spell. The summoning of the departed. The materialization of the apparition. The thrall of the visitation.

●

Xenie's illuminated mouth enunciates the lyrics with relish.

I'll forever love you for the rest of my days.

The banal words take on a new quality. It's not the baritone of the singer or the shimmer of the accompaniment, but the emphatic movement of Xenie's lips tracing the contours of the words that supply their meaning.

I'll never part from you or your loving ways.

During the stately piano solo, she takes a tube of glycerin and squeezes a drop into each eye. Her irises turn an agitated red through the final verse, and tears stream down her cheeks. Her lips form the words:

May this fire in my soul, dear, forever burn.

●

The end of the performance is met with silence. For several seconds, the only sound is the rattle of blank magnetic tape threading a path through mechanical spools. Xenie presses STOP, steps off the stage, and withdraws into the darkness.

●

Nobody wants to be the first to break the silence. Applause feels too disruptive for this delicate moment. Instead, a reverberating hiss spreads throughout the club. People steadily add their voices to the low whistle, an intensifying ovation of spooked appreciation.

I can't believe those idiots are impressed.

The lights flicker on. Backstage they illuminate the figure

of Florian, curled on the floor and clutching his pulverized foot. His pain is doubled by the migraine throbbing in his temples. His bandmates call to him, but their mouths seem to move at a different speed than their voices. The entire room feels out of phase. When the words finally reach him, they deliver what's either an ironic salute or a sincere curse: *You're still alive.*

●

Randy and Derek D. pull on their clothes. They're too pissed off to comfort Florian, who refuses to get dressed. He now sits perched atop the sofa, leg dangling, completely nude except for the bloody napkin cinched around his foot. He smears the red splotch in the middle of his forehead and stares at the runny residue on his fingertips. A compound of sweat, grease, lipstick. There's some significance to this mixture, but he can't summon it. Everything has been emptied of meaning.

●

People filter into the cramped backstage. Randy pumps each outstretched hand and accentuates the show's virtues. They bought bulletproof plastic and wanted us to play behind it, he brags. But we totally refused. Several dudes nod their heads in muted appreciation. Florian hopes the show's drama counted for something, but people avoid mentioning the most obvious aspects of the performance. They offer half-hearted congratulations and half-assed compliments. Their praise is like wet confetti.

Lisa-Lisa is the only one who references what happened onstage. She appears with a fat roll of duct tape. My God, she says, how many toes did you break?

Everyone's too embarrassed to talk about the show.
They actually pity me.

—I really fucked up, Florian says.

Eddie awkwardly rolls his shoulders into what might be construed as a shrug. It was fine, he says.

—C'mon, Florian says. Don't bullshit me.

Eddie says: It was fine.

—It was fine in sound check, Florian says. After the amp shorted, my sound was screwed. That's when it all blew apart.

Eddie won't make eye contact. It was fine, he repeats.

—Even you? Florian says. Even you can't say it?

If someone would dare to tell him the truth, it might puncture his black mood, but Eddie simply pats him on the shoulder. The obvious kindness of the gesture will leave a bruise.

•

B.C. appears with a black marker. Randy and Derek D. tag their names alongside the hallowed graffiti that covers the club's walls. Florian refuses his part in the ceremony. His migraine tightens the grooves in his head another turn. All the signatures are just ink. They resemble the tired obscenities carved in bathroom stalls, each stroke the equivalent of the forged phone number, the exhortation to rim someone's mother, the cannon spew of a scribbled cock.

> *Maybe I tried too hard.*
> *Maybe I should've paid tribute to Shaun with some bullshit karaoke.*
> *Everyone seemed to love that.*

Most of the crowd has dispersed through the parking lot and into the night. Florian watches as A.C., Randy, and Derek D. strike the drum kit, break down the microphone stands, loop ovals of black cable around their elbows.

—Hey, B.C. says. Why don't you make yourself useful.

He extends a broom to Florian, who ignores him. He can't even summon the emotional energy to shake his head. The tide of dirt can rise, and the filth can choke them all.

The pock-faced kid lurks at the edge of the stage, trying to remain incognito inside his hoodie. He presses his fingers into the battered indentations of the trapdoor, as if absorbing the evening's emotions through these fissures.

Florian's guitar lays nearby, neck wobbly, frets cracked. The chipped enamel reveals the raw wood beneath, but somehow the instrument remains intact. It's an absurd artifact, a rebuke to his powers of self-destruction.

Faces turn as Xenie enters the room. She's shed the wig but still wears Shaun's clothes. Something uncanny clings to her appearance. Even with her shock of blonde hair, she seems less herself than somebody performing the role of Xenie. People approach her with a half-reverential look in their eyes. Derek D. offers his unaffected applause. Randy quietly suggests that she should perform more often. A.C. and B.C. both bend down to kiss her on the cheek. We knew you'd do something great, they say. Florian stays silent. The sincerity of this praise intensifies his migraine. He's consumed with jealousy watching her collect the accolades he imagined for himself.

A man with a graying beard, a local music critic, claps Xenie on the back. Here's the real talent, he announces. How did Shaun feel about the fact you were better than him?

Xenie looks like she's been kicked in the throat. Embarrassment is scribbled across her face. That's fucked up, she rasps, trying to catch her breath. That's a seriously fucked-up thing to say to me.

The congratulations continue, but Xenie refuses to revel in the attention. She acts more dejected with every compliment, waving them off with a stern glare. Florian can't decide whether this is a highly sophisticated form of gloating or she genuinely feels like shit.

The pock-faced boy makes his move. Florian braces as the boy approaches, but he's headed for Xenie. He holds out his small sweaty hand. That was so cool, he stammers. I just had to say something. As he exits the club, the boy cinches the strings of his hood. He nods familiarly at Florian, as if they were former accomplices.

●

Randy peppers Xenie with questions about her performance. His candid confusion is the highest form of praise. Why did you lip-synch? he asks. You got a bad voice? Scared you can't carry a tune?

—I wasn't scared, Xenie says.

—Anybody can open their mouth, she says, and sing a fucking song.

—That would've been worthless, she says. That would've missed the entire point. I never even considered singing.

Xenie rubs her face. It's as if her features have gone numb and she's trying to massage the feeling back into them.

—Besides, she says, who could ever sing that song better than Johnny Ace?

—Never heard that tune, Randy says.

—It's an old rock-and-roll ballad, she says. The last song Johnny Ace recorded. He was shot in the head a few days later.

—Somebody shot him? Randy says. You're serious?

Xenie says: He shot himself. He was playing poker and somebody challenged him to a game of Russian roulette. His eyes filled with blood, his limbs convulsed, and he died there at the table. The next month "Pledging My Love" became his first number one hit.

—People say he's the ghost that haunts rock and roll, she says. They claim that song is cursed and bad things happen to people who perform it.

—Of course, she says, it's also a love song.

She thinks she's fooled everyone.

Florian coughs several times to draw everyone's attention. He hikes a pair of jeans higher on his hips, balancing on one leg like a drunken flamingo.

—If that story is true, he says, then you forgot the most important thing in your performance: the gun.

Xenie takes her time turning to Florian, as if she's only now registering that the sounds from his corner were aimed in her direction. Her face is purged of all emotion.

She says: Maybe the gun was part of my original plan.

—What changed your mind?

She says: Maybe I didn't need it.

—Was it going to be loaded?

She responds by sucking her teeth.

—Because that would've been a real act. That would've been real commitment. But don't worry, I'm sure Shaun appreciated your empty gesture.

Xenie says: I guess you'd have gone farther. I guess I should be taking notes from you.

She says: You're like all the others. Looking for any opportunity for exposure. You don't have the guts to be Johnny Ace. You don't even have the guts to be Shaun. You're not even Bruce.

She says: You're nobody.

●

Florian takes several seething steps toward Xenie, but then he's staggered by a realization. Maybe it's spurred by the clenched intonation of her speech. The sight of her quivering nostrils. Her flushed cheeks. Her despairing stare. Or maybe it's those things in concert. He turns on his heel and heads for the bathroom.

●

Xenie tries to back out of the room, but she bumps into Eddie. He wraps his arms around her, thinking she's looking for comfort. Her body starts to tremble. She can't face the discovery of her secret. I brought it, she whispers. I brought the gun, but I couldn't pull the trigger. Her lips trace the shapes of words, but they produce no sound. She's losing track of where her thoughts end and the world begins, everything becoming a spiral of fear and shame, rushing into the black hole that she calls herself. Eddie holds her tighter and murmurs comforting phrases, but she doesn't register a syllable. Nobody in the room is paying attention to anything spoken. They're listening with their eyes. Their attention is locked on the bathroom door.

●

That faraway night, Johnny Ace sitting at the poker table, shuffling the deck, cutting the cards, considering the wager.

●

He's fresh off a sold-out show, his latest song climbing the charts.

●

He can still feel the applause.

●

Florian flips over the toilet lid, unpeels the silver duct tape, strips away the newspaper. The revolver is untouched. He releases the weapon from its ceramic cradle. Freshly cleaned and polished. More slippery than he imagined. He brandishes it, ready to march outside and confront everyone with Xenie's contraband and show them what she's capable of. Then he thinks to check the weapon. He slides open the cylinder and rotates through the chambers. He's shocked to discover they're fully loaded.

> *She wasn't planning to play Russian roulette.*
> *She was planning to kill herself.*

Florian empties the bullets. He rolls them round his palm and registers their weight. When he tilts them into the sink, the metal shells make a rhythmic clatter as they tumble into the trough. The sound isn't musical, it's music.

●

He withholds a single bullet, inspecting it between thumb and forefinger. The rounded nose is slightly darker than the smooth cylinder. It seems almost benign. He wonders if his prints have blemished the powdered metal, but the light is too murky to tell if it's greased with his whorls. He slides the bullet into a chamber and tries to spin it. The chamber sticks. Even this he can't do right. He gives it a harder twist and it whirls. He spins it again. And again. His hands know what they're doing even if his mind hasn't caught up.

●

Florian centers his reflection in the bathroom mirror. The word JEANETTE is still scrawled on the surface. It's comforting to see those eight letters obscuring his own pathetic features, and he wonders if the presence of his mother's name will protect him. The floorboards whine under his weight. Dirty water sloshes around his feet. The night quietly offers one last opportunity for redemption.

No more playing for applause.

He gives the chamber a final spin. He should be seizing with fear, but the tension in his head feels lighter. The odds are stacked in his favor, he only needs to supply the courage. Florian's thinking clearly, if coordinated actions count as thoughts. He places the gun against his head. He braces himself for the chill of the round tip of the barrel, but it feels comfortable, the exact temperature of his temple.

I'll do what Xenie couldn't do.

Don't make a face in the mirror. Don't even look at yourself. It's too easy to transform a moment of truth into a cheap performance. Florian shuts his eyes. The inside of his mouth is coated with the taste of licorice and stomach acid. He tries to spit but can't summon any saliva. He's not sure what he wants to happen. His index finger releases the safety.

Steady now, Bruce.

He can hear the incremental increase of pressure in the trigger, the springs growing taut, the interlocking parts preparing to lurch into action.

He wonders if whatever he hears next will be able to measure up to the sound in his head.

Easy does it, son.

THE BIRDS

Evening. As the sun retires, the flock of white-throated sparrows grows silent. Their numbers expand as more birds return to the grove of trees, quietly alighting on the branches. There's no call-and-response against the darkening sky. They now crave silence. The only sounds are the crack of cartilage in flexing wings. The murmur of beaks cleaning sooty feathers. The steady blink of hooded eyes. No song erupts from their trembling throats, but let me assure you, son, even these movements are part of their singing.

chapter
five

THE EMBERS

THEY'RE LISTENING. Ears perked straight up. The big buck raises its head to register the noise from the woods. The does stop chewing grass. The three deer stand motionless in the meadow. Their ears are fur sleeves, individual hairs etched in fernlike patterns, prickling in reaction to every shift of the environment. The exhalation of trees. The fidget of leaves. The stereophonic hum of insects. The capering clatter of squirrels. After several moments, the deer warily return to eating. They're acutely aware of the reverberations made by their own teeth as they rip mouthfuls of green stems from grubby roots. They catalog each sound with their entire bodies.

●

Their enormous eyes all lift and stare in the same direction. The three deer face into the wind, noses sifting the breeze. They stare into the bushes at the edge of the woods and wait to see if the sound will recur. The soft metallic click of a shell being slotted into a cylinder. The noise isn't natural, but it's familiar. Their bulging muscles are tensed. Their posture is perfectly immobile. Only their triangular white tails twitch. There's a long silence. The sides of the animals press in and out, though no breath can be heard. The cries of several crows break across the sky, but nothing stirs. The entire forest frozen in the moment. The creatures can see themselves being seen. It feels like there's an eye in every leaf. Each one lidless.

●

The buck breaks into a sprint. As it darts across the meadow, a rifle shot rings out. A thunderous echo ripples through the woods. Sparrows and finches scatter skyward. More shots. The other deer gallop after their compatriot and hurtle through the forest. For the moment, they're still together. Pursued by spent shells tumbling to the ground. Careening around trees without a backward glance. Heartbeats pulsing in their eyeballs. Blurred hooves barely alighting on firm ground.

> *This is a mistake.*
> *I shouldn't be here.*

The overcast afternoon bears down on them. A moist chill saturates the air, and heavy clouds sink lower every few minutes. A couple tramps along the dirt road leading toward the woods. They resemble a pair of listless, derelict troubadours. The girl has a guitar case slung over her shoulders and the boy hefts an oversize backpack. Xenie registers a series of signs tacked along the trees and keeps turning to Eddie, awaiting some reaction. He trudges doggedly ahead, fogged in by some concoction of pills that he claims are the only way he can muddle through this miserable day. The way ahead is choked with traffic cones. Men in orange flak jackets stand clustered in conference. One of them spots the couple and thrusts his rifle into the air. It's not a salute, but a signal to halt.

●

A caravan of pickup trucks is parked up the road. A single dead deer lies lashed atop each hood, limbs splayed and stretched, hooves clasped together, heads wrenched in the same direction.

●

The forest is off-limits this weekend. Xenie reads the poster nailed to the bole of a nearby oak that states the habitat can no longer support the overpopulation of deer. The animals are short of food, and disease is spreading, so hunters have gathered to cull the herd.

—It's not safe out there, explains a white-haired man in camouflage. The hunting club announced a reward for whoever kills the most deer, and more people showed up than anybody bargained for. It's become a free-for-all. Even getting back, you'd better wear these.

The white-haired man passes orange flak jackets to Xenie and Eddie. She puts on hers, but Eddie examines the fabric as if it's something an extraterrestrial just crapped in his hand.

Xenie slips the jacket over Eddie's shoulders, but he barely registers its presence. She shakes his skinny biceps to snap him from his stupor.

—The area is closed, she says. We've got to turn around. We'll come back and do this another time.

—No, he says. I know a different way.

In the distance, a hunter takes aim at a buck that's wandered from the edge of the forest. There's a deafening recoil, then the animal's front legs collapse under it. The deer kneels awkwardly as another shot strikes a bloody blow to its head. As the animal tumbles to the ground, there's a chorus of whistled appreciation.

●

They backtrack until they're out of sight of the hunters. Then Eddie hunches his shoulders and leads them across a muddy field. He hums beneath his breath, an unconscious sequence of soft keens. Xenie finds it oddly reassuring that his noises stumble into a recognizable rhythm, echoing the sucking sounds of their boots as they lumber across the scrubby mire. She watches Eddie scratch the stubble on his chin. His face is speckled with stray hairs. This morning was the first time he wouldn't let her shave him. The past two weeks he's lived at her house. He's been almost catatonic, barely responsive to her affectionate caresses. She'd wind him in an old blanket as if that might hold him together. Now he's plodding toward the forest in a determined trance and she's the one reluctant to follow.

●

The guitar case bounces awkwardly between Xenie's shoulder blades. It contains Shaun's guitar, the one she stole the night he was shot. She's only brought it along because Eddie insisted. For his sake, she swallows complaints about the strap cutting into her back and chafing her chest. She worries how far she'll have to take this to make things right.

—Hey, she calls. This isn't safe. We're miles from town and surrounded by hunters. Can't we talk about this?

Eddie sets the backpack at his feet and unzips the front pouch. He removes a shiny black cylinder. Florian's ashes. Some violent emotion fights its way to the surface of his cloudy eyes, but his voice maintains its druggy monotone.

—I promised Florian I'd do this, he says.

—I know, she says softly. I know.

—So I'm doing this now, he says. You don't have to come.

I do. It's my fault we're here.

A massive tree lies diagonally across the entrance to the woods. She tries to read the green paint sprayed across its leprous bark. It's impossible to tell if the words are vestiges of an urgent municipal message or a vandal's sloppy tag.

—How far is the cemetery? she asks.

Eddie shrugs.

—I sometimes went this way with Florian when he'd visit his mother's grave, he says. He loved the old family plot in the middle of nowhere. I could never stand this place.

Before going any farther, Eddie unpeels his flak jacket as if it's a hair shirt and heaves it into a puddle. Despite the danger, she adds her jacket to the murky water, the two pieces of fabric floating atop each other, a gesture of solidarity.

●

The path is a tunnel of green. Fallen leaves slick the soft ground. There's the cloying smell of fresh rot. Eddie maintains a steady pace, ducking under thorny branches, shaking through thick brambles. Xenie keeps getting snared, vines ripping the wool of her purple sweater. She feels guilty as she listens to him mumble a monologue of amputated phrases, the static of his private thoughts taking shape. If she could trace the signals to their source, she's sure this sad broadcast originates with her.

●

. . . Sometimes you have to teach them a lesson . . . hide in the forest . . . talk me out of going home . . . make sure I stay the night . . . be more vocal about the show . . . need my help to convince the guys . . . teach them a lesson . . . seriously damaged . . . terrified by every sound . . . I'm in over my head . . . teach me a lesson . . .

●

Xenie unwraps two hard-boiled eggs from a sweaty napkin. She offers one of the white orbs to Eddie, but he either doesn't hear or doesn't want it. Or then again, maybe he's pissed at her. During the past two weeks, they haven't talked about what her revolver was doing at the club. She hopes there's no reason to talk about it now. She figures Eddie must know. Or he can guess. Or he knows enough to guess that no good can come from talking about it. She can't muster the courage to put her shame about that night into language. Those words are an avalanche she's waiting to call down upon herself. A weight from which she'll never be unburied.

> *That night, if I'd stopped him from going to the show, Shaun would still be alive.*

> *That night, if I'd had the guts, Florian would still be alive.*

> *I should've shot myself.*

Eddie is quiet now. The only sounds come from the thrash of his limbs as he clears the way. Xenie turns her attention to the birdsong volleyed from tree to tree. She alternately tries to pick out the individual strains and listen to the diverse voices as a unified tune. The refrains are faithfully recorded and redoubled by the mockingbirds, their echoes added to the insistent chorus. Tucked inside her sweater, a sheet of song lyrics and chords itches against her like a rash.

●

Black clouds of gnats whine around her face. Knee-high ferns and scrub hardwoods press closer. Unseen creatures patter and rustle around them. Xenie can't shake the feeling that she shouldn't be here. There's an uneasy sensation her presence is being monitored. Even the pine needles seem to be conversing. Each needle a tongue too small to be seen.

●

She dreads arriving at the cemetery because she's going to have to keep her promise. The path ahead is scored and banded by heavy shadows. As the branches sway, the specks of brightness dotting the forest floor shrink. She stares up at the dark canopy. Trees eat light.

●

She stops to stretch her spasming back. As she slings the case over a different shoulder, she jostles Shaun's electric guitar. They're both spooked to hear it emit a few fugitive twangs. A panicked expression bobs to the surface of Eddie's face.

—You have the song? he asks.

Xenie produces the yellow sheet from inside her sweater. She unfolds the legal-sized page and holds it out as further proof. There's a precocious neatness to the penmanship of the lyrics and chords. It's one of the first songs Florian and Shaun wrote together as kids. She remembers how rapt Shaun became when he talked about these early tunes, describing them as if they'd been conjured supernaturally.

Eddie discovered the song combing through Florian's things at the Bunker. He asked Xenie to sing it as part of the last rites, and she agreed out of a crippling sense of guilt. There's so much guilt spread across the living and the dead that she isn't sure to whom she feels most beholden. Though she's resigned to this performance, even touching the paper fills her with nausea.

I should have ripped up the song the first time he showed it to me.

As Eddie leads them along the winding curve of a creek, they're jolted by a gunshot. Xenie realizes he's sobered up enough to be worried, though stoned enough to keep moving. He shuffles through the rank, spreading weeds and stalks of burrs. She lets him round the bend a few steps ahead of her.

A hunter stands on the bank over a young doe. It looks badly wounded, its hooves twitching feebly at the air. He keeps circling it, rifle barrel extended, and pumps a fresh shot into its small belly. He maintains a wary perimeter, as if afraid to get too close to the dying animal.

As Eddie and Xenie approach, the hunter removes his cap and flashes a bashful grin. He's a scrawny teenager decked out in baggy secondhand camouflage. He has a bulging Adam's apple and cheeks full of tobacco. His bland green eyes glitter in his thin face. They're as opaque and empty as jewels.

He has the same expression as the other shooters.

The so-called zombies.

Maybe it takes someone like me to recognize it.

The boy stands the barrel of his rifle in the dirt and spits chaw on the ground. He says: You hunting deer?

—Not us, says Xenie.

—Neither of you is wearing the orange.

—No, says Xenie.

—Sure you're not hunting deer?

—Absolutely, says Xenie.

—That's my trick for sneaking up on deer, the boy says. Not wearing the orange. But it isn't working so well. They're hiding from me. Except this one, but it was hurt when I run across it. Any deer the way you came?

—No, Eddie says. He stares quizzically at the boy, like he's having trouble pulling him into focus.

—Actually, I think we heard a few, says Xenie. In fact, I'm pretty sure we did.

She stares meaningfully over her shoulder and waits to see if the boy will set out on the trail of her hint.

—I can see the sickness that's ruining these creatures, the boy says. It's a gift I got. Somebody has to put them out of their misery.

—Somebody has to do it, says Xenie.

—There's a cash reward for the person who kills the most, the boy says. I'm thinking maybe I'm going to burn down the woods and smoke the deer out. They'll have to come running. That way I'm sure to get every last one of the herd.

The boy smiles, a lopsided contortion reminiscent of the aftereffects of a stroke.

—You're funny, Xenie says.

—You all are the funny ones, he says. Look like you're aiming to serenade the furries.

—We're here for a funeral, Eddie says.

—I didn't see no dead people, the boy says.

—They're everywhere, Eddie says.

The boy's laughter sounds like leaves crackling underfoot.

—As long as you're not hunting, he says. I can't have no competition.

He hoists up his rifle and heads in the direction they came.

—Don't you want this deer? Xenie calls.

—It's too small, he says. You can have it.

●

Eddie and Xenie stand over the doe. Its stomach has been blown open, displaying slick and viscous inner organs. Its body radiates warmth. Xenie kneels next to the animal and smooths its blood-matted fur. She strokes its neck and looks into the large wet stones of its eyes. A reflection of herself swims in the black expanse of its pupils. Then the deer seizes, a sudden jerky exhalation, a spasm of its nervous system and a final rasping breath. Its last shudders shake loose a white rope of intestines and Xenie screams.

> *I'm the last thing it saw. I watched it change*
> *from something living to something dead.*

She bends over the creek, wrings her hands in the water, and frantically tries to slough off the warm blood. She watches as the ruby hues and musky smell dissipate into the current and disperse downstream. Let's get this over with, she says.

●

Eddie says it'll be quicker to walk up the shallows of the creek. They hang their shoes round their necks by the laces, roll up their jeans, and tighten the straps on his backpack and her guitar case. Eddie wades out a few yards and establishes a foothold in the slippery sediment. He helps Xenie take the first awkward steps into the bracing water. As they start upstream, neither lets go of the other's hand.

The water laps at their shins. As the weight on their backs shifts, they strain to stay balanced while striding against the current. As she sloshes alongside Eddie, she tries to imagine Shaun carrying out this sort of pilgrimage and has a hard time picturing it. Maybe her mind balks simply because time doesn't flow that way. She keeps her eyes on her feet, maneuvering around loose branches, moss-slicked rocks, rubbery strands of lichen. The creek bed feels terraced, a series of silt steps. Each movement leaves a wake imprinted on the water.

●

The creek turns a muddy emerald green, full of dubious sediment, an augury of the coming seasonal change. A chill breeze whisks their bodies. Xenie hugs her sweater tight. Eddie's unruly hair rustles across his forehead, revealing his recently retouched blond roots. She kept fumbling with the dye, but it turned out halfway decent due to his patience. She's grateful he still trusts her after everything that's happened. She kisses the back of his neck, turned on by the faint odor of ammonia that clings to him.

●

Eddie has become increasingly alert, swiveling his head to acknowledge the landmarks along the shore.

He says: Florian's mom belonged to this church that believed music should only be used for important ceremonies. That way it'd keep its power. Anything else was a waste. When we sang at the funeral, it was so intense that Florian passed out.

—His mom believed music could guide the dead person's soul on their journey, he says. Let them know they weren't alone. Sing them home.

—I guess that's what Florian wants us to do for him, he says.

> It's always about paying tribute to the dead.
> It's never about trying to make the living feel better.

Xenie spots a noose tied to a branch, dangling over the water. Then she realizes it must be the remnant of a rope swing from when this used to be a swimming hole. They stand in an expanse of water whose glassy surface is undisturbed. The only suggestion of current is the slight tickle between their toes. Yellow leaves tumble from surrounding trees, and their reflections hurry to meet them out of the watery depths. Xenie snares one of the spinning leaves and is surprised how it crumbles beneath her fingertips.

—These leaves must've been dead a long time, she says.

Eddie isn't listening. He's scrambled onto the grassy bank and is headed toward an expansive clearing. She moves after him through the shallows, the song a persistent itch in her pocket.

The hinges of the cemetery gate are rusted shut. They swing their legs over the knee-high iron fence that encircles the graveyard. The rows of burial mounds spark uncomfortable memories of the mound they encountered in the homeless encampment. Their bare feet register the warm terrain, the sodden ground stretching out a soft carpet of grass, dotted with spongy moss and mulched leaves. Nature has overrun everything. The plaques, the marble crosses, the angels with upturned eyes are swaddled in coats of orange lichen. The epigraphs have been scrubbed away by obstinate years and insistent weather, so it's impossible to make out more than the inscribed echo of family names.

●

Despite herself, Xenie is affected by the defiled beauty of the place. She can understand why Florian loved to come here. There's a serenity to the effaced stones and sunken rot. The only thing that hasn't been reclaimed by the earth is the black granite marker of the most recent resident. Eight letters are emphatically etched into the center of its shiny surface: JEANETTE.

●

They stand before the grave of Florian's mother. The headstone is ringed with cherub dolls, plastic bouquets, and half-melted candles, alternately bleached and blackened by the weather. Xenie stares at the ornamental rose chiseled into the granite tombstone. The sculpted lines of its petals are already becoming smooth. Soon the stone will express nothing about its resident and signify only its own resilience.

—Who was she? Xenie asks.

—Florian didn't talk much about her, Eddie says. I remember her being calm and kind. She had a lisp, but it disappeared whenever she'd sing and play the piano. I thought maybe she was practicing hymns, but Florian said she made up most of the songs.

—Her death was a big deal in town, he says. Even people who didn't know her well came out for the funeral. This whole place was filled with mourners and wreaths of flowers.

—The burglar who killed her was just a kid, he says, but he shot her in the face. People were shocked by the brutality of it. They had to have a closed casket.

The swirling wind clears some leaves from the raised mound of earth and reveals the translucent grass underneath.

Neither of them mentions Florian, who has no casket at all, only a canister of ashes in Eddie's backpack.

●

Xenie wishes there were some words she could say to Eddie about his friend, but she worries they would only make things worse. She wishes she could apologize to the ashes. She wishes it wasn't too late for language.

●

There's a volley of gunshots. They go off like fireworks, waves of explosive pops that ricochet through the atmosphere. It's hard to tell whether the hunters are coming closer. Eddie and Xenie brace themselves, but nothing stirs in the forest.

—We should hurry, Eddie says.

He unzips his backpack and places the cylinder of Florian's ashes on the ground. Then he removes a folding shovel and snaps it into shape. He sinks the blade into the dirt and scoops a chunk of topsoil from Jeanette's grave.

—What the hell are you doing? Xenie says.

—Florian wanted his ashes buried with his mother.

—So you're digging up her grave?

—How else are we going to put his ashes with her casket?

—That's going to be a lot of work.

—You can't bury bodies very deep here. The water table is too high.

Eddie shovels with manic ferocity. Sweat darkens his hair and perspiration pools in his eyebrows. He stubbornly blinks away the wet. Xenie inhales the smell of upturned earth. A fecund mix of moss, moist dirt, musty spores. Soon a pile has been amassed next to the grave.

Soft clods of turf, flecked with brown clay. The ground proves surprisingly easy to move.

●

A fresh rifle salvo rattles through the air like approaching weather. Xenie tries to blot out images of crows rooting in the sockets of deer that have been shot and tagged. Visions of hunters artfully stacking dead bucks, shaking plastic cans of gasoline over their hides, and setting them alight. The pyramids of flesh burning bright.

> Why not build shrines and organize memorials for the
> dead deer?
> It wouldn't be any less absurd.

A flock of sparrows gathers in the top of a nearby tree. They titter as they shift from branch to branch, their anxious song riddled with warnings. Xenie sets the guitar case across her lap and reluctantly moves the zipper around its edges. She stares down at Shaun's violet-hued electric guitar. Its plastic coating is a codex of scrapes and scratches, scarred pickups and bent tremolo bars. She runs her fingers over the stickers, lingering over the residue left by ones worn away or peeled off. To her these scrapes represent a secret history of Shaun, but to him they were insignificant, an inconvenience. Now that inconvenience is all she has left.

●

Eddie stops digging. He stands in the center of the hole. Face and arms spackled with dirt. He ventilates his sweaty shirt and wipes the brown streaks from his glasses. For several moments, he stares at the soil beneath his feet. Then he sends the shovel whirling into the graveyard.

—It's not here, he says. The casket is gone.

●

—I've dug deeper than I should've had to, he says.

—Maybe there never was a casket.

—I could've sworn they lowered it into the grave, Eddie says. I was at the ceremony. I was standing where you're standing. I'm pretty sure she was in the ground.

—Maybe you're remembering wrong? Or maybe they had to move the body? The flooding was threatening to wash it away?

They both look down at the empty space.

—Whatever happened, Eddie says, she's not here now.

●

Xenie wonders if it's the same for all these graves. Maybe they're less holes than trapdoors. Escape hatches down which dead bodies vanish. Maybe these corpses did just that and left the entire cemetery untenanted.

●

She watches Eddie circle the gravesite. His fragile poise breaks into beads of perspiration. We can still do this, he repeats, but it's clear he has no idea how to execute whatever comes next. He removes a candle from his backpack and places it at the foot of the grave. He lights the wick and stares into the modest flame as if it might provide some guidance. Then he arranges the cylinder of Florian's ashes so it's upright in the hole. The shiny surface returns their gazes, an expressionless shell offering neither accusation nor understanding.

●

This is the moment Xenie has been dreading: Eddie lifts the electric guitar from the case. Handling it like a prop, he begins the task of tightening the strings. He looks at her expectantly. She finds it almost endearing how he tries to wrestle the acerbic strums into a recognizable tuning. The wind carries off the mangled notes, but not far enough.

●

Xenie removes the song and unfolds the paper to its full length. She scans the writing for the first time, encountering the familiar slant of the script and the fastidious flourishes. Her heartbeat swirls in the ridges of her fingerprints. Her breath grows choppy.

One day you'll crawl back to me, she reads to herself, *with a mouth full of ash.*

As her eyes soundlessly navigate the lyrics, she pays extra attention to the end rhymes. She can hear the chord changes and experiences the hurtling pulse of the tempo, the plaintive voice of the singer ringing in her head, making certain to stretch the vowels the way Shaun loved to do.

When your heart shatters, the refrain goes, *it makes a beautiful sound.*

The song is a tingle in her skull. The melody thrums in her throat. She plays with adding her own pauses, then catches herself.

Her lips stop moving.

●

Xenie's eyes burn. Her shoulders quaver. Her tears collect in a single scalding mouthful.

●

It's a love song. She can't keep pretending it's not a love song.

●

—I can't do this, she says. I know I promised you, but I can't sing.

—This is for Shaun, too, Eddie says.

—There's no way to connect with them. I thought performing at the concert would help, but it made things worse. Everything with Florian never would've happened if I hadn't done that.

Eddie removes his glasses and leaves them off, as if he doesn't want to witness her distress.

—This is your chance, he says. Your chance to make up for all that.

Xenie stares into the empty hollow. She pulls the sweater tighter against herself. The harsh scratch of the wool helps to maintain her resolve.

—I keep getting stuck deeper and deeper, she says. After that show, I went home and I had to face the hard drive full of music that Shaun left me. All those songs he'd written and recorded. They'd been haunting me for months. I couldn't think straight. Finally I realized I had to delete them.

—You didn't.

—They're part of the problem, she says. Why hold on to those recordings if I'll never listen to them? Nobody will. They're more clutter. More noise.

—You shouldn't have done that.

—You know what? she says. As soon as I did, there was this huge sense of relief. It's the only thing I've done that's made me feel better.

Xenie looks down at the yellow sheet crumpled in her hand. Her index finger has gouged a hole through the first verse.

> *This song is suffocating me.*
> *Shaun is suffocating me.*
> *I need to scour it all away.*

Eddie says: It's awful to see you keep punishing yourself.

He says: You can run away from it, but you're a natural performer. Everyone in the club felt it as soon as you stepped on the stage. They couldn't take their eyes off you. People would sell their soul for that talent.

He says: You were singing the first time we met. You were walking toward the woods and thought nobody was around. But I heard you. Your voice was beautiful.

He says: You're itching to sing. Just now I saw how you held that song. I saw how you read the lyrics and the way your lips moved.

He says: I see you, Xenie.

●

Xenie picks up the guitar. She adjusts the tuning pegs until there's a melodious strum, then executes a few chords and a fluid progression of notes. She notices how surprised Eddie seems that she can play. She plucks the thin high string, evaluating the trebly sound, then snares it between her fingers. She snaps it off. Methodically she pulls off the other strings, one by one, until she finally grasps the bass string. She rips hard, red faced and resolute, her hands crisscrossed with blood. As the coiled thread snaps, the instrument emits a metallic alien cry.

●

—Shaun always wanted me to sing, she says. He kept asking me to make recordings with him.

—I kept begging him to quit music, she says. He thought I was crazy, but it turns out I was right.

—I stole his guitar because I thought it'd stop him from

playing that show, but I should've known better, she says. I got drunk by myself at a bar that night and refused to answer his calls. I have so many regrets they're choking me.

> *You think I've let go of too much, but I haven't let go of enough.*

—Maybe you're right that I want to sing, she says. But that's something I have to let go.

—You're making a mistake, he says.

—Not everything has to be a performance, she says. That's what ruined music. That's why the epidemic had to happen.

—Forget about those people, he says. You need to do this for yourself. Otherwise you're just silencing yourself. If everyone followed your lead, there'd be no music at all.

—I'm sorry, she says. I can't. Please don't ask me to do it. Some things I need to be private. Some things should stay pure.

Eddie turns away, trying to conceal the disappointment that flashes across his face. He says: But you're destroying something that's part of you.

●

She can't deny the song is still in her mouth, the hum of those words, the thrill of those imagined tones.

●

She holds the crumpled yellow sheet over the candle. She expects a spark, but nothing happens. The page damp, the flame curdled. She holds it closer. Closer still. For an incandescent instant, the tongue ascends, and the fire and the song are one. Xenie holds on to the burning page until it singes her fingers, then lets it drop into the grave. She blows out the candle and tosses it into the hole after the blackened paper. Last, she adds Shaun's unstrung instrument. Maybe in the grave these musical totems will relinquish their hold on her. Maybe they'll become refuse, discarded, dead. Clapping her hands, she shakes loose the final sooty flecks of the song.

•

—I didn't come here for Shaun, she says.

—I trekked into the middle of the woods for you, she says.

—One of the reasons I like you, she says, is you understand why I can't sing.

•

The song slips down her throat, dissolving inside her, unsung.

•

Eddie stares at his muddy toes for some time, unable to hide his sadness. He watches the pupae wind paths through the damp soil. When he turns back to Xenie, he manages to meet her eyes.

—Okay, he says. If that's what you really want.

He shovels the loose earth back into the pit, until all that can be seen is more dirt, until the hole itself starts to rise. He tamps down the burial mound with his bare feet. Xenie feels a surge of relief once it's sealed with the arched oval pattern of his soles.

There's still more to let go.

With shaky hands, Xenie strips off Shaun's purple sweater, struggling to pull her head through the top. She's not sure what to feel without it. Her exposed body looks unspeakably vulnerable. Her prickled flesh breaks out in bumps and she tries to welcome the chill. Her naked breasts feel strange in the air, her pores unaccustomed to being free from the wool, the slight itch that for so long has been her skin.

●

Xenie takes off Eddie's jacket. She loosens his shirt and pulls down his jeans. He helps her out of her pants, their hands simultaneously unbuttoning and unzipping. Fabric pooling around their ankles. Mouth on mouth. They tumble to the muddy ground, paused face-to-face, her fingernails combing through the blond roots of his hair. Then she straddles him and pushes him into the dirt. His tongue licks between her breasts. Her hands explore his ass. She arches her back as he penetrates her, their legs knotted, thrusting together. They kiss between shudders of breath. For a few moments, the spasms of their thoughts are wiped blank.

•

They lie together, arms entwined, coated in a patina of grime. They're imprinted with indentations of pebbles, pine needles, twigs and moss, the landscape mapping itself onto their pale bodies. Ants and gnats crawl over them, but they don't mind. They explore each other with their fingers and inspect their pubic hair for insects. Xenie finds a tick, and they watch transfixed as she squeezes it, a blotch of blood popping between her fingers.

•

Xenie props herself on her elbows and kisses Eddie, relishing the sour taste of his saliva. Her tongue licks away the bits of soil smeared like a bruise across his cheek. As she rolls over, she's greeted by the fire.

•

A strip of orange undulates across the far horizon. An exquisite cleansing curtain of flame. The entire clearing has been transformed. Xenie feels as if she's awakened on the shoals of a new world.

She points at the distant fire.

—The forest, Eddie says.

—It's beautiful, Xenie replies.

She's mesmerized by the sight. They stand without bothering to put on their clothes. Tongues of flame wave in their direction, a series of dazzling hues smeared against the sky, a gentle set of guiding signals.

Easy does it.

Around them, hundreds of sparrows explode into the air. The birds fly in swooping arcs, twisting and torqueing in formation, carving a practiced geometry in the sky before breaking apart in loose spirals, scattering into paths too numerous to trace.

●

They take a few hesitant steps toward the fire's beckoning flicker, coaxed closer. Fronds of faraway smoke drift into the atmosphere of low-hanging clouds. The glow of flames further tints the firmament. The sky is a shimmering violet.

●

The fire spreads in slow sighs. The conflagration continually fades and sharpens. The air is perfumed with the sweet smell of char. It won't be long before the deer start to flee the forest. Hunters will soon be kneeling at the edge of the meadow with rifles propped on shoulders. But right now, it's remarkably serene. Do you hear it? Xenie asks. Her head crackles with a strange music. The whisper and sizzle of smoldering bark, blistering leaves, blazing boughs. She's entranced by the intricate slivers of this delicate symphony. They stand naked in the clearing, listening to the rapturous sound of everything burning.

JEFF JACKSON

DESTROY ALL MONSTERS

Jeff Jackson is the author of *Mira Corpora*, a finalist for the Los Angeles Times Book Prize. His short fiction has appeared in *Guernica*, *VICE*, and *The Collagist*, and six of his plays have been produced by the Obie Award–winning Collapsable Giraffe theater company in New York City.

DESTROY ALL MONSTERS

KILL
CITY

SIDE B

DESTROY ALL MONSTERS

THE LAST ROCK NOVEL

JEFF JACKSON

FSG Originals • Farrar, Straus and Giroux • New York

FSG Originals
Farrar, Straus and Giroux
175 Varick Street, New York 10014

Copyright © 2018 by Jeff Jackson
All rights reserved
Printed in the United States of America
First edition, 2018

Library of Congress Cataloging-in-Publication Data
Names: Jackson, Jeff, 1971 July 16– author.
Title: Destroy all monsters : the last rock novel / Jeff Jackson.
Description: First edition. | New York : Farrar, Straus and Giroux, 2018.
Identifiers: LCCN 2018011509 | ISBN 9780374537661 (softcover)
Classification: LCC PS3610.A3518 D47 2018 | DDC 813/.6—dc23
LC record available at https://lccn.loc.gov/2018011509

Designed by Richard Oriolo

www.fsgoriginals.com • www.fsgbooks.com
Follow us on Twitter, Facebook, and Instagram at @fsgoriginals

1 3 5 7 9 10 8 6 4 2

Gratitude for advocacy and sage advice: Jaida Temperly, Jo Volpe, Devin
Ross, and the New Leaf Literary team, Jeremy M. Davies, Alethea Black,
D. Foy, Frank Lentricchia, Phillip Larrimore, Darragh McKeon, Giorgio Hiatt,
Michael Kimball, John Schacht, Gregory Howard, Sean Madigan Hoen, Irini
Spanidou, John W. Love Jr., Jim Findlay, John Cochrane, Scott Adlerberg,
Duvall Osteen, Virginia Center for the Creative Arts, MacDowell Colony,
Hambidge Center, Ben Marcus, Dennis Cooper, and Don DeLillo.

For Stephanie.

in memory of
JENNIFER MARX

Fire seeks its own form.

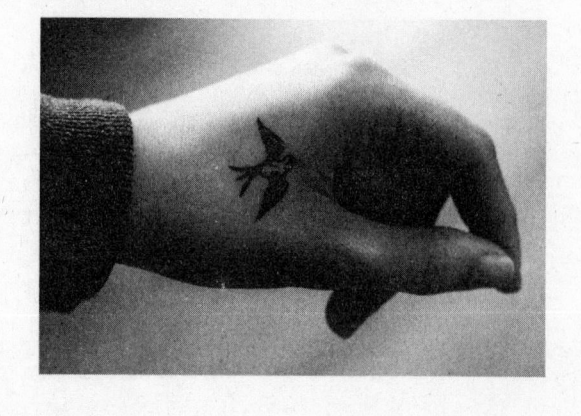

Often we write the word *execution* and
pronounce it *song*.

—OSIP MANDELSTAM

CITY
KILL

THE DESTROYERS

"How did the epidemic start?" Xenie asked. "How did we get here?"

"It started with the first shot," Shaun said.

"Before that," Xenie said. "What sparked the idea? How did it take root? There's always something before the beginning."

DAY ONE

NORTH CAROLINA ● HE FOLLOWS THE MUSIC.
The boy heads in the direction of the sound, drawn to the dim repeating throb emanating from down the street. Like a sleepwalker in a trance, he shuffles down the sidewalk in search of the source.

With his blank expression and rumpled clothes, the boy has little in common with the people around him. The animated drunks clustered outside the bars bumming cigarettes and perfecting their monologues. The college students in skinny jeans pasting flyers along the blank canvas of the construction fence. These posters are adorned with the photo of a bloody panda, but there's no time to ponder the image's possible significance because the boy keeps moving.

The pulse grows louder as he passes the rows of telephone poles coated with weathered concert notices that rustle in the breeze like dried leaves. He marches past the clothing boutiques and thrift shops, tapas restaurants and pizza joints. At the end of the block, he crunches across a

gravel parking lot toward a windowless concrete building. The home of the music.

A trio of girls hovers in front of the veterans hall. They're dressed in matching purple, purses poised on hips, necks arched, eyes narrowed. As the boy approaches, they talk about him in theatrically loud voices, tossing out their words like taunts, as if he isn't standing close enough to hear them.

—Here comes another one, the first girl says.

—Him? says the second girl. He's not a musician.

—Might be, the third girl says.

—Come on, the first girl says, rolling the whites of her eyes. I was obviously joking.

The first girl steps forward and hands him a printed notice about the concert, already in progress. It's a battle of the bands and the list of performers looks endless. The bubbly handwriting at the bottom indicates another group added to the bill. While the boy examines the flyer, the girls pay closer attention to his shaved head and the empty spaces where his eyebrows used to be.

—Is he drunk? one of the girls whispers.

The boy takes the flyer and folds it in half, in quarters, in eighths. He makes the creases perfect and the proportions exact, reducing the paper to an immaculate square. Then he tosses it onto the ground. The move is so swift and precise that it's clear he hasn't been drinking.

Bathed in the echoing rumble of the music, the boy pauses at the entrance. He stares at the elderly vet positioned behind the plastic folding table with a metal cash

box. He hesitates, hands plunged in pockets, reconsidering. Or perhaps he's just having trouble fishing out the few dollars required for admission. He finally produces the crumpled bills, purchases a tear-off ticket, and crosses the threshold.

He steps into a darkened foyer stacked with folding chairs and collapsed circular tables and tracks his muddy footprints across the linoleum floor. Distorted sounds beat around the room like a trapped bird. Looking up, he's startled by the plastic banner strung along the ceiling. It's probably been hanging here for decades, greeting successive waves of veterans. The boy's lips twitch and his eyes shine as he repeatedly mouths the words printed across it.

As he enters the main space with its wood-paneled walls, the boy spots the source of the music: a trio of guys in bowling-league shirts, high-top sneakers, and matching flattop haircuts playing a frenetic brand of garage rock that harkens back to an earlier era. They throttle their instruments and crank up their vintage amps, straining to suggest a dramatic crescendo. They finish the song with the guitarist half-heartedly hopping into the air.

The boy takes a seat at the bar, which is adorned with oxidized award plaques and faded photos of uniformed men in front of fighter jets. Totems of a bygone age. He pulls out a suspiciously shiny driver's license and orders a beer. The bartender sets a sudsy glass in front of him, then notices the trail of dirt in his wake.

—How the hell'd you get so muddy? the bartender asks. It hasn't rained here in weeks.

The boy doesn't appear to understand the question, then he looks down at his soil-encrusted sneakers. He seems genuinely confused. I don't remember, he mumbles.

For some reason, the boy can't bring himself to watch the band furiously riffing away on the small wooden stage. Instead his gaze is directed at the hunting trophy mounted on the wall above them. Something about the wood duck, hung upside down with its wings outstretched and beak open, entrances him. The glass eyes embedded in the slightly worn feathers preserve the bird's final moments, a flux of alertness, confusion, fear. No matter how long he looks, the expression refuses to settle.

The boy scans the packed room. The audience seems mostly composed of musicians. A motley assemblage of jam bands in tie-dye shirts and denim jackets, unbathed punks with ratty coifs and ripped jeans, bearded indie rockers with headbands ironically coordinated to the color of their drainpipe pants. There are even a few long-haired kids immaculately adorned in corpse paint. Some strike poses to indicate polite engagement, while others watch with slitted lids and pursed lips. None of them really hear the music. They all await their turn to perform.

Onstage, the guitarist windmills his arm while the lead singer strangles the microphone stand in time to the beat. The drummer launches into a spastic solo, pounding each part of his modest kit in turn. The band finishes another purposefully sloppy tune and pauses to collect some listless applause. The boy runs his hand across his shaved head, as if trying to loosen his thoughts. On a napkin, he

scribbles a string of vowels that adds up to little more than a wordless moan. His beer glass sits on the counter untouched, the beads of perspiration becoming imperceptibly engorged.

The boy takes a few steps toward the stage. His hand slowly reaches into the small of his back. The movement looks rehearsed, but it acquires a new meaning in the context of an audience. The singer does a series of awkward high kicks, but most likely the boy misses this. His eyes have been closed for several seconds. He produces a revolver from the waistband of his pants, points it in the direction of the band, and pulls the trigger. A single shot is all he can muster. His lids remain shut, his lashes as tightly entangled as a Venus flytrap. Slowly, his irises appear and absorb the scene.

It must have been a lucky shot because the guitarist stutter-steps across the stage in a crabwise stagger, clutching his shoulder. The wound soaks his shirtsleeve in a spiderweb pattern. There's a quizzical look on his face. Nobody else in the room seems able to process what is happening, either. The sound of the blast is smothered by the spiraling feedback. The boy squeezes the trigger again. A series of small thunderclaps issue from between his hands.

The band is suspended midsong. The drummer tumbles backward, and there's blood on the wall. A bullet brings the lead singer to his knees. His puckered lips seem to be forming a phrase, or maybe mechanically completing the final syllables of the song.

The boy stands in the center of the room. It's empty now. Maybe he's been standing here for a while. The power has been cut and the music has ceased. He continues to face the stage, now populated by slumped corpses, half-drunk beer bottles, a notebook of handwritten lyrics. Droplets of blood are spattered across the grille cloth of the amp. Everything is silent except for the repetition of the boy's index finger pressing the trigger, the steady rotation of the empty chambers, the rhythmic click of the hammer. Those three interlocking sounds, in continual sequence, again and again and again.

Something about the poster bothers you. It's one of a series taped up along the mirrored panel of the back wall, part of the club's makeshift calendar, announcing an upcoming concert. This full-color flyer features the preening portrait of some established musician. As you run your hands along your freshly shaved head, you keep coming back to the musician's faraway gaze, his forged half smile, his brooding aura of manufactured mystery. You're so repelled that you can't look away. Without thinking, you swipe a pen from the bar and start to scrawl out his smug face. You scrub over the features with frenzied black lines, the tip of your pen pressing so hard that it breaks clean through the paper.

DAY NINE

OHIO ● THE WOMAN STUMBLES DOWN THE FRONT steps of the theater. She lies sprawled in the street, her skirt ripped up the calf seam, panting under the soft glow of the marquee. Her face is a mask of glistening tears and smeared mascara. She pulls herself up and sprints down the vacant sidewalk, vanishing into the shadows. She reappears in the pooled light of each lamppost, materializing and evaporating, a frantic apparition.

Across from the theater, the boy with the scraggly beard watches to see if others flee the venue. He adjusts his baseball cap and wipes his hands on his denim overalls. He could've come from work at the gas station around the corner, if it hadn't shut down months ago. The recently restored theater is the only active business in this desolate neighborhood.

The boy with the scraggly beard saunters up the red-carpeted steps to the gilt-trimmed ticket booth. The cashier takes his money without a word. His bored features betray nothing about any possible drama inside.

The theater's lobby is eerily unoccupied. Nobody sits on the plush black ottomans. Nobody stands behind the glass counter stocked with T-shirts, screen-printed posters, limited-edition vinyl. The plaster walls hum with the muffled sound of preshow music. The only movement comes from the clink and sway of the chandelier, the tear-shaped crystals chiming in reaction to unseen activities overhead.

The boy climbs the staircase to the main floor. The room is ringed by a balcony reserved for VIPs whose dim faces peer over the balustrade. The band hasn't taken the stage, and most of the audience mills around the bar. He orders several beers in quick succession and empties the glasses without seeming to taste the contents. Flecks of foam collect around his beard and shining wet lips.

The crowd gives the boy a wide berth, appraising his appearance with sidelong glances. He stands out among these impeccably groomed creatures costumed in vintage smoking jackets, silk skirts, and fishnet stockings, conversing over cocktail glasses and strategically arranged scarves.

The lights dim. There's a fanfare of blaring trumpets, then the band strides onto the stage. The boy studies the musicians as they launch into their opening number. In addition to guitars and drums, they're armed with violins and cellos, theremins and other antiquated electronic instruments. The men sport tuxedos, top hats, white face paint. The women wear patterned sequin dresses, a peacock plume speared in their hair.

The crowd surges forward, swept up in the flamboyant churn of the music. Band members bounce on the soles of their white leather shoes in time to the beat, pressing their painted lips against the microphones in perfect tandem. There's an unabashed irony to the lyrics about partying as the world ends, but that only makes the audience repeat back the words more passionately.

The boy's gaze settles on the accordion player, whose instrument is hot in the mix. He seems to be the band's maestro: his hand gestures cue the backup singers, pantomime the lyrics, call for another chorus. The rest of the band seems to fade so far into the background that they're little more than excess glitter in the streamers hanging along the rear wall.

The boy with the scraggly beard moves closer. In the corner, a set of stairs leads up to the stage. He ducks under the velvet rope and ascends the first few steps. He observes the accordionist working the bellows, generating a barrage of melodic gusts. The boy's fingers open the flap of the leather pouch attached to his tool belt.

As the next song begins, the boy sprints across the proscenium, his hands a sharp silver glint. He lunges at the accordionist and stabs him in the neck. The music falters. Band members drop their instruments and start to scatter. They bump past one another, sprinting offstage in different directions, entwined in cords, trampling the abandoned cello, stumbling over the upturned theremin.

The accordionist remains standing upright, the static center of the action, until the boy yanks the hunting knife

from his neck. There's a spurt of blood as he collapses onto the stage.

The boy straddles him and continues to stab. A dark wet pattern spreads around the squeeze-box, soaking the musician's shirt, as if the instrument itself were hemorrhaging. The accordionist parts his lips, perhaps attempting to pose a question, but he only manages to display his gritted yellow teeth. They're not as bright as they appeared in the spotlight.

As the audience shouts and stampedes over one another, an invisible stagehand drops the curtain. It tumbles from the ceiling and the red cloth pools along the rim of the stage. The rippling fabric obscures the ongoing scene from view, but the convulsing wheeze of the accordion continues to blurt through the speakers. It resounds throughout the theater, echoing along the corridors, pursuing those who are clambering down the stairs, throwing open the fire exits, fleeing into the night.

The band's set seems to last weeks. You're one of a dozen people crammed into the swampy basement, perfumed by the acrid smell of laundry detergent and sweaty feet, listening to the group stumble through another meandering tune. You feel trapped and try to escape by sinking deeper into the faded floral pattern of the mildewed sofa. You know most of the musicians who are standing only a few feet away. Their preening expressions remind you of the poster in the club, and you wish you could scribble over and obliterate their smug faces. Everyone else here seems to wish the performance was over as well. They fidget and scratch, shut their eyes, shuffle their feet. As the band launches into another fumbling jam, a redheaded boy walks over to the wall. You watch how he calmly unplugs the various cords connected to the amps, his hands disconnecting them one by one, until the electrified noise evaporates from the room. Even the drummer

stops playing, his sticks held aloft, midbeat. It's a revelation—the ease with which the music is expunged. You want to applaud, but the silence feels too precious. Instead, you stare down at your hands.

DAY
27

OREGON ● **THE BOY IN THE SWEATSHIRT IGNORES** the shouts. He focuses on the band instead. Four women in black dresses perform at the end of the outdoor patio. Their pummeling riffs ripple the night air. A video is projected on a sheet behind them, twilight shots of a pine forest, frantic sparrows flying in swooping arcs, skittish deer with red eyes, hunters dressed in orange flak jackets. The boy moves closer, like he's trying to step inside this landscape. But the shouts continue. Somebody in the crowd keeps calling him.

—Hey! a kid with curly hair shouts. It's Lawrence. I was waving at you. Guess you didn't recognize me.

The boy lowers the hood of his sweatshirt. His unblinking eyes flicker in Lawrence's direction. His lips shudder into a shape that might be construed as a greeting.

—Never thought you'd be at something like this, Lawrence says. I mean, it's cool you're into this stuff. My friend ditched the show for some chick, so I drove here myself. No chance I was going to miss this.

The boy in the sweatshirt remains silent and his head swivels back toward the band. Probably he's being purposefully rude, but either it's too dark for Lawrence to pick up the insult or he doesn't care.

—I'm starting this band, Lawrence says. I've recorded some backing tracks and now I'm looking for members. The guys who run this place floated the idea of opening for an upcoming show.

The boy scrutinizes the musicians like he's trying to decode a message contained in the stray pulses of light glinting off their instruments. They're locked into a groove, cranking up the distortion with every repetition. The crowd rocks on its heels, bobbing in time to the bracingly loud music.

—You have any interest? Lawrence asks. In joining? You play an instrument, right? If not, no big deal. It's easy enough to figure that out.

The video projection now shows a dirt road running through the woods. The camera glides along an empty trail lit only by a pair of headlights. The boy's eyes are stretched wide as if he's trying to absorb the entire forest. The musicians must seem like little more than extra pixels, obscuring bits of distortion.

—What do you say? Lawrence asks. We could be what this place needs.

It's impossible to guess what emotion animates the boy's puckering face. His hands squirm inside the pouch of his sweatshirt. His voice is hoarse and strained.

—What this place needs, the boy says, is a good fire.

—That's sick. Lawrence laughs and slaps him on the back.

Something clatters to the floor and Lawrence scoops it up. His hands cradle an object of bewildering weight as if it's a shard of space debris. The flashing video briefly illuminates the polished barrel of a handgun.

The boy snatches it back and spins around to see if anyone noticed.

—What the fuck is that for? Lawrence says.

—Self-defense, the boy says. Then he points the gun at the stage and pumps the trigger.

He braces for the recoil, but nothing happens. Lawrence screams at him, unintelligible sounds, voice shrill like a siren. He flaps his hands madly, trying to wrestle the gun away without actually touching it. The boy makes evasive maneuvers, and their flailing hands perform an awkward dance around the weapon. All the while, the boy clutches the polished metal. Then his fingers find the safety.

The boy fires the gun without taking aim. It discharges directly into Lawrence's face. A spattering combustion of flesh and bone. A sickening sucking thump. Somebody seizes the boy from behind and the weapon goes off again. The boy in the sweatshirt squeals, twisting away from his captor and hopping madly across the darkened space. He's shot himself in the foot.

Most of the crowd tries to flee the patio, bodies churning for the rear exit. A few people point at the maniacally bouncing figure. A woman grabs a fire extinguisher and

clocks the boy in the back of the head. He staggers, hands instinctively clutching his vibrating scalp. At some point, he must have dropped the gun.

Throughout, the band keeps playing. The image behind them remains the same. The video must be on a slow fade because its edges grow steadily darker, but the boy can still make it out: the twilight woods, the bobbing headlights, the vacant dirt road, the endless path whose destination remains forever a few paces ahead.

Your mother sits in her wheelchair and hums to herself. It's an irritating children's tune whose name you can never remember. You kneel in front of her and spread streaks of shaving cream on her calves. You try not to let it bother you that she's so withdrawn she barely notices your presence. There's no acknowledgment as you gently shave her legs with a razor. When you accidentally draw blood, you watch the red bead bloom on the surface of her skin. Then you wad a piece of tissue and place it over the cut. Your mother can't feel anything, but you always look up to make sure she's not in any pain. She absently strokes your shaved scalp. Why'd you cut off all your hair? she murmurs. You don't reply. She's talking to herself anyway. Her eyes remain fixed on the television screen, absorbed in some stupid show about running. A coach is seated on a bench in the locker room next to a skinny boy in a track uniform. The coach scolds the boy for missing

practice. *You never show up,* he says. *Why don't you quit?* The boy doesn't reply and stares obstinately at his shoes. You recognize his expression. *Why don't you quit?* the coach repeats. You know how the boy should answer, so you say it for him: *Because I'm not a quitter.*

DAY
45

NEW YORK ● **THE BOY IN THE BAGGY WINDBREAKER**
is late. He stands in the stalled line, shuffling his feet,
advancing every available inch. In his frustration, he
plucks out an eyelash. It's an involuntary reflex he keeps
repeating, seemingly unaware of the collection of fine
black squiggles amassing on his sticky fingertips. Finally
he enters the glass lobby, claims his ticket, and hops on the
escalator that descends below street level. Standing on
the languidly moving metal staircase, he yanks his baggy
windbreaker tight, hugging it to his chest as if it's a security
blanket. He plucks another eyelash.

When he reaches the main floor, the boy brushes past
the fans with the macabre tattoos and metal piercings
gathered at the bar. He hastens down the terraced steps,
past the merchandise table where two men with long
black hair autograph embossed posters of winged de-
mons. He's almost running toward the entrance of the
concert hall. The music is a seismic rumble beneath his

feet, a slithering symphony of electric current. The doors are within sight.

A uniformed security guard halts the boy and instructs him to place his arms behind his head. Routine inspection, the guard says, as he ferrets through the windbreaker. In one pocket, he discovers a lighter. From the other, he produces a glass bottle filled with translucent yellowish liquid whose top is stoppered with an old rag.

—That's my soda, the boy mumbles.

—Like shit, the guard says. You're another one of those psychopaths.

The guard is marveling over the Molotov cocktail when the venue's doors burst open. Masses of bodies stampede for the exits. People knock past one another, elbows maneuvering, voices strafing. The guard briefly maintains a grip on the boy's shoulder, then he wades into the swarm of seething bodies.

The boy in the baggy windbreaker looks perplexed. The show should have just begun. He shoves through the pandemonium into the darkened hall. A deafening maelstrom of feedback fills the air, gales of distortion gust from the speaker stacks, but the musicians aren't playing. The spotlit stage is a gory frieze: the long-haired drummer slumped over his kit, the robe-wearing bassist contorted with a head wound, the leather-clad singer draped across one of the screeching amps.

The room is shrouded in tendrils of mist from a smoke machine. It takes the boy a few seconds to register the

teenager in the black overcoat who stands near the stage, cradling a semiautomatic weapon, surveying his handiwork with a stately sense of detachment. The shooter turns to the boy, and the pair lock eyes. A moment of recognition. The muscles around the shooter's mouth spasm into what might be described as a smile.

You lock yourself in the bathroom and tune out the off-key song your mother is warbling to herself in the hallway. Staring into the mirror, you admire the pair of headphones that resemble the ear protectors worn at shooting ranges. Your hands form the shape of a gun and you aim your fingers at the mirror. Your reflection still seems incomplete. You rustle through the supplies in the medicine cabinet until the razor gives you an idea. You soap your forehead and meticulously etch away your eyebrows. Soon they're both obliterated. This blurs your features, leaving only a foggy familiarity, but it's not quite enough. Before you leave the bathroom, you reach over to the mirror and wipe your face clean off the glass.

DAY
63

NEVADA ● **THE DREADLOCKED BOY IS CLEARED.**
The bouncers trace the contours of his body with a metal wand. They pat down his shirt, investigate the inseams of his crotch, make him remove his shoes. They rifle through his backpack and discover only a bottle of water that they empty onto the ground. The routine is exhaustive everywhere, even on the edge of the desert, and there's nothing to find on the boy. He walks up the concrete ramp into the cavernous darkness of the warehouse.

The dance floor ahead is a sea of massed shadows, strobing explosions of white light, rumbling bass frequencies, but the dreadlocked boy veers away from the music. He traces a path along the edge of the venue toward the bathroom. He pushes open the door with unexpected urgency. Inside, the fluorescent lights are wrapped in purple gels, lending the lavatory a sickly glow. He walks past the empty urinals to the row of stalls. Two are open, but the farthest one is occupied.

The dreadlocked boy retreats to the sink and washes

his hands. The throbbing dance music is recalibrated by the insulated walls into a thrum of hushed rhythms, and he taps his feet in time to the woozy beat. He maintains his station at the sink for several minutes. In the haze of violet light, it's difficult to make out his expression. He continues to wash his hands, over and over, his eyes locked on the farthest stall.

Finally, the door swings open. The boy almost collides with the bald man vacating the stall. He slips inside, slides the metal latch shut, double-checks that it's secure. Blackened scum is frescoed into the tiles, and kidney-shaped islands of urine pool on the floor. He sits on the toilet without removing his pants.

He swivels behind him and carefully removes the toilet lid from the water tank. He flips it over. The underside of the lid is crisscrossed with silver duct tape, encasing an object wrapped in newspaper. A thick lump of gray material stuck with strands of multicolored wires. He carefully places it in his lap, attaches the two red wires, and presses the plastic display. The numbers begin to race in reverse.

The dreadlocked boy slides the bomb into his backpack. He lowers his head between his legs and takes several raspy breaths, as if he's about to hyperventilate. His fingernails dig deep into his kneecaps. Then he replaces the lid, flushes the toilet, and exits the stall. He doesn't bother to wash his hands.

As he steps onto the dance floor, the music fades and the lights cut, immersing the crowd in blackness. Knew they'd be on time, a voice says. Almost on time, someone

corrects. Maybe it's the same voice. Maybe it's even the voice of the dreadlocked boy.

A spotlight snaps on. The audience applauds as a musician in a silver tracksuit tips his visor and takes his place behind a bank of keyboards and computers. A large man in a seersucker suit picks up an electric bass and plucks the strings. Beneath the scrim of glitchy electronic textures, the stirrings of a soulful ballad emerge. The musicians initiate a loping groove that signals a woman in the wings to make her way to the microphone. She wears a red satin dress that sets off her radiant coffee skin.

As the boy presses toward the front of the stage, he studies the singer's movements. She shakes her metal braids in time to the sultry rhythm. She repeats a single phrase, shifting the stress of the syllables, steadily transforming it into an incantation. Her hand guides the microphone toward her mouth in fixed increments. Each intonation, each gesture, entwined.

The boy stands enraptured, backpack clutched to his chest. The singer's movements seem perfectly synched to his own internal clock. The crowd appears equally in thrall to the performance, to the seductive pulsations of the song, to the shimmer of fitted red satin. They're all clasped in the same moment, unknowingly held together by the boy's beguiled lips, moving in silent countdown.

You kneel in the basement, under the only functioning light fixture, and take apart the weapon. The carpet is mildewed from past flooding, so you work over a flattened sheet of newspaper. You're determined to ignore the rusted frame of your mother's first wheelchair and the moldy plastic bedpans tucked into the surrounding shadows. You won't let them shame you. Your attention is focused on your tools. You've lined up an assortment of toothbrushes, rods, oils, solvents. You disassemble the guts of the handgun while softly chanting the names of the mechanical parts. The frame, the slide, the barrel, the chamber. You remove the buildup of caked carbon and unburned powder, then wipe down the components. The smell of ammonia stings your nostrils, but you like it. The sharper the burn, the better. You slot a fresh round of ammunition into the magazine, but there's no satisfying click. The parts grind against one

another. Even this doesn't work. You hurl the weapon across the room, where it's promptly swallowed by the shadows. You stand up to retrieve it, but you're halted by an earsplitting shriek—your own—though you don't recognize the voice.

DAY 81

MISSOURI ● **THE THREE BOYS REMAIN SILENT AS** the freight elevator rises with a slow rumble. They each remove large handkerchiefs from the pockets of their jeans. Or rather these are white ski masks. They stretch the masks over their heads and watch the dingy lights for each floor blink to life, one by one. The lift finally sighs to a halt, and the metal doors slide open. They're greeted by an enormous poster featuring a bloody panda lying in a pile of bamboo leaves, but the three boys move past it before any of the names listed below can come into focus. They march swiftly into the sprawling loft.

They each grab a plastic cup of red wine from a serving tray that's been left atop a wooden crate. In front of them, a variety of performances are under way, a cacophony ricocheting from different rooms. The hyped-up rockabilly duo, the couple whose electronically wired bodies generate humming frequencies, the troupe of pajama-clad dancers fucking teddy bears in time to a frisky beat. For a moment, the three boys stall before these colliding

spectacles, then walk straight ahead, following the dotted yellow line painted on the concrete floor.

As the three boys weave their way through the swarming crowd, nobody acts surprised by their appearance. They trail the yellow line around the corner, entering a sparsely lit space where the music is so loud it rattles their teeth. People twitch their limbs in time to stammering jackhammer beats. The sound bumps a cluster of silver helium balloons across the ceiling.

A slim man in a tailored pinstripe suit struts across the modest stage, whooping into the microphone. The edge of the singer's frizzy hair is haloed in the stage lights. Behind him, the other musicians hunch over banks of keyboards and vintage electronics. They're all wearing white ski masks.

As the three boys move closer, they let their cups drop to the floor. The wine splatters across the concrete and splashes their sneakers. They step over the quivering red pool, leaving behind an intricately shaped stain, the dark liquid shimmering in the dim light, uncongealed.

You're not sure what you're doing at the concert. You barely remember driving here and now you're standing in the middle of the crowd, watching an unfamiliar band perform. Their music is deafeningly loud but it feels inert, a gauzy hive of sound that's not unlike the noise in your head. It makes you feel queasy. The audience around you also seems half dazed, listlessly watching the musicians move between their effects pedals. People keep bumping into you as they cut a path toward the bathrooms. Nobody apologizes. You look around the cramped club, not recognizing the fishing nets dangling from the ceiling, the ship's wheel tacked above the door, the flag with the skull and crossbones draped behind the band. Behind you, the translucent shelves of the bar are lit from below, suffusing the rows of liquor bottles with a murky glow. You decide you need a drink, then discover you're already holding a beer. The band lets the song slowly wind down, leaving the

singer alone to croon the final ethereal phrases. She thanks the crowd, kissing her fingertips and planting the kiss on the tip of the microphone. The audience wakes up and starts to offer their applause. This is your cue to reach under your shirt and grab the cold metal tucked in the small of your back. But instead you find yourself sitting alone in the parking lot, sobbing in the front seat of your car, staring at your hands where a bright gun barrel shines with your tears.

DAY
100

FLORIDA ● THE MUSIC IS A GHOSTLY ECHO. A faint hint of instruments being tuned, amps turned on, levels adjusted, but these sounds are lost in the crowd. The pulse and push of tightly packed bodies. The tanned teenagers, sunburned parents, elderly couples in matching wide-brimmed hats. The street is closed to traffic, and people amble past the metal hot-dog carts, the stand of home-made necklaces, the Realtors hawking vacation rentals, the tarot-card reader offering discounts so low they're supernatural. Banners strung from streetlamps announce the beach town's annual fair.

People shuffle by food trucks selling fish tacos and falafel sandwiches. They admire the larval dough of fun-nel cakes taking shape in bubbling oil. Flocks of pigeons swoop onto the sidewalk to choke down stray popcorn kernels. The ring-toss operator bellows a list of prizes into his megaphone and shakes a stuffed giraffe at pass-ersby. Pyramids of trash rise in the metal trash cans. As

everyone flows toward the end of the street, heads swivel to take in each fresh sight.

In front of the entrance to the beach, musicians in flower-print shirts, shorts, and sandals stand on a raised platform. These middle-aged men adjust their mirrored sunglasses while they test microphone levels. They observe the exodus of tanned bodies, the sand-flecked families carrying folding chairs, wet hair plastered to scalps, eyes marked by white ovals in the shape of sunglasses. Seagulls drift in placid circles overhead. The sun is setting and the clouds turn shades of pale pink, crimson rose, plasma red.

The band announces their first number, a song promising an endless summer. The singer strums a few chords on his acoustic guitar, then launches into a winsome melody. The rest of the group adds amiable doo-wop harmonies. A few people sing along, but most are distracted by phone screens and scampering children. They're busy knocking sand from the folds of clothes and congealed tar off the soles of shoes. Someone here in the crowd is awaiting his moment, weighing the timing against the tang of salt in the breeze and the vibrations of the unseen surf.

You find yourself following a sound that might be music. You shuffle along the sidewalk like a sleepwalker, weaving through the evening crowd, locked into the dim throb repeating from somewhere down the street. You have no idea who's creating this echoing sound. You don't stop to ask the college kids who are pasting up concert flyers featuring the photo of a bloody panda. The posters stapled to the telephone poles are too old to offer any clues. You keep walking, past the rows of coffee shops, tapas restaurants, thrift stores. With each step, the pulse of the music grows louder. As you approach the veterans hall, you realize this must be your destination. Three girls stand outside the entrance and squint in your direction like they're having trouble bringing your features into focus. Maybe it's your shaved head and missing eyebrows. They talk about you as if you're not there, probably hoping that you'll leave, but you're no quitter. One of them presents you

with a sheet of paper about the concert, which turns out to be a battle of the bands. There are so many names printed on the page that your head starts to swim. You watch as your fingers make the words disappear, patiently folding the announcement into a perfect square and tossing it onto the ground. The old man behind the table mumbles the ticket price and you start to get the money, but your hands hesitate. They go numb in your pockets like they've got a mind of their own. You wait to see what will happen and soon your hands reappear with a few crinkled dollar bills. As you enter the building, you stumble into a foyer stacked with folding chairs and collapsed tables. You stand in the center of the darkened space. The nearby music is a rumble in your chest. The distorted sounds beat around the room like a trapped bird. You're unsure if this is really the place you should be, then you spot a banner strung across the ceiling. Reading the phrase printed on the plastic, the cold metal tucked in the small of your back feels lighter. You move your lips, soundlessly forming and re-forming those two words, feeling the warm tingle of their syllables on your tongue: WELCOME HOME.

part two
THE DEVOTED

"I've been reading about the different ways to reach the dead," Xenie said. "Mediums, séances, Ouija boards, fire rituals."

"Any of them work?" Shaun asked.

"Hard to tell," Xenie said. "I wonder if the dead ever feel like they're being haunted by the living?"

HE ASKS THEM TO OPEN THE CASKET. Standing in the funeral parlor in his borrowed black suit, face roughly shaven, long hair combed into a ponytail, Shaun hopes to appear more authoritative than his twenty-one years. He hides his trembling hands behind his back, embarrassed by how badly he needs this. Neither the funeral director nor the aunt replies, so he asks again. His words barely float above a whisper. Please, Shaun says, struggling to keep his voice from shattering. Please.

●

Shaun tugs at the cuffs of his suit that's at least a size too small. He feels swallowed by the pastel hues of this private reception room with its plush carpet and overstuffed furniture. He offers the elderly funeral director a solicitous

smile and speaks in his most confidential voice, hoping his usual charm won't abandon him.

—Listen, Shaun says. This doesn't have to be a big deal. This isn't for the service, it's just for me.

—I'm sorry, the funeral director says.

Shaun loosens his suffocating tie while he speaks. His nose twitches from the sharp smell of antiseptic. Come on, man, he says. I'm her boyfriend. We were together for three years.

—I'm sorry, the funeral director repeats.

—You don't understand, Shaun says. She's going to be cremated.

He tries to maintain eye contact with the funeral director, but he keeps being distracted by the casket and the sight of his own warped and wavy reflection bobbing inside the black lacquer polish.

—I haven't seen her since that night, he says. I want to see her one last time.

He feels the pitch of his voice rising and his control slipping away.

—I just need to share the same space with her, he says. A few moments to see her body lying there.

Maybe if I see you, it'll finally feel real.

Shaun keeps waking in the middle of the night and nothing's changed. Then his outstretched hand encounters the empty side of the bed. His fingers furrow under her pillow and find his oversize black T-shirt that she slept in.

Bunched up exactly as she left it. And everything comes back, not in a flood of memories, but as a searing knot in his stomach. He somehow resists the urge to smell the shirt, but her scent is smeared all over the sheets, so he starts to choke anyway.

●

Shaun focuses his beseeching gaze on the aunt, the matronly woman in the black pantsuit who served as his girlfriend's longtime guardian. Her red-rimmed eyes blink incessantly, too sensitive for even the room's diffuse lighting. She stares at the powder-blue carpet, as if expecting some revelation to emerge from the woven pattern.

—Mary, he says, we've always gotten along. Help me out here. Say something to this man.

Aunt Mary stirs from her trance. She tenderly strokes the top of the coffin, as if smoothing her niece's unruly hair.

—We're doing you a favor, she says.

Her voice sounds like a kitchen drain that's partially clogged.

—You don't want to see her like this. Nobody should ever see her like this.

●

The funeral director places a large bouquet atop the casket. Pink carnations wrenched into the shape of a heart and encircled by a sash that reads FARE FORWARD,

VOYAGER. Summoning his most officious tone, he announces: The casket of Jennifer Marx remains shut.

It takes Shaun a full second to recognize the name.

Xenie. Her name was Xenie.

●

Shaun can't decide whether to sink to his knees and beg like an animal or grab their shoulders and shout demands. He doesn't believe Aunt Mary's excuses for an instant. He wonders how Xenie would've handled this situation. He keeps having conversations with her in his head. He keeps sifting through his memories like they're questions. And he keeps expecting an answer.

> *Would you even stick around for this ridiculous*
> *scene?*

Shaun remembers the totem tucked inside his suit jacket. He spent hours combing through Xenie's music collection, hunting far-flung favorites, attempting to distill her complicated personality into a single potent playlist. He's mostly spent the days since the shooting entombed in his apartment, existing in a semiconscious fugue state, hours evaporating without a trace. This is the only thing he's managed to accomplish. He hoped it would prove cathartic, but each new selection wrung him inside out.

—Here are her songs, he says, producing a compact disc.

As soon as the funeral director sees the shiny object, he shakes his head so vigorously the wattle under his neck flaps back and forth.

—I've got them on my phone if that's easier, Shaun says.

—The service won't include anything like that, the director says.

Shaun is stunned into silence for several seconds.

—You're not playing her songs? he says. At all? You've got to play at least one. At the beginning or the end.

The funeral director starts to stammer an excuse, but Aunt Mary intervenes.

—I don't care about some fad that's taken off at these funerals, she says.

—Xenie would've wanted this, Shaun says.

—I won't allow it, Aunt Mary says, clutching her purse with both hands, her grip so tight that he can see the bones of her knuckles. That music is the reason she's not here now.

●

Shaun steps to the aunt and glares down at her. Her puffy face is adorned with more makeup than usual, rouge and eyeliner applied with violent disregard. He prides himself on his genial ability to let things slide, but this is too much.

—This is fucked up, he says. The cremation, the closed coffin, now this.

Aunt Mary returns his stare, undaunted.

—I don't expect you to understand, she says, but her spirit can't go on without a righteous ceremony. She'll be trapped here. It's our duty to give her a proper send-off.

Shaun thinks she's putting him on, but then remembers Xenie talking about her aunt's unusual spiritual beliefs.

—Is the cremation part of the send-off?

Aunt Mary nods.

—It was also Jennifer's wish, she says. It came up several times, and she was very clear.

She reaches out and pats Shaun's shoulder. He's unprepared for the glints of genuine kindness in her gray eyes.

—I'm sorry she never told you.

●

The funeral director is flanked by several imposing men in black suits. The service is about to start, he says. An usher takes Aunt Mary's arm and escorts her through the side door to the chapel. She proceeds with halting steps, compulsively tightening her black head scarf, her bottom lip quivering.

Shaun finds himself standing beside the casket, his body flush against its form, his fingers running along the grain of the wood and toward the seal.

—We have to move that into the chapel, the funeral director says.

Ushers grasp the polished brass handles on both sides of the box.

—*Her,* Shaun says. You have to move *her.*

He keeps thinking about their first meeting at the cele-
bratory homecoming concert for the Carmelite Rifles and
their mutual obsession with music. Their drunken dates at
the laundromat. The shallow indentation of her navel. The
bottle of hair dye they'd pick out every month and rub into
each other's scalps over the bathroom sink. The matching
scars on their wrists, desperate mementos they rarely discussed but weren't surprised they shared. Those twin inci-
sions were their bond. Xenie is the only girl he's ever loved.
The only person he let witness the clinical depression he
stubbornly hid from everyone else. The waxing and waning despair. She understood him without explanation.

The wooden pews of the chapel are sparsely filled. As
Shaun takes a seat, he scans the crowd and finds he doesn't
recognize a soul. Everyone at this private service is old. It
looks like an assembly of old school secretaries, old town
administrators, old payroll clerks, old church deacons. It
dawns on him Aunt Mary has only invited members of her
spiritual sect, maybe a scattering of friends and distant
relatives. Sitting among the wrinkled flesh and unfamiliar faces, surrounded by their stoic demeanor and formal
attire, Shaun feels like he's slipped inside somebody else's
dream of his girlfriend's funeral.

Xenie, did you really want to be cremated?

Two women in long black dresses march along the perimeter of the chapel, carrying metal bowls of burning incense. Smoke trails behind them, accompanied by the stinging scent of sage. This must be preparation for the ceremony. He's handed a program with a photo of a grinning young girl, hair in pigtails, holding an empty birdcage. She bears practically no resemblance to the girl Shaun loved. Somehow he manages not to rip it in half.

He wishes his friends hadn't been shut out and were sitting here with him, though maybe they're suffering funeral fatigue. Every day there are a few more. The public services for Xenie's bandmates were yesterday. The city's official memorial is scheduled for later in the week.

The shooting in Arcadia was one of the worst of the entire epidemic. The sickening body count put the small industrial city on the national map. A photograph of the plastic body bags lined up along the sidewalk outside the theater has already taken on iconic status. The casualties were so high the paramedics kept losing count. It was a record release party for Xenie's band.

The killer was a part-time employee who avoided the usual security protocols. He stood in the wings with an automatic assault rifle, waited for the band to reach the bridge of their first song, and mercilessly unloaded round after round until—

●

He can't think about that anymore. It's not the shots and screams and splattering blood that haunt him, but the mo-

ments right before. The anticipation in the sold-out theater as the lights dimmed. The heat of the bodies massed around him. The stickiness of spilled beer underfoot. The beads of sweat stinging his eyes. The surge of brightness from the back of the stage as the musicians' silhouettes strut toward their places. Xenie positioning herself at the front of the platform. Adjusting her microphone stand. Tilting it to her mouth. Counting to three.

●

The sound of her voice booming out of the speakers, reverberating through the room as she chants the first lines of the song.

●

The sound of her voice.

●

Her voice.

●

Shaun never caught a solid glimpse of the killer that night, but he can't stop picturing the police mug shot snapped after the boy was in custody. The round chubby face, hair shorn almost to the skull, pallid blue eyes, empty expression. Down his left cheek, a zigzagging puffy pink scar that looks like it might be self-inflicted. This face flashes so often before him that he wouldn't be surprised if it materialized here at the funeral.

He should be the one in the casket, not you.

The funeral is about to start when she enters. Heads swivel as she parades down the center aisle. A tall redhead in a green strapless gown, her glamour slightly undercut by her lanky frame and storklike gait. Shaun recognizes her immediately: Florence, Xenie's best friend since grade school. She always struck Shaun as aloof and bookish with an air of superiority, the sort of person who avoids shitting in public toilets. Maybe because they were the two people who knew Xenie best, they mostly avoided each other's orbit. But in these circumstances, he's relieved to see her. Florence takes a seat a few pews ahead. He leans forward and stage-whispers her name, but she doesn't stir. He can't tell whether she's purposefully ignoring him. The back of her bobbed red hair and the pattern of acne across her bare shoulders offer no clues.

●

Shaun scowls at the minister who stands at the lectern, adjusting a black fur hat on his head. He removes the compact disc from his jacket and snaps it into several pieces. The mirrored shards gleam in his palm. This is when Xenie's music should be playing. As the killings gained momentum, families began to play the victims' favorite songs at the start of their funerals, a small gesture that swiftly took root as ritual. Now the music is often blasted at deafening decibels, leaving mourners with a cathartic buzz in their eardrums. It's an act of defiance in the face

of the epidemic. It makes the silence of the chapel feel obscene. The slightest noise seems amplified: rustling programs, murmured gossip, blown noses. Each insignificant sound is another death.

How can you have a proper send-off without music?

The gray-bearded minister speaks in a gravelly monotone. He opens a tattered leather book and recites from his notes, describing the tangible presence of the deceased among them, like a color tinting the air, awaiting release. In the front pew Aunt Mary sobs, her body rippling in soft spasms, her ragged voice repeatedly addressing a person she calls *Jennifer*. Shaun keeps himself together by focusing on the oil painting hanging at the front of the chapel, an otherworldly forest scene at sunset, trees burnished by orange sky. He can't figure out the smudges of black paint murmuring around the edges, violent black swirls that vaguely resemble birds in desperate flight.

●

Shaun slowly takes in the sight of the casket, surrounded by urns of lilies. He imagines her laid out inside, slipped between the satin lining, dyed blonde hair sheared on the sides and pomaded on top, skin even paler than usual, small hands crossed atop her chest. He wonders whether they put her in one of her typical eclectic thrift-store ensembles: calico dress, black tights, combat boots. He hopes they didn't use makeup to obscure her scar. He wishes he

could see that mark one last time. Before it's all consumed by flames.

•

He's struck by a sickening realization. It's so simple and obvious, he can't believe it didn't occur to him sooner. He wasn't allowed to look in the casket because she's not inside. The cremation is a ruse and they've already done away with Xenie's corpse. There's no body there.

•

The woman seated next to Shaun taps him on the shoulder. She stares at him with the candid concern of a schoolteacher for a badly bruised student. You okay? she whispers. Shaun feels clammy and discovers his white dress shirt is soaked through with sweat. I'm fine, he says, though the words are little more than a rattle in his throat.

•

He runs his index finger along the scar on his wrist, tracing the livid line of raised flesh.

•

Everyone in the chapel suddenly stands and starts to speak. Their voices meld into a single sound, chanting in unison, locked into a lugubrious cadence. It's startling until Shaun realizes that they're reciting the text of the

archaic liturgy printed in the program. Though he has no interest in this ritual, he rises to his feet.

●

The organist plays dolorous chords to accompany the call-and-response between minister and congregation, somber tones that mask the sound of Shaun's footsteps. As he walks down the aisle, he tries to appear calm, a natural part of the proceedings, planning to peek inside Xenie's casket and return to his pew before anyone can register what's happened.

●

The casket lid won't budge. He grips it with both hands. While his fingernails search for a purchase in the seam, the organist falters and the reciting voices trail off. He grunts as he tries to wedge the rubber apart, but the seal remains stubbornly intact.

●

Shaun is aware of the growing commotion, but he just needs a little better leverage. He climbs atop the flower urns and leans over the casket. He strains at the lid with all his strength. The minister attempts to say something but instead convulses into an uncontrollable coughing fit, the microphone amplifying his percussive bark. Aunt Mary waves her hands in a frenzied semaphore. From the back, the funeral director whistles through his fingers.

Xenie, open up.

Two enormous ushers exert a firm grip on Shaun's arms and elbows, though he's too humiliated to offer any resistance. The mourners on both sides of the aisle goggle in stunned silence as he's marched from the chapel. His head hangs low. His face is wet. The casket remains unopened.

●

Shaun sits on the curb outside the entrance to the funeral home. He unknots his tie, undoes his ponytail, shakes loose his long hair. He takes a deep breath. The evening feels unfinished. His mind keeps returning to the words about Xenie's trapped spirit. During the past few days, he's been visited by the uncanny feeling she is still nearby, somewhere slightly beyond his vision, on the flip side of this reality. The sun slides below the horizon and tints the fading light a vivid violet. He finds himself immersed in the color, telling himself it isn't real, its presence a trick of perception.

●

Florence takes a seat on the curb beside him. The green fabric of her dress shimmers in the diffuse light. Reflexively, Shaun straightens his green tie. Xenie's favorite color.

—That was some show, she says.

He can't tell whether she's impressed or disgusted. Her arched eyebrows and pursed lips give away nothing. Maybe she doesn't know herself.

He says: It's not my fault. I wanted to do it before the service, but they wouldn't let me.

—After the shooting, he says, they took her away in the ambulance before I could get to her. And you had to be family to get into the morgue.

—I never got to see her, he says. There was no time to say goodbye.

Across the parking lot, the funeral home's plastic sign lights up. It emits a gentle buzz, mimicking the sound of the insects that will soon be swarming around it.

—Fuck, Shaun says. I really lost it.

He lowers his head between his knees, too embarrassed to blush. He waits for Florence to ream him out for ruining the ceremony, but she swallows her words and stares at the rows of parked cars. As the night settles around them, she removes a small metal flask from her pocketbook and passes it to him.

—I guess we're the only ones Mary invited, he says, taking a drink.

—Who was invited? she says. I crashed.

He finishes the final mouthful of vodka and returns the flask.

—You didn't get kicked out, he says. Why don't you go back in?

She traces her fingernails along the surface of the empty flask. The fading metal is engraved with two cursive letters. Xenie's initials.

—Those people don't know her, she says.

From the pronounced way Florence slurs her words,

Shaun guesses she's heavily medicated. He recognizes the crumpled expression behind her eyes and the cold despair in her voice. He wonders if she also wakes in the middle of the night gripped by a sort of vertigo, simultaneously nauseated and hollowed out.

—We need more to drink, he says as he gets to his feet. There's a bar down the street.

Still seated on the curb, she hesitates. They've never spent any time together without Xenie.

Shaun extends his hand. Come on, he says. This isn't the night to be alone.

●

There are only the briefest stares as they enter the bar. It's a blue-collar establishment, filled with workers making the most of their time away from the tire warehouses and construction gigs. Her shimmering green dress and his black suit and long hair stand out, but it's a testament to how thoroughly the killings have sunken into every particle of Arcadia that nobody acts surprised to see them. Shaun suspects the place is seedier than Florence prefers, but she says nothing. They take seats at the bar and discover their first round of drinks is on the house. In the dim light, they listen to the bank of televisions tuned to classic football reruns. Florence produces a small pillbox from her purse. Mama needs some more medicine, she murmurs. But there's nothing left, and she stares in dismay at the emptiness. Shaun focuses on his whiskey. The bartender selected a high-quality blend, but the superior

flavor is wasted on him. He'd happily swallow wiper fluid or witch hazel. All his throat craves is the burn.

●

Normally Shaun chats up the people around him at a bar, but tonight he's withdrawn. He has no idea how to act around Florence and realizes how little he knows about her. Their limited rapport was largely based on competing for Xenie's attention, a rivalry that now seems petty. Sitting here together, her absence is even more pronounced. They resemble strangers who recently discovered a blood tie, only now realizing how intimately they're bound.

They find themselves staring at the Wurlitzer jukebox stashed behind the pool table, partly obscured beneath a black tablecloth, the refuse of a distant epoch.

—I think I could've made it through the service, he says, if they'd played the songs. I bet the music would've made it more bearable.

—I put together a really good playlist, he says. All her favorite tunes.

—I need to do something for her, he says.

●

Shaun's reflection stares at him in the murky mirror behind the bar. He wonders how long the black dye will last, how long before the roots begin to show, before the last evidence of her hands running through his hair is expunged.

Florence stirs her White Russian with her pinkie until a little whirlpool appears in the milky liquid. She doesn't pause to take a sip.

—I know what you mean about doing something for her, she says.

—I was in her first band, she says. Not many people know that. We were in junior high, messing around in our bedrooms, barely able to play any chords. We wrote and recorded a few tunes. I was totally hopeless, but you could already hear her talent. The way she loved to get lost inside a song.

—I found that old cassette, she says, and added it to the shrine in front of the theater. It was my tribute to her. I thought it'd make me feel better, but as I walked away I realized it was meaningless now that she's gone. I was just like everybody else, adding more trash to the sidewalk.

•

Florence stares at her hands and chips away at the green nail polish. Shaun watches her expression fluctuate as memories flicker across her face, catching a glimpse of a younger girl who fleetingly possesses her features.

—I wasn't at the show that night, she says. I was going to go, but—

She intends to say more, laying out the reasons, but she's overwhelmed by her own words, swallowed by the magnitude of her confession. Her eyes are glazed, still she

holds back the tears she knows haven't earned the right to fall.

Shaun reaches over and places his hand next to hers on the bar.

—Florence, he says.

—Call me Flo, she says. That's what Xenie always called me. Tonight, I'm Flo.

●

Somebody has also bought their next round. The bartender gestures to the booth in the corner where a skinny girl with a nest of brown hair sits nursing a tall can of beer. Edie, the unofficial manager for Xenie's band, offers a shy wave. There's something rehearsed in her greeting that gives Shaun the odd sense she's been expecting them.

Neither of them knows Edie well. Shaun is familiar with her mostly in the context of various backstage scenes, offering his congratulations after shows and a helping hand with the equipment. She's always struck him as exceptionally careful and quiet.

She walks over and gives both Shaun and Flo an awkward hug.

—I'm sorry, she says. It doesn't seem real. I know everybody says that when people die, but it's true.

She acknowledges the shimmering green fabric of Flo's dress with a nod. Although Edie favors a tomboy style with a tatty cardigan sweater and jeans, her lipstick is also a conspicuous shade of green.

—It was today? she asks.

—Yeah, Shaun says. Her aunt kept it private.

—That's too bad. I really wanted to be there.

He suspects she knew all the details of the funeral and has been drinking at this bar precisely because of its proximity.

—You didn't miss anything, he says. It was a horror. A complete horror.

●

Flo downs her White Russian in a single swallow and pushes the glass toward the bartender for a refill. Actually, she says, she had a memorable funeral.

At first Shaun thinks this is a malicious dig, but then he realizes it's spoken as a compliment, a gesture of camaraderie.

—I tried to open her casket, he says. I got kicked out.

Edie looks confused and waits for a punch line. None is forthcoming. She pushes her oversize glasses closer to the bridge of her nose to bring Shaun into sharper focus.

—I needed to see her, he says simply.

None of them can bring themselves to say her name.

●

—I tried to talk her out of playing the show, Edie says. I wanted you to know that. I tried, but none of the girls listened to me. They thought the epidemic was fizzling out. They thought it wouldn't come here. Or they just didn't care.

—Even if I'd canceled the show without telling them, she says, they would've played it somewhere else.

—I know what I know, she says. But I still feel like shit.

●

The evening of the concert, Xenie couldn't decide on an outfit. She tried on shredded jeans, drainpipe trousers, a short black skirt. Shaun lay on the bed while she asked his opinion of each ensemble, and he kind of loved how she didn't give his words much weight. As she surveyed her reflection from every odd slant, he worried that she might be growing addicted to the crowds and the applause. He wanted to beg her not to perform, but she made it clear that she'd never cancel the record release show. So, stupidly, he stayed silent. Before she left the bedroom, Xenie tossed a purple guitar pick into the air. It was like she was flipping a coin to decide whether to play. She caught the pick in her palm and examined it closely, even though both sides were the same.

●

His mind won't stop replaying the purple guitar pick twisting in the air.

●

At the back of the bar, on a tiny wooden stage, a woman starts to sing. She nervously grips the microphone with both hands and presses it against her lips. Shaun wonders if she's performing on a dare or because she lost a bet. She

stands there petrified, eyes pinned to the karaoke video monitor. Though she wears gobs of mascara, a tight mini-skirt, and spike heels, the words pouring from her mouth sound ancient and apocalyptic. *Love is a burning thing,* she sings. *It makes a fiery ring.* Her hesitant high-pitched voice throws the phrases into sharp relief. Shaun feels an eerie kinship with the song. *I went down, down, down,* she sings. *And the flames went higher.* The woman's barely inflected warble floats atop the synthetic rhythms and simulated mariachi horns, insinuating itself into the prerecorded backing track, until voice and machine vibrate on the same frequency, sharing the same tremulous breath. *When hearts like ours meet,* she sings. *Bound by wild desire.* This was always one of Xenie's favorite songs. Shaun had forgotten it's also a love song.

I should be the one singing this song.
I should be singing it for you.

The entire bar is transfixed by the tune's hushed spell. Despite herself, the woman has become a vessel for the song. Shaun remembers when Xenie sang there were glimpses of this alien aspect, as if her body was tuned to a foreign frequency and she was host to a sound separate from her. *I fell into a ring of fire,* the woman intones. *It burns, burns, burns.* It reminds Shaun of the incantatory language of the funeral litany, except these lyrics have their own fatalistic power. The woman's stoic presentation transforms the song, making it seem as if she has already

been consumed by the flames, though the fire continues. She has already fallen, though her descent is perpetual. *A ring of fire,* the woman sings. *A burning ring of fire.*

●

Shaun stands up and keeps applauding even after the karaoke machine is switched off and the woman returns to her table. Edie orders them a fresh round and insists on paying. Flo pours a shot directly into her flask and immediately orders another. Around them, casual flirting resumes and friendly bets are placed on games of pool, but he can tell the mood has shifted. The air seems curdled with smoke. The hazy lights radiate a reddish glow. The heightened atmosphere of the song has infected the bar and opened up the possibilities of the night.

●

The pool games grow increasingly spirited. Balls are racked and rolled. Stripes and solids scatter in unexpected configurations. Pockets are called and angles calculated. Slowly Shaun registers the sullen teenage boy who leans against the wall. There's something odd about how he continually chalks his cue but never joins a game. His eyes fixed on the clock behind the blue felt table.

●

Shaun tries to work out the details of the boy's appearance in the gauzy light. His brown hair is shorn almost to the skull. His pasty cheeks are chubby. His gray tracksuit is so

thoroughly matted with dirt that he must have been crawling through mud. As the boy turns in profile, Shaun's scalp begins to tingle.

•

The clamoring conversations around the bar, the clack of the billiard balls, the unconcealed stares of pity, Aunt Mary's purposeful send-off, the old people lining the pews, the photograph of the pigtailed girl on the program, the closed casket—all the incidents of the evening coalesce around the darkened line of flesh that slaloms down the boy's face.

•

Shaun leans toward Flo and whispers to avoid attracting attention. He maintains a neutral tone and refrains from making eye contact, careful not to influence her in any way.

—See that boy standing against the wall? he says. Does he look like anyone to you?

For several long seconds, Flo squints into the halo of light generated by the glass fixture above the pool table. An involuntary shudder ripples up her spine that makes her skinny shoulder blades flutter.

—Look at the face, he says.

—That does look like his face, she says.

—Look at the eyes, he says.

—Those do look like his eyes.

Shaun is relieved this isn't some drunken hallucination.

—But it's not him, right? he says.

—It can't be, she says.

They keep staring. The possibility proves too potent to shake.

—Is that a scar on his cheek? he says.

—It looks like a scar.

—A zigzag shape?

—Looks like, she says. Looks like a zigzag shape.

They're locked into the moment, their minds humming on the same wavelength.

—It's not him, he repeats.

—It can't be, she says.

But they can't stop looking at him.

●

Edie returns from the bathroom to find Shaun and Flo focused with unnerving concentration on the pool game. She's alarmed by their feral expressions, perspiring faces, lunar pallor.

—What are you guys staring at?

Shaun tips his chin toward the teenage boy. He has just propped his cue against the wall and is rubbing his hands together, sloughing the powdery residue of blue chalk from his fingertips.

Edie blanches.

—Oh, she says.

—But that's not him, she says. You know that, right?

—That's not the killer, she repeats. The killer is in jail.

Shaun and Flo don't reply. They're perched on the edge

of their barstools, their attention absorbed entirely by the boy, who steps away from the pool table. He winds his way past the booths along the back wall, head low and shoulders hunched, aiming for the exit.

●

They watch the boy push open the front door and slip out of sight like a mirage. Shaun isn't sure whether he feels relieved or distressed. The encounter seems incomplete. Flo stares at him with a stricken expression, and he realizes how deeply they've committed to their unspoken conspiracy.

—What do we do? Flo asks.

—Follow him, Shaun says.

—What are you talking about, Edie says. He's not the killer.

—For a few blocks, Shaun says. To see what happens.

He pours his remaining whiskey onto the bar and slams down the glass. Flo does the same. The alcohol floods across the counter, causing the regulars to jump back and the bartender to curse as he lurches for his towel.

—Come on, Edie says. Be reasonable.

But their barstools are already empty.

Is this what you want?

They spot the boy a few blocks ahead. He's the figure whose footsteps thread the dotted yellow line down the center of the road. The streets have been unusually empty since the

massacre. Edie jogs after Shaun and Flo, still pulling on her jacket as she joins them. Hope I'm drunk enough for this, she says breathlessly. Shaun wonders if she's spurred by a crush on Flo, or a manager's instinct for keeping people out of trouble, or some cocktail of regret and anger about missing the funeral. Or perhaps some part of her wants to believe they're trailing the killer. Shaun sets the tempo, keeping them from encroaching too close to the boy. This pursuit seems like something plucked straight from his subconscious, and he finds himself standing on the precipice of his own daydream.

●

The boy leads them past the strip of sporadic businesses on the edge of Arcadia. The check-cashing agency with the polished metal bars on the windows, the pawnshop stocked with ancient radios and stereos, the insurance office advertising the final days to take advantage of low prices on a term life policy. There's something uncanny about walking among these dormant establishments, enveloped in darkness. Shaun notices how the erratic lighting from the streetlamps and shuttered stores shifts the boy's shadow in size and proportion every few steps, as if it belongs to several people at once.

●

Shaun recalls Xenie's obsession with the killers and the epidemic. She seemed simultaneously disgusted and intrigued. She'd muse aloud about the motivations of the

very first shooter, the mundane incidents that might've incited him on his path, the fraught family situation that could've included being caretaker for his wheelchair-bound mother, how he spent the months leading up to loading his weapon and walking into the veterans hall during the battle of the bands. Shaun pretended not to notice the faraway expression that crept over her face as she imagined the various scenarios. Her speculations increasingly seemed like questions she was asking herself. As much as he doesn't want to consider it, maybe some part of her welcomed the violence, reenacting the courtship of the circling moth and flickering flame.

What fascinated you about the killers?

The bearded killer with the hunting knife.

The black-overcoat killer with the semiautomatic weapon.

The dreadlocked killer with the backpack of explosives.

The trio of killers in the white ski masks.

The boy stops in front of the window of a sporting-goods shop. The gently glowing display highlights hiking boots, camping tents, and orange flak jackets. He presses his

palm against the illuminated glass. Standing across the street, submerged in the shadows, Shaun wonders if he's testing its resistance against a possible break-in.

—You know what they sell in that store? Shaun says.

—Sports stuff, Edie says. Obviously.

—Guns. You can get assault rifles.

—That doesn't prove anything, Edie says.

Flo thrums her fingers against her pocketbook, creating an insistent rhythm, steadily ratcheting in intensity.

—Maybe he's out on bail, she says.

—Maybe he escaped, Shaun says.

—How? Edie asks.

Neither answers. They're both watching the boy lick his index finger and inscribe a set of circles in the dust on the windowpane, an increasingly tight series of spirals, one inside the other. The pattern resembles a target.

●

Shaun says: Maybe he escaped from prison a few hours ago. His gray tracksuit looks an awful lot like a prison outfit. Maybe his clothes are so dirty because he was crawling through some drainage pipe, splashing through an inch of muddy water, navigating toward a pinpoint of light.

He says: The prison is close to town. Maybe he was waiting at the bar until he could safely head to a friend's house. Or maybe even his own place.

He says: Maybe that's where he'll lead us.

The boy picks up the pace as he turns down a side street lined with shabby bungalows. He must be close to his destination. Shaun wants to believe his story. From Edie's and Flo's intense expressions, he guesses they do, too. Flo bites down on her bottom lip, as if she's trying to draw blood. Her eyes remain locked on the boy while her fingers knead the satiny green fabric of her dress. Edie walks with her hands plunged in her pockets and hums under her breath, a sequence of soft sighs that matches her footfalls on the pavement. They each absorb and expand the narrative in their own way.

The killer you never imagined.

—If it is him, Flo asks Shaun, what'll you do?

In her resolute gaze, he can make out reflections of the boy's bruised face, his body cowering on the floor, kicked to a pulp, tied to a chair, squealing in pain.

—It's not what I'll do, he says. It's what we'll do together.

●

A series of loud shots. It could be a car backfiring, except the detonations issue in deliberate succession. They originate from a nearby block, the echoes rippling through the night, slow to dissipate. Shaun lets his long hair obscure his face and tries to maintain his cool. Edie turns her

head every few feet, anxiously scanning the surrounding houses for clues. Flo acts unflustered. Don't worry, she says. It's probably fireworks. But the arcing blackness of the sky is unburnt.

●

The terrain grows unfamiliar, but none of them suggest turning back. The boy leads them past bulldozed plots, now weed choked and overgrown. He taps a small stick against the windows of the rust-mottled sedans parked along the street. Shaun worries the boy knows he's being followed and is purposefully pulling them deeper into this sketchy neighborhood.

●

In the distance, they're serenaded by the keening wail of an ambulance siren. Shaun wonders whether this is connected to the earlier gunshots. He pictures the emergency vehicle careening toward the hospital and the condition of the person inside, perhaps another blood-soaked girl, twitching on a stretcher, rasping for every breath, two bullet holes in her chest.

I should've been there with you.

They watch the boy veer into an overgrown wooded lot. He heads toward an oak tree and casually shimmies up the trunk. Crawling out on a low branch, he lies flat against it and extends his hand toward a bird's nest. His

fingers squirrel through the thatched twigs and produce a silver key.

•

The boy walks to a ranch-style home framed by a stand of overgrown boxwoods. The house is dark. He lingers on the front porch, as if listening for something, then quietly inserts the silver key in the door and vanishes inside.

Shaun exhales and stands up from behind the parked car. When he turns to Edie and Flo, his face is beaded with sweat.

—We can't let him get away, he says.

—If it is him, Edie says, we need to call the police.

Flo shakes her head.

—Fuck that, she says. I know what Xenie would do.

•

Shaun remembers Xenie in bed, perched on her elbows, wearing nothing but his oversize black T-shirt. They were arguing about the epidemic, and Xenie playfully shaped her hand into a gun, thumb as the hammer, extended finger as the barrel. She straddled his chest and aimed the weapon at his head. He can still feel the pressure of her index finger against his temple. He can still hear her whispering: I'll protect you.

•

Shaun's knees wobble as he leads them down the brick path toward the house, but the night pushes him onward.

There's no bell, so he raps his knuckles against the translucent glass door. No reply. He knocks harder, the blows convulsing the wooden frame. No reply. The house remains still. The only sounds come from the itchy pulse of the cicadas. Edie keeps swiveling around, attentive to every stray shadow, on the lookout for anything unexpected. Flo stands directly behind him, her fingertips grazing his shoulders, determined not to let him back down. Shaun discovers he's standing on a doormat whose cursive letters spell out the greeting WELCOME HOME.

●

Shaun smooths his long hair and places his mouth next to the door. He turns on his charm, speaking in the calm and coaxing tone of an old friend whispering confidences into the boy's ear.

—Hey, man, he says, everything's cool. We'd like to see you for a minute. We just want to talk.

—Maybe you can help us, Flo adds, in a voice that has an unexpected authoritative purr. We've got a question about our friend.

Behind them, Edie has removed her oversize glasses and paces in a tight circle. She traces the same conflicted steps, clockwise, then counter. Her fingers worry holes in her cardigan sweater, poking through the loose weave of the wool, widening the fissures until they resemble exit wounds.

Finally, she stops and confronts the door. She thumps her skinny fists against it and emits a series of wordless

shrieks. She acts possessed, her face a mask of pure ferocity. A wild scarlet pucker.

—Open up, motherfucker! she shouts.

•

Somewhere inside the house the boy switches on a lamp,
brightening the glass door and throwing a rectangle of
light onto the front porch.

•

They stand back and stare at the pale light. White moths
fly frantic circles around the illuminated door. No shadows
darken the frame. No voice from within replies. Shaun kicks
at the walkway, dislodging several loose bricks. Edie applies a fresh coat of lipstick and hands the tube to Flo. Their
mouths are bright emerald smears. They shine like iridescent battle scars. As they stand together in the taunting
glow, Shaun has a better appreciation of why Xenie liked
them. Down the street a dog starts to yowl, joined by others
in succession, protesting against an unseen moon.

You were always drawn to people like you.
Savagery hidden in their hearts.

Shaun uproots a brick from the walkway. A surge of adrenaline courses through his cells, and he's surprised how
much he craves this violence. He balances the brick in his
palm. It's lighter than he imagined.

The air feels electric, and the girls' expressions alter-

nate like a current between excitement and alarm. Flo suddenly pales and her puckered mouth begins to twitch.

—You're absolutely sure it's him? she whispers.

Shaun's face is clenched. His eyes are numb. His voice is a flattened croak.

—It doesn't matter, he says. Xenie's dead.

He takes a few stuttering hops and hurls the brick at the door, propelling it with all his energy, a week's worth of despair compressed in a single throw. The glass shatters with a high-pitched cascading crash.

●

Shaun stares into the gaping hole. An emptiness defined by its jagged edges.

●

They wait for approaching police sirens or an alarmed neighbor to appear with a shotgun, but nobody seems to care. There's no response from inside. In a frenzy, Flo scoops up a brick and hurls it at the door, shattering another portion of the glass. Edie lobs a brick with both hands and widens the hole with a piercing smash. Shaun's next volley obliterates the rest of the pane. They're granted a fugitive glimpse of the foyer and its long hallway, then the light is extinguished.

●

Shaun signals the others to follow him. They step over the threshold of the wooden frame, through the border

of broken glass, and into the house. They're greeted by splintered shards that glimmer across the floor. They walk through the foyer, each clutching a brick. Their steps slow and measured. Their eyes wide and wild. Their ears scanning for any sound that isn't their own shallow breath. Their noses are attuned to every stray scent. The musk of stale sweat. The fumes of fresh paint. The faint tang of piss.

●

Something keeps them from calling out to the boy. As they progress down the darkened hallway, they hear rustling noises deeper in the house. He must be close, Shaun whispers. They enter the living room, which is empty except for a stack of metal folding chairs in the corner. The parquet floor is stripped and scarred, gashed with haphazard grooves. In the corner is a balled-up and blood-soaked athletic sock. Scrawled chalk marks cover one wall, an ongoing tally, arranged like a scoreboard. Somebody has spray-painted a large black circle on another wall. Above it, in stylized block letters, is the phrase KILL CITY.

—What's Kill City? Edie whispers.

—Haven't you heard? Flo says. It's gone viral.

—We are, Shaun says. It's Arcadia.

●

They creep down a hallway that leads to several bedrooms, where the boy must be hiding. The smells become stranger, cloying incense, formaldehyde, burnt hair. They slink into the first room and use their phones to illuminate the

space. Plastic folding tables are arranged to resemble workstations. One holds a pile of surgical masks and aerosol paint cans leaking thick black gobs down their sides.

Another table contains cardboard cartons filled with bird eggs. Black and white speckled, green with brown spots, brown and tan, bright blue. Most of the eggs are cracked open and hollowed out.

The final table is covered with rows of small mason jars containing a clear viscous fluid. Shaun picks one up to examine it. He's pretty sure it's filled to the brim with gobs of spit.

●

The next room is stacked with molting mattresses bearing a faded pattern of roses. They stand upright along the walls, blocking out the windows. A clothesline is tacked across the center of the space, hung with tattered T-shirts, muddy pairs of jeans, and a moth-eaten flag with holes cut into the stripes and stars to form a poncho. Drooping from the end of the line is an assortment of threadbare training bras. Shaun wonders how many people live here. On the far wall, he spots another painted black circle. As they edge into the room, something crunches underfoot like brittle confetti. The entire floor is carpeted by bits of broken eggshells.

●

In the hallway, Flo discovers something attached to the baseboards. Unpeeling strips of silver duct tape, she finds

herself holding a revolver. It's freshly polished and slippery to the touch. She feels dizzy and feverish. She's about to present the weapon to the others as proof, or protection, or provocation—but she stops herself. Instead, she slides open the cylinder. The chambers contain only a single bullet. Rolling it round her palm, she registers its weight. She places the empty gun on the ground, but feels compelled to keep the bullet, pocketing the powdered metal shell as her private memento.

●

The last room is bare. The wooden floor is eerily pristine and recently must have been scoured clean. The emptiness feels like its own ritual. In a shadowy corner, they spot a box of condoms and a topless jar of lubricant, but the focal point of the space is another black circle. Shaun wonders what this primal mark means to these people. Was it something they created or something that created them? This one is significantly larger than the others. It sits dead center on the white wall, perfectly round except for trickling drips at the bottom, spray-painted so many times its blackness shines.

●

As Shaun looks closer, the black becomes so deep he starts to see purplish hues. It might be a trick of vision, but the circumference of the circle seems to radiate. It pulses with totemic power.

The longer he stares, the larger the circle grows, swelling like a portal, preparing to swallow him.

Is this what happens when you die?

They enter the kitchen to find the sliding glass door flung open. They stumble into the backyard, sprint across the grass, and confront an expanse of trees. The boy must've fled into the woods that run through this part of town. The area has a reputation for being a haven for unstable homeless, the site of gruesome rapes, a dumping ground for stolen corpses. There's even an infamous rumor about a black market in human organs. None of them are eager to pursue the boy there. Shaun feels immobilized. For the first time tonight, he registers the encroaching cold and begins to shiver. He lets the brick he's been brandishing fall to the ground.

They've all been having nightmares about the killers marching through a forest. Dozens of them armed with a variety of weapons, pushing past clinging vines, ducking under thorny branches, steadily tramping closer until you feel yourself surrounded by their vacant stares. It's a common dream that's circulated since the epidemic started, variations spreading across the country, infecting the

national subconscious. Shaun can't help replaying the unsettling scenario in his mind and suspects the others are doing the same.

> You had the same nightmare.
> You'd thrash around in bed and I'd wake you up.
> It took you a while to shake it off.

As Shaun stares into the forest, he's seized by a vision of fire, a massive conflagration of smoldering bark, blistering leaves, blazing boughs. A consuming blaze that smokes out all the potential killers and sends them fleeing into the open. He pictures scores of them running from the towering flames, pursued by the waves of heat and the deafening roar.

●

Edie produces a wallet constructed from purple duct tape. I found this on the kitchen counter, she says. He must've dropped it. They gather around and comb through the meager contents: several dollar bills, a crumpled note scribbled with addresses, and a driver's license. Behind scuffed layers of laminate, the boy's sullen face stares out at them. Shaun inspects his features more closely, comparing them against the killer's memorized mug shot. There's a definite resemblance, but that's not a scar on his cheek. It's a birthmark. Then there's the name. The name isn't even close. He feels queasy. Shit, he mutters.

●

Shaun realizes the boy must have been terrified and desperate to get away from them. He catches a glimpse of himself from the boy's perspective, the cold brutality of his expression in the midst of the dogged pursuit. But still he feels no remorse.

●

They pass the wallet from hand to hand as if it's a stranger's soiled underwear, an unwanted intimacy. Flo looks like she's been kicked in the windpipe. Edie's mind is churning, but Shaun can't tell whether she's relieved or concerned.

—This creepy house is almost exactly how I imagined the killers would live, Flo says. There's something deeply sick about the place.

—Maybe we shouldn't have broken that window, Edie says.

Flo removes the boy's ID. In a fury, she tries to rip it in half but only succeeds in twisting the plastic into a misshapen spiral.

—Maybe we should break some more, she says.

●

Shaun says: I really wanted it to be him. After that fucked-up funeral, it would've been something. Something I could've done for her.

He says: Her aunt has this theory that Xenie's soul can't move on. She has to have a proper send-off or she'll be trapped here.

He says: I can't stop thinking about that.

The others wait for him to continue, but his words have exhausted themselves. He looks up at the sky. The clouds obscure all but a scatter of stars whose pale light is probably posthumous.

•

—So let's do something for her, Edie says.

She polishes the lens of her oversize glasses with the hem of her cardigan while racking her brain for the proper tribute.

—A special concert, she says. For Xenie and the rest of the band. We could do it at a local club and get the entire scene involved.

Shaun shakes his head.

—It's too much, he says. Too complicated. Anyway, it would ultimately be for everyone else.

He sighs and walks back toward the road. Half the light poles seem busted, and the street's shadows have taken on more substance than the surrounding houses.

•

Somewhere in the night, people have gathered in front of the theater to add candles, stuffed animals, and bouquets of roses to the sprawling shrine for Xenie and the other casualties. Shaun wonders how long before he

becomes like one of those strangers, offering their store-bought mementos, performing an empty gesture with solemn reverence.

●

Shaun heads back in the direction of downtown, though he doesn't exactly remember the way. Mostly, he follows the downward slope of the road. There's no sign of fire, but he smells smoke. The air is perfumed with the sweet smell of char. The scent is oddly intoxicating.

Edie and Flo walk a few steps behind, accompanying him while allowing some space, letting his mood settle. Flo shudders from the deepening chill and Edie wraps her jacket around Flo's bare shoulders.

—Those eggs freaked me out, Edie says.

—I bet he eats them, Flo says. Cheap meal. Super organic.

Edie laughs a bit, but Shaun doesn't break a smile.

> *I've changed so much in the few days since you died.*
> *I've become so serious, you wouldn't recognize*
> *me now.*

Navigating the backstreets of Arcadia, they keep encountering the forest, as if it's traveling alongside them. Shaun isn't sure whether they're retracing their steps or walking in circles. He can't seem to escape the spooky sound of the wind whisking through the trees. The whispering leaves call to him, trying to lure him closer.

He pictures the boy huddled there behind a pile of broken branches, cowering in the darkness, not sure if it's safe to return home.

At the next corner, Shaun turns toward the faint rumble of the highway overpass. As they cross some railroad tracks, Flo pauses to press her palm against the steel. She lingers for several moments, as if sensing some far-off vibrations relayed through the line. They continue on past a run-down condo complex that looks foreclosed, though a three-tiered fountain still burbles in the concrete courtyard. The rails were cold, Flo says. Nothing's come through here for a while.

—When we were kids, we played chicken with the freight trains, Flo says. We'd press our ears to the rails and listen for locomotives. We stood on the tracks to see who could hold their ground longer.

—Xenie liked to challenge the conductor, she says, to see if she could make him use his emergency brake. She loved the high-pitched scream it made and she wouldn't step away until the last second. Sometimes I worried she secretly wanted to get hit.

—She always won, she says. I could never come close to matching her. I still feel bad about that.

•

Night creates confession. They feel no need to comment. The longer they walk, the more attuned they become to one another's sounds, until even their breathing is in synch.

•

Edie speaks in a soft and halting voice as if she's talking to herself.

She says: A few years ago, I ran away from home. My parents never liked music, never liked me being involved with bands, among other things. They used to . . . Let's just say they're terrible people.

—I didn't know where else to go, so I went to the diner, she says. I spent the evening there drinking coffee and eating pie. Xenie was working a long shift, and that's when I met her. She talked me out of going back home to my parents. She insisted at least I stay away for the night. Teach them a lesson. Take a stand. She let me come home with her and crash on her couch.

—I moved out of my parents' place for good a few weeks later, she says. It was all because of her. I owe her. I owe her everything.

•

The street feels like an index of their emotions. The carcass of the dead sparrow in the road, feathers blackened, tiny body imprinted with tire tread. The shards of glass on the sidewalk, illuminated by a stuttering streetlamp, mapping

a shattered archipelago. The graffiti tagged on the mailbox that commands: BREAK UP YOUR BAND.

•

Flo's and Edie's expressions remain concealed by the shadows after they finish their stories, but something torn in their voices broadcasts how they've been branded by the experiences. Shaun has a lot of friends, but these are the only people whose wounds go as deep. Xenie was irreplaceable for each of them.

> *All our memories of you put together, it still*
> *isn't enough.*

They're stopped by a sound floating down the street. Beseeching voices carried by the breeze. As they approach, they realize this must be people singing, several drunken soloists, overlapping snatches of a single chanted melody. They instinctively feel drawn to the sound and quicken their pace up the incline of the hill. The sound grows louder until they realize the voices aren't singing, they're sobbing.

•

As they crest the hill, they spot a trio weaving up the sidewalk toward them. Two young men support an older woman in a black head scarf and red dress who's bereft, staggering every few steps, face spattered with tears. She wails between gasping breaths and waves her arms while the men take turns consoling her in low tones. As they

pass, Shaun tries to catch their eyes to show he understands their grief, but they don't look up, consumed by their own tragedy.

●

Unsure what else to do, they continue walking toward the site the trio was fleeing. They pass a medical-supply warehouse whose flags tout an assortment of wheelchairs and a sheet-metal storage facility with a mural of a herd of deer, their upper halves nothing more than outlines, as if they've been absorbed by the bricks. Several cinder-block buildings are enclosed behind a barbed-wire fence. A pair of silver high heels dangles from a sagging telephone wire. Soon they arrive at a discount supermarket that's shut for the night. The empty parking lot is lit by sodium lamps, irradiated by a harsh glow that scrubs away every silhouette. In the far corner, Shaun spots yellow ribbons of tape undulating in the wind, cordoning off a crime scene.

●

Inside the triangle of police tape rests a chalk outline. It's the contorted-but-unmistakable form of a human body. Almost certainly the victim of a shooting. The arms and legs are spread wide. The white lines contain dark splotches, like someone has rubbed red into the asphalt. Shaun tries not to stare at the bits of hair and congealed clumps. There's less to a dead body than he imagined. It's as if it vanished through the ground, and the chalk marks the edges of a trapdoor.

•

The outline pulses with a certain presence, like it's caught something within its borders. He can tell Edie and Flo sense this as well. As they stand on the cusp of the murder scene, it's as if they've managed to summon her specter. The contours of Xenie's gutshot spirit.

•

They duck under the tape, compelled to get closer to the chalk figure. Shaun removes his suit jacket and rolls up his shirtsleeve to reveal his scar. He remembers right after he slashed his wrist, that suspended moment of observing himself in the bathroom mirror. He was disappointed by his familiar reflection, hoping something about himself would look different so close to the end of his life.

When I told you, you kissed my scar.

Shaun holds out his wrist to Flo and Edie. He's never talked with anyone else about this, and he's surprised to realize how fully he trusts them. Under the scalding lights, the raised pink flesh of his scar seems to simmer.

—Xenie had one just like it, he says. A few years before we met, we'd both tried to kill ourselves.

—She told me how she felt after she made the cut, he says. She said she calmly put down the razor and looked at the incision. She watched the blood begin to spill out,

these rolling waves of red, and it seemed like it was happening to someone else.

—She was sure that she was looking at somebody else's blood, he says.

Are you being cremated now?

They stare, unsteady, at the residue of recently spilled blood.

—I never knew, Edie says.

—I'm sorry, Flo says.

There's more to say, but words feel like another broken part of the night. He needs to do something, so he bends down and touches the form. Feeling the chalky residue on his fingertips isn't enough.

Is your body burning up?

Shaun kneels on the ground and lies in the outline. Ignoring the cold dampness, he fits his limbs between the lines and matches the contorted position as closely as possible. He shuts his eyes and remains stationary. It feels like he's finally been able to open her casket and climb inside.

Will the scar tissue be the last to blister away?

He stills his breath and slows his pulse. Maybe this is how he can finally give her a proper send-off. He tries to let his posture mold his state of mind and help him understand

what Xenie might've felt that night, to make her death real, to release her.

Your ashes too hot to touch.

Flo and Edie stand over his motionless body. They're overcome by the sight, their bodies quailing, holding each other's hands for support. In the distance, a passing freight train rumbles along the track and lets loose a piercing whistle. Flo begins to quietly cry and Edie breaks down as well, a knot of sorrow buzzing in their throats until it turns to bile.

Love is a burning thing.

Shaun lets his body go limp and surrenders. He sinks into Xenie's final moments, picturing her body strapped to the ambulance stretcher, her wheezing breaths becoming shallow, her hiccupping pulse slowing to a crawl, until he can feel the world around him begin to blacken, flaking apart and falling away, till nothing is left. Lying on the hard asphalt, he suddenly understands her spirit's passage from this sad plane. It's nothing more than a sensation of shifting into a different space, or slipping into a new story. A mental maneuver occurs, a lidless eye opens—

Another way to see.

THE DREAM

"Sorry to wake you up," Xenie said. "You were having a nightmare."

"It was the same dream you had the other night," Shaun said. "I was dreaming your dream."

"Now it's our dream."

YOU'RE BACK IN THE WOODS—DEEP IN THE GREEN— pushing past vines, ducking under branches, shaking through brambles—surrounded by the stickiness of spiderwebs and the pulsations of insects—the sporadic path keeps vanishing, but you're not discouraged because you know the way—you perk up your ears—listen closely to the wind whispering through the leaves of the trees—the unseen creatures rustling through the underbrush—the sparrows repeating their sequences of shrill calls—there's an uneasy sensation your presence here is being monitored—even the pine needles seem to be conversing—you pass a series of dirt mounds adorned with small round stones and feel a cold rush of recognition in your veins—these are graves—venture farther into the forest—the trees squeeze together and the light filtering through the canopy pales—the trail ahead is banded

by heavy shadows—slowly you realize other people are nearby—you catch flickering glimpses of them through the foliage—hear the thrash of their limbs as they clear a rough route through the woods—maybe they're hunters here to thin the deer population, though none of them seem to be wearing camouflage—as you tramp across the fallen boughs and knobby roots, you spot a boy with a shaved head and missing eyebrows—he clutches a revolver—you wish you didn't recognize him, but his blank expression is unforgettable—soon you can clearly make out the silhouettes of his companions—they're closer than you imagined—the trails start to converge and you find yourself surrounded by a dozen boys shuffling along like they're snared in a trance—armed with an array of weapons—handguns, shotguns, assault rifles—hunting knives, Molotov cocktails, backpacks of explosives—and they share that telltale uninhabited expression—soon you're all walking together along the same path—its edges ornamented with refuse from a children's party—crinkling candy wrappers, handfuls of soggy confetti, plastic bases from a kickball game—swallow your fear as more people join the swarming procession—boys and girls filing into formation from the far ends of the forest—a tree lies alongside the path, an urgent message tagged across its bark in purple spray paint, but the letters are smeared together and there's no time to decipher them—you have to keep moving—the killers maintain a steady pace—nobody speaks—the only conversation is the birdsong volleyed from tree to tree—it's difficult to pick

out the individual refrains because they're redoubled by mockingbirds whose echoes add to the confounding chorus—up ahead, the path forks in two distinct directions, one route curving right and the other left—everybody pauses to assess these options—then the killers walk straight ahead, forging their own trail, tramping down the scrubby underbrush—follow them deeper into the darkening woods—listen to the dead leaves crackling underfoot—inhale the smell of fresh rot—the improvised passage progressively transforms into a smoothly furrowed thoroughfare—the vegetation thins and odd flowers peek out among the weeds, their twisting stems culminating in strange and suppurating blooms—the killers accelerate the pace—you can sense their increasing agitation—your own heart beats faster and your forehead is crowned with droplets of sweat—as you crest a hill, a building rises into view, emerging a few steps at a time— the familiar structure of a theater appears in this clearing in the middle of the woods—its façade is lit up like a beacon and its radiance illuminates the forest floor—the walls teem with thick shingles of ivy—the windows are scabbed over with multicolor band posters, illustrated concert schedules, official venue announcements—but the glowing white marquee showcases no performer names and remains pristine in its blankness—you can't shake the feeling that you shouldn't be here—a current bristles through the treetops and the atmosphere feels amplified, the charged air crackling and threatening to feed back—the theater's doors are flung open and you find

yourself standing on the cusp of the entrance—the parade of killers is assembled behind you, clutching their
weapons, their vacant expressions awaiting your
signal—you walk together into the theater, greeted only
by the sagging strands of red bulbs suspended across the
ceiling—there are no people—the bar is empty and the
merchandise tables unmanned—enter the auditorium
where the overhead lights are dimmed in preparation
for a performance—there is no audience—instruments
are set up on the stage, a ring of gleaming guitars,
basses, keyboard, and drum kit—plus a lonely row of
microphones—the surrounding speaker towers emit a
gentle buzz that ripples through the room—but there are
no musicians—all of you stride down the sloping floor
toward the stage to investigate—as you clamber onto the
raised platform, the footlights slowly brighten—revealing
a hole in the middle of the stage—a trapdoor—an escape hatch whose hinges have been triggered, leaving an opening large enough to swallow several
people—peer into the hole—watch the spinning dust
motes drift downward, though it's impossible to determine any bottom—there's only a yawning absence—all
of you cluster tightly around the trapdoor—dismayed by
the disappearance of the band—the boy with the shaved
head and missing eyebrows begins to stamp his feet—
maybe trying to generate a reaction—or to flush the musicians out into the open—a few others join him—and
soon you're all stamping your feet in tandem, the noise
growing louder, the rhythm more syncopated—the blows

reverberate through the wooden boards of the stage—the sound both sinister and alluring—there's a heady intoxication as the stomping becomes more insistent, escalating toward a crescendo, enveloping you in its rapturous din—until the thunderous pounding rings in your ears—until your heart swells from the beat—until you realize that it sounds like applause.